E.R. PUNSHON
THE BATH MYSTERIES

Ernest Robertson Punshon was born in London in 1872.

At the age of fourteen he started life in an office. His employers soon informed him that he would never make a really satisfactory clerk, and he, agreeing, spent the next few years wandering about Canada and the United States, endeavouring without great success to earn a living in any occupation that offered. Returning home by way of working a passage on a cattle boat, he began to write. He contributed to many magazines and periodicals, wrote plays, and published nearly fifty novels, among which his detective stories proved the most popular and enduring.

He died in 1956.

Also by E.R. Punshon

Information Received
Death Among The Sunbathers
Crossword Mystery
Mystery Villa
Death of A Beauty Queen
Death Comes to Cambers
Mystery of Mr. Jessop
The Dusky Hour
Dictator's Way

E.R. PUNSHON

THE BATH MYSTERIES

With an introduction
by Curtis Evans

DEAN STREET PRESS

Published by Dean Street Press 2015

First published in 1936 by Victor Gollancz

Cover by DSP

ISBN 978 1 910570 61 6

www.deanstreetpress.co.uk

CONTENTS

CONTENTS

INTRODUCTION

On 23 March 1915, Scotland Yard formally charged George Joseph Smith with the murders of Bessie Williams, Alice Smith and Margaret Lloyd. After nine days' trial Smith was found guilty on 1 July and hanged six weeks later, on 13 August. Justice (and sometimes, it must be admitted, injustice) was swift in those days, but although Smith's legal ordeal was brief, his infamy is imperishable. Today, a full century after his trial, Smith remains one of England's most notorious killers, the man who executed the infamous "Brides in the Bath" murders. Each of Smith's victims was a woman he had bigamously wed, then drowned in a bathtub. The sensational case was referenced in works by Golden Age mystery writers, including the Crime Queens Agatha Christie, Dorothy L. Sayers and Margery Allingham; but in 1936, E.R. Punshon--who the same year published, in the Detection Club true crime anthology *The Anatomy of Murder*, an essay on the infamous French serial killer "Bluebeard" (Henri Desiré Landru) --devised an entire detective novel that pivoted on the plot device of a sinister succession of bathtub deaths. In this novel, *The Bath Mysteries*, Punshon mentions not only the Brides in the Bath Murders, but the Rouse burning-car killing and the Brighton trunk slayings, further evincing his interest in true crime. It is one of Punshon's most interesting works of detective fiction, despite the fact--or perhaps, indeed, because of it--that it is a challenging book for the period, difficult to pigeonhole, as we are wont to do, into a convenient genre mystery category. The plot of the novel is interesting, to be sure, but it is the quality of Punshon's empathy for his victimized characters that makes *The Bath Mysteries* exceptional for its time and still resonant today.

The first couple of chapters in *The Bath Mysteries* raise the reader's expectation that what she has in her hands is a witty manners mystery in the fashion of the detective novels of Sayers, Allingham and Ngaio Marsh, yet something rather different soon emerges. The tale opens with Punshon's series sleuth, Detective-Sergeant Bobby Owen, visiting a London conclave of his aristocratic family held at the Lords of Hirlpool's decayed white elephant of an ancestral abode, in which none of them could afford to live since the 1850s. As Bobby surveys the mansion's grand hall, from which arises the majestic double stairway, Punshon writes amusingly, in a passage reflective of the waning of England's traditional landed aristocracy and the waxing of crass commercial enterprise, that with all its marble and gilt "it would have done credit to almost any tea shop or cinema in the land. Indeed, one well-known provincial department store had recently made a tempting offer for it, though, unfortunately, trust deeds prevented its sale." Here in this magnificent ruin Bobby encounters his grandmother, the dowager Lady Hirlpool, whom loyal Punshon readers had already met in the previous Bobby Owen mystery, *Death Comes to Cambers*; his uncle, Lord Hirlpool; Christopher ("Chris") Owen, Bobby's cousin and an antique dealer who is "the heir to the title and the family mortgages"; Cora Owen, wife of Bobby's other cousin, Ronald ("Ronnie"), vanished for the last three years after being named as a party in an especially scandalous divorce action; and Dick Norris, who though strictly speaking is not family, was a close friend of the missing Ronnie Owen.

The family has recently learned that a man giving his name as Ronald Oliver, whom there is reason to believe may have been Ronnie Owen under alias, was found dead in his bath, apparently "from the effects of boiling water coming from a lighted geyser during approximately thirty-six hours." (The inquest concluded he was "the worse for drink" when he ran the bath.) Oliver's—or Owen's—life was insured for 20,000 pounds, which was duly collected by a woman claiming to be his wife. Sometime afterward the same woman pawned a signet ring—Ronnie Owen's signet ring, bearing the family crest of three dolphins. Lord Hirlpool and the family want Bobby to investigate the matter personally, and Lord Hirlpool complacently informs his nephew: "I had a chat with the Home Secretary yesterday. He rang up the Commissioner while I was there, and you're to be seconded, or whatever you call it in the police, to look into the thing and find out what really did happen to poor Ronnie."

Bobby, who is acutely embarrassed within the police force by his aristocratic connections, desperately resents these elite behind-the-scenes machinations and prays fervently that the next general election will "hurl this Government and all connected with it into outer darkness." Until that fine day arrives, however, he has yet another investigative job to do, in what proves a singularly bizarre case. It turns out that the gruesome demise of "Ronald Oliver" in his bath is only one of several such fatalities that have taken place over the last few years, all of them involving obscure men whose lives have been insured for 20,000 pounds. Have these men been ground up in a kind of remorselessly efficient "murder factory," Bobby begins to wonder, some "carefully prepared, widely spread organization of death, working in a strange and fearful secrecy"? Bobby's investigation takes him into the pits of London, exploring life among the down-and-outs in a decade overtaken by what the prominent socialist intellectual and detective fiction writer G.D.H. Cole in 1932 aptly termed "world chaos" (see *The Intelligent Man's Guide to World Chaos*, published by Victor Gollancz, who also, not altogether incidentally, published the detective fiction of Cole's Detection Club colleague E.R. Punshon).

The characters of greatest interest in *The Bath Mysteries* are not found among the genteel sleuth's aristocratic family members, as one might expect in a novel from this period by, say, Ngaio Marsh (see *Surfeit of Lampreys*, for example), but rather are drawn from the ranks of the downtrodden. For these people Punshon memorably conveys sympathy in the most striking passages of the novel, with words, no doubt partly inspired by his own past personal circumstances (see my introduction to *Death Comes to Cambers*), that are powerfully condemnatory of human exclusion and exploitation:

> Leaning against the parapet with his back to the river, Bobby watched how, in the darkness of the night that now had fallen, there drifted by a shadowy procession of the lost, of the outcast, of the disinherited, of those who had fallen or been thrown from their places in a society that knew them no more—men and women shuffling by like ghosts of their own past, like phantoms of the dead waiting only a signal to

> return to the graves they had deserted….Perhaps in the gloom of some other night another had leaned as he was doing upon the parapet, back to the river, and watched the shadowy line of the lost trailing aimlessly by, and watched them with the appraising eye of the butcher searching out the fattest sheep for the slaughterhouse.

It is in this netherworld of vice and despair that we catch glimpses of such striking individuals as the elderly sneak thief Magotty Meg, a colorful personage of whom Punshon readers were soon to see more, and the coffee-stall keeper George Young, nicknamed "Cripples" on account of his missing left arm and right leg. The arm was lost in a Durham coal mine accident, we learn, the leg from the impact upon him and his stall of an inebriated young gentleman's space-hurtling sports car. "Lucky…it was a left arm and right leg," reflects "Cripples" phlegmatically, "keeps you from being lopsided like."

It is between two denizens of this dark place that we find what Milward Kennedy, another of Punshon's Detection Club colleagues, in his *Sunday Times* review of *The Bath Mysteries* called "a love-interest…as moving as any which I can recall in a detective story." More about this element of *The Bath Mysteries* cannot in good conscience be divulged by me to the neophyte reader of the novel, so I will simply conclude by urging that you read it posthaste.

Curtis Evans

CHAPTER I

FAMILY CONFERENCE

DETECTIVE-SERGEANT BOBBY OWEN, leaving the Park, crossed Carlton Lane. Through the dark shadows cast by a cliff-like block of flats opposite he passed on, round the mews, into stately Carlton Square itself, where on the north side, No. 1, the ancestral home of his race, sprawled its interminable and depressing length.

Bobby surveyed it with a sigh, thinking what a difference would be made in the family fortunes if only legal complication, jointures, mortgages, reversions, Lord knew what, permitted it to be pulled down, and a new block of spacious, super-luxury, one-room flats erected in its stead. But that could not be—at least, not without a special Act of Parliament whereof the expense would eat up all possible profit; and so Bobby sighed again, and then cast a glance of professional interest at the third window from the south-east corner on the top floor, that of the room where legend told that, a hundred and fifty years ago, a servant-maid had been murdered in mysterious circumstances never cleared up. Then, ascending the steps leading to the huge front doors, he knocked; and as from the very bowels of the earth a thin voice floated up to him.

"Beg pardon, sir," it said, "I can't get them doors open; they haven't been used so long they've stuck someway, or else it's the lock. His lordship was proper vexed."

Descending to the street-level again, and peering over iron railings, Bobby saw, far below, the ancient retainer of the house whose services had been rewarded—or punished—by the job of caretaker of this mansion, which none of the Lords of Hirlpool had been able to afford to inhabit for three-quarters of a century past.

"Do you mind coming this way, sir?" quavered again the voice from the depths. "His lordship had to, and proper vexed he was, too."

"Righto," said Bobby, and accordingly descended the long flight of steps that led down to the area door, where the old caretaker waited. "Bit of a climb," he commented; "if uncle had to, I can believe he didn't like it. Do you have to climb those steps every time you want to go out?"

"Oh, no, sir," answered the caretaker, "there's the back door, sir, opening on the mews, but it's nearly ten minutes' walk to get round there from here. This way, sir."

Bobby followed the old man through a series of grim, dark, chill, dust-strewn chambers, compared with which the vaults of the Spanish Inquisition would surely have seemed cheery, homely abiding places. They came to a spot whence steep and narrow stone steps led both up and down, though whether to a gloom more intense above or below was hard to say. But it seemed to prove that even beneath these depths there stretched depths lower still.

"Good Lord," Bobby said. "Are there cellars under these?"

"These aren't the cellars, sir," answered the other rebukingly. "This is the basement floor. Over there's what used to be the kitchen, and that's the door of the old servants' hall. Very spacious apartment, sir, and very different everything looked when there was a staff of twenty or more busy here."

"It's a wonder they didn't die of T.B. or rheumatism," observed Bobby, peering into the dark cavern that once had been a kitchen. "Probably they did, though. What about the breakfast bacon? How long does it take to get from kitchen to dining-room?"

The caretaker considered the point carefully.

"I don't think it would take more than ten minutes," he decided; "not much more, anyhow. His lordship will be waiting, sir," he added; "her ladyship, too."

"Oh, has granny got here already?" Bobby said. "All right, I'll cut along. What about Mrs. Ronnie? Has she turned up?"

"Yes, sir, she came the first. They're all there except Mr. Chris. Mr. Norris came immediate after Mrs. Ronnie. It's the small room to the right at the top of the big stair."

"Right, I'll find my way; don't you bother," Bobby said, and began to ascend the steps leading to the upper regions of the house.

As he went he wondered again what could be the meaning of this family conference to which his uncle, Lord Hirlpool, had summoned him; his grandmother, the dowager Lady Hirlpool; his cousin by marriage, Cora, who was Mrs. Ronald Owen; his other cousin, Chris Owen, the heir to the title and the family mortgages, debts, tithes, income-tax, and all the rest of the financial encumbrances that went with their old and historic name; and finally Dick Norris. He wondered, too, why Dick Norris had been included, since Norris was not one of the family, though he had been a very intimate friend of the vanished Ronnie Owen. It was a friendship that had been formed and consolidated on the links, for Norris was a famous amateur golfer, known to a wide circle through the articles he contributed to the golfing press under various pseudonyms, as "B. Unkert," "N. B. Luck," and others, all jn the breezy, healthy type of humor that made him so popular a writer.

"Hope," Bobby thought uneasily, as he groped his way up the dark, twisting steps, "Ronnie hasn't been up to something they think I can hush up because I'm at the Yard."

But he did not think this very likely, as, though Ronnie had been wild and reckless enough, and had been badly involved in that disastrous and scandalous divorce case after which he had vanished from the ken of all his former friends and acquaintances, including his justly offended wife, he was not likely to have mixed himself up in anything of a criminal nature—at least, not unless he had been more badly drunk even than usual.

"Must be something pretty serious, though," Bobby told himself, as he emerged from the stairs and discovered he was by no means certain which was now the right direction to take.

However, after one or two attempts that brought him back to his starting-place, he arrived at last in the huge sepulchral entrance-hall, a bare, desolate void ringed round by possibly the worst collection of statuary in the whole wide world.

From the center of this hall there rose the great double stair; so magnificent in marble and gilt, it would have done credit to almost any tea shop or cinema in the land. Indeed, one well-known provincial department store had recently made a tempting offer for it, though, unfortunately, trust deeds prevented its sale.

At the top of these stairs Bobby turned to the right, and,

guided by the sound of voices, found his way to a small room at an angle of the building. Its door was open, and into it daylight streamed through one open and unshuttered window. At a second window a tall, thin, elderly man, with a long, thin, melancholy face, a very short body, and very long legs, was engaged in a free-for-all struggle with shutters that seemed as fixed as the decrees of fate. A woman's voice said:

"Chrissy, dear, if they won't open, get Mr. Norris to swot 'em with a chair or something."

"My dear mother," answered gloomily the man at the window, "maintenance and repair are ruining me as it is."

He made a final effort, retired defeated before those immovable shutters, and turned round as Bobby entered the room.

"Morning, uncle," Bobby said to him. "Hullo, granny," he said to the lady who had advised the "swotting" of the difficult shutters, and he dropped a kiss upon her hair, that would very likely have been gray had either she or her maid ever dreamed of permitting such a thing. To a dark, tall, slim, somber-looking, youngish, very handsome woman who was smoking cigarettes opposite, he said: "How do, Cora?" With a big, loose-limbed, brown-faced man in plus fours who was Dick Norris, and who was seated in the background, straddling a chair with his face to its back and his arms resting thereon, he exchanged silent nods, and again he wondered why Norris was there. Most likely there was nothing in it, but there had been stories that Norris, too, had been a competitor for Cora's hand, and that the disappointment had been bitter when she bestowed it upon Ronnie Owen.

Bobby's uncle, Lord Hirlpool, the tall, thin man, mumbled an indistinct reply to his greeting. The dowager patted his hand absently. Cora took not the slightest notice, but lighted another cigarette, though the one she was smoking was but half finished. Bobby asked himself whether it was quite an accident that her back was turned to Norris, while Norris, in his reverse position on the chair he straddled, was exactly behind her, his curiously expressionless, light blue eyes fixed full upon her. Of a feeling of tension, of expectation, in the room, Bobby was at once aware, and he began to think that perhaps Cora and Dick Norris were intending to get married—or, rather, to do without getting married, since Ronnie's disappearance only dated from about three years back. No denying that Ronnie had treated Cora disgracefully, and perhaps there had been some foundation for the stories representing Dick Norris as a disappointed rival, though there had never seemed to be any breach in his friendship with Ronnie. Even when the scandal broke upon a London most delightfully shocked, Dick had still stood by Ronnie when others of his friends deserted him. Emerging abruptly from deep thought, Lady Hirlpool said:

"If only we could let the place—even if there's no one left in England with money enough to live here, surely some American millionaire . . . ?"

"American millionaires," her son answered bitterly, "think of nothing but bathrooms. The last one wanted nine put in, five for the family and four for the servants. Imagine the miles of plumbing . . . "

"Why not," suggested Bobby helpfully, "flood the basement and call it a swimming pool? Very likely you would catch a film star then."

Lord Hirlpool did not seem to think much of the suggestion. He looked at his watch and mumbled:

"Chris ought to be here by now. He's always late."

A slow and hesitating step sounded without, paused as if in doubt, and then came on, and there entered languidly a youngish man of middle height with the long, melancholy face and legs too long in proportion to the body that often characterized members of the family of Owen of Hirlpool, and that Bobby himself was thankful some trick of Mendelism had allowed him to escape. The newcomer was Christopher Owen, eldest nephew to Lord Hirlpool, who was a childless widower and to whom, therefore, Chris was heir-presumptive. It followed that he was also grandson to the dowager Lady Hirlpool, cousin by marriage to Cora Owen, cousin by blood to the missing Ronnie Owen and to Detective-Sergeant Bobby Owen, and anything but friend to Dick Norris, with whom he had had in the past certain complicated financial relations which had ended in a common loss and mutual ill-feeling. He was the proprietor of a small antique shop, of which the extremely fluctuating profits afforded him his means of livelihood, and he had the reputation of often picking up for a pound or two in the houses of his friends and acquaintances bits of china, drawings, old furniture, and so on, that afterwards he disposed of on trips to America at a fantastic profit. But it was also believed that most of what he gained in business he promptly lost again, gambling on the Stock Exchange. He had a considerable reputation as what is vulgarly called a "lady-killer," since his long, melancholy face had its own attractiveness, his eyes could take on a look of infinite appeal, and many women seemed unable to resist the languid and melancholy indifference of his manner that seemed positively to challenge them to relieve it. Often they managed to convince themselves that that was a breaking heart which was in reality only wonder whether an offer of a couple of guineas for the bit of Sèvres—worth ten—on the mantelpiece would be accepted or resented. He spoke with a slight, indeed very slight, stutter, intermittent and at times scarcely perceptible, and yet, in a general way, oddly noticeable. Slight as it was, it had had a great effect on his life. It had made impossible for him a stage career to which he had been strongly drawn and for which he had real aptitude, and at Cambridge it had been the cause of his having been sent down without taking his degree. Absurdly sensitive always to what was a very trifling defect, he had resented so strongly a mocking imitation of it given by a fellow-undergraduate, at a party at which the cocktails had been frequent and strong, as to express that resentment in terms of a carving knife. A serious criminal charge had been narrowly averted; there had even been a few hours when a death and a charge of murder had seemed a possibility; in the end the injured man's lie that he had inflicted the injury himself had been accepted. But the incident had brought Chris's university career to a conclusion, and with it his hopes of entering the Civil Service with an eye upon the Foreign Office. Now, the moment he entered the room he announced gloomily, his little stutter more marked than usual:

"T-t-those Chippendale chairs I bought at the Lawes sale are all duds—made in Birmingham year before last. R-rather a bore—means I shall drop a couple of hundred on them."

"Hard times all round," agreed the brown-faced Norris.

"It's hardly any good writing anything about golf—every editor you try has a drawerful of stuff already. All they want to know is if you've won the Open, and, if you haven't, then yours goes down the drain."

"You shouldn't buy duds, Chris," his grandmother told him tartly. "Antique dealers sell duds, they don't buy 'em." Having delivered herself of this aphorism, Lady Hirlpool turned to Norris: "Why don't you turn pro, Mr. Norris?" she demanded. "They make plenty of money; they charge you a guinea for advising you to buy one of their own clubs at twice what they paid for it."

"I know," sighed Norris, "but if you're a pro you have to compete with pros—not good enough."

"Got any tips to give away?" asked Chris, dangling eyeglasses of which he had no need, since his sight was excellent—the eyeglasses were in reality powerful magnifiers, enabling him to give a close examination to objects on which he seemed to be bestowing a merely casual glance.

Norris answered this inquiry for tips by a dismal shake of the head.

"The last three blokes I wasted a spot of coaching on stood me one dinner, one week-end invite, and one 'Thanks awfully' between them," he said dejectedly, "and one of them knew jolly well what was going to happen to 'Emmies' and never said a word."

"Too bad," murmured Chris, more sympathetically than believingly. To Cora, Chris added: "I don't know when I shall be able to pay back that couple of thou."

Cora took not the least notice of this remark. She might not have heard, and yet they all felt in her a kind of hidden heat of attention, as though no word was spoken but was fuel to some secret fire in her. Chris's remark had reference to a sum of £2,000 Ronnie Owen had lent to him in a mood of unusual benevolence, affluence, and less unusual intoxication. That, of course, had been before the crash, and Bobby remembered the occasion well, for he had chanced that night to be in his cousins' company; had had made to himself, but had not accepted, similar generous offers; and had admired a fur coat in ocelot skin Ronnie had happened to see in a shop window, taken a fancy to, and bought then and there for Cora. She had been less grateful in that she had already two fur coats, and did not care for ocelot fur or consider that it suited her. The loan to Chris had been for the purpose of buying out an unsatisfactory partner in the antique business and for extending it, and the windfall which had permitted Ronnie to display such all-round generosity had been the result of a highly successful speculation in gold-mine shares, undertaken on the strength of information passed on by Dick Norris that it was commonly said he had failed to act on himself since he had not believed it reliable—otherwise he would not have passed it on but kept it to himself, was the unkind comment generally added when the story was told. By an added irony of fate, it was only this lucky hit, resulting in such unusual affluence—for the £2,000 lent to Chris had been a comparatively small part of the gain—that had put Ronnie in a position to propose to Cora. Chris said to her now:

"No news yet of Ronnie, I suppose?"

"Yes," she answered. "I believe he's been murdered."

CHAPTER II

A TASK FOR BOBBY

THE LAST WORD fell like a stone into a quiet pond. One could almost see the slow ripples of surprise, horror, incredulity, spreading in each listener's mind—but incredulity predominating. Lady Hirlpool was the first to speak. She said protestingly, a little with the air of thus finally disposing of the matter:

"My dear Cora!"

Cora picked up the half-smoked stump of one of the cigarettes she had discarded and put it between her lips without appearing to notice that it had long been extinguished.

"I expect I shall begin to scream soon," she remarked dispassionately.

"Oh, I say . . . Cora," exclaimed Norris, his first expression of blank disbelief changing to one of acute alarm.

"When people start to scream at the Yard," observed Bobby as dispassionately as Cora, "we just let 'em. Then we go on when they're through."

His grandmother turned on him with a flash of genuine indignation.

"I call that simply brutal," she declared heatedly.

"So do they, granny," agreed Bobby.

Lady Hirlpool snorted, and took refuge in her lipstick.

Lord Hirlpool said:

"It's because of this idea of Cora's that I asked you to come along here. Mother's flat is too small."

"'Tisn't," snapped Lady Hirlpool, still indignant. "I can get two bridge tables in quite easily, and three if some-one sits in the lobby."

"Besides, it's in West Kensington," Lord Hirlpool added clinchingly. He still thought of West Kensington as others think of Central Africa, and, before his mother could frame another angry protest, he went on: "At my hotel one can't be private, so I thought it would be better to meet here to talk."

"If I had known," interposed Norris, "I would have suggested my place. I've a flat in Park Lane now, you know," he added with a certain complacence, since this suggested an affluence altogether new and the more unex-pected in view of his recent lament over the present diffi-culty of selling articles about golf in a world in which possibly not everyone played golf, but certainly everyone wrote about it.

"But . . . murdered?" protested Chris, as if the word had only just sunk into his mind. "Old Ronnie . . . mur-dered . . . ? Oh, come. . . . "

"If Cora has any facts to go on," Bobby pointed out, himself incredulous, "she ought to give information to the C.I.D."

"Well, you're the C.I.D., aren't you?" asked Chris. "Jolly good, too; people like it, when you're buying bits of things from them, if you tell them you've a cousin in the C.I.D. Makes them feel so safe," he added, his voice the soft purr of a cat lazily absorbing a saucerful of cream.

Bobby, very indignant at this shameless use of a family connection, tried to think of some effective protest, but failed. All he could do was to grumble out:

"I'm not the C.I.D. I'm a detective-sergeant, and a detective-sergeant is just an errand-boy running about where he's told. It's the big hats upstairs do the brainwork. If Cora's got anything to show . . . "

"I've this," said Cora, and put a signet ring on the table. "It was Ronnie's."

"It was offered me," explained Lord Hirlpool, "by a dealer who had noticed the crest and motto and thought I might like to buy it for family reasons—it was a man in quite a small way out in Islington," added Lord Hirlpool, explanatory, since it was obvious no West End dealer would ever have thought of Lord Hirlpool as a likely market for the purchase of anything whatever. "I thought the ring must be Ronnie's from the description, but to make sure I went to see. It had been pawned."

"Oh, well, nothing in that," observed Dick Norris as the speaker paused; for, indeed, to Norris, in spite of his present remarkable Park Lane affluence, the pawnshop still seemed the natural and indeed inevitable home for all unattached jewelry.

"Ronnie would never have parted with it," Cora said, her long-extinguished cigarette still between her lips.

"Oh, well, when a chap's put to it," Chris observed tolerantly. He himself was not without experience in such matters.

"Ronnie would have starved first," Cora insisted.

"It was not Ronnie who pawned it," Lord Hirlpool said. "It was his widow."

"Widow?" repeated Bobby, a little uneasily.

"Widow," repeated Cora. "But not me."

"The pawnbroker made inquiries," Lord Hirlpool went

on. "The ring is of some value—he advanced £30 on it, and I suppose rings worth that much don't often turn up in Islington. He found it had been the property of a man on whom an inquest had been held a few days previously. The name was given as Ronald Oliver. If any of us saw the report of the inquest in the paper, that name wouldn't suggest anything. It was mentioned in the evidence that Mr. Oliver had recently taken out an insurance on his life for £10,000, as well as an accident insurance for another £10, 000. Both amounts were paid."

"Well, that couldn't have been Ronnie," Chris pointed out. "Rotten heart, always getting knocked up, daren't even run for a bus. No company would have insured him for ten thousand pence."

"Then why had he Ronnie's ring?" Cora asked, looking with an air of surprise at the cigarette-end she had just taken from her mouth, as if wondering how it had got there.

"When pawning the ring," Lord Hirlpool went on, "Mrs. Oliver explained that the insurance was all taken up by business liabilities. Mr. Oliver was described at the inquest as a stock and share dealer, but apparently not a member of the Stock Exchange."

"Well, that's nothing against him," said Norris, somewhat defiantly. "Just as straight blokes outside as inside—straighter, if you ask me."

"As well as the life policy there was an accident policy—both for ten thousand," Bobby repeated thoughtfully. "Do you know if they were recent?" he asked.

"The accident policy had been taken out only three months before," Lord Hirlpool answered.

"Nothing in that," observed Norris. "I took one out myself for £20,000 only the other day." He smiled, and seemed inclined to wink, but did not. "Useful in business sometimes, and blokes don't always spot the difference between an accident and a whole-life policy. You can always raise a bit of coin on a policy with a good company."

"I suppose the company made some inquiries before they paid?" Bobby remarked. "What was the verdict at the inquest?"

"Death by misadventure."

"What caused it?" Bobby asked.

Lord Hirlpool hesitated, and looked at Cora. She put both hands on the table before her, holding them firmly together. In a loud, clear voice she said:

"Boiling."

"What?" said Bobby, thinking he had misunderstood.

Cora got up and walked out of the room.

"Boiling," repeated Lord Hirlpool.

"But, good Lord," protested Chris, "you mean he scalded himself . . . kettle of boiling water . . . ?"

"No, I don't," said Lord Hirlpool. "The evidence showed he died in his bath from the effects of boiling water coming from a lighted geyser during approximately thirty-six hours."

"I think I'll go and see what Cora's doing," said Lady Hirlpool, getting up and following her niece.

"She means she's going to be sick somewhere," said Lord Hirlpool gloomily. "It does make you feel a bit like that."

"Yes, but hang it all," spluttered Chris. "Well, I mean . . . how could it—happen?"

"The evidence," said Lord Hirlpool, "was to the effect

that Ronnie—Mr. Oliver—was the worse for drink when he returned on Saturday night to the flat he occupied alone. The charwoman he employed didn't come on week-ends. It was only when she arrived on Monday morning that what had happened was discovered. The flat is in a big new building, meant chiefly for working people, and the overflow from the bath ran off into a main waste-pipe, so there was nothing to attract attention there. Neighbors said that 'the gentleman often came home jolly.' They thought nothing of it when he was seen like that on this occasion. It seems quite clear Ronnie was alone. There was a half-empty whisky bottle in the bathroom. The suggestion adopted was that Ronnie had decided to have a bath, possibly to sober up on; that he got ready—his clothing was lying about the room—and that he lighted the geyser and then, overcome by the steam perhaps, had managed to fall in his intoxicated condition into the bath in which the boiling water from the geyser continued to pour continuously for a day and a half."

"I suppose it might happen like that," Bobby said slowly.

"The jury thought so," answered Lord Hirlpool. "The police were called in, and found papers showing that he was living separated from his wife, to whom under the deed of separation he had to pay £7 a week. The insurance policy was in her favor, to assure her a continuance of that income in case of his death."

"I thought the money had to go to pay business liabilities," interposed Bobby.

"There seems an inconsistency there," agreed Lord Hirlpool. "The wife's name was given as Mary Oliver, at a Bournemouth address. The police communicated with her, she came to London, seemed decently distressed, made all necessary arrangements, collected the £20,000 insurance, and that's all."

"Why does Cora think it was murder?" Norris asked. "It might have been a genuine accident."

"Had Cora heard from him at all since—since the scandal?" inquired Bobby.

"Yes," answered Lord Hirlpool. "At the time she told him she would never forgive him, and never wanted to see or hear of him again. He had the grace to be thoroughly ashamed of himself, and he went away accordingly. He took nothing with him except a few clothes and a little ready cash—not more than £50 at the most. He saw his lawyers and instructed them that Cora was to have everything else, and signed the necessary papers. Apparently as Mr. Oliver he took up some sort of stockbroker's business, and was doing quite well at it. He wrote once or twice to Cora. He gave no address. He said that was so she wouldn't be able to return his letters unanswered. He said he supposed she would never forgive him but he always read the *Announcer,* and if one day he saw his name in the agony column, with the word 'Return' with it, he would give her a week to make sure she meant it and then, if there was no other advertisement to cancel the first, he would take it she was willing to have him back and he would come."

Cora had returned to the room. She had been listening intently and smoking furiously. Abruptly she said:

"Father hated cigarettes; he said they were poison."

Her father had been a doctor, and she herself, chiefly to please him, had begun medical studies. But she had never made much progress with them, and on his death she had abandoned them. A lingering regard for his teaching made her a rare smoker, but today she was helping herself to one cigarette after the other, though indeed it was more a case of burning them up than of smoking them. Bobby reflected her abrupt remark probably meant she was longing to have again her father's presence and advice. He said:

"Did the pawnbroker give any description of the woman who pledged the ring?"

" 'Tall, dark, slim, wearing a leopard-skin coat,' he said," Cora answered. "I had one in ocelot fur once. I got rid of it long ago. It was one Ronnie gave me. I went to the shop. The man said it was someone like me but not me—someone older and darker, much darker skin. There was no one Ronnie knew like that."

"Did you do what he asked about the advertisement?" Bobby inquired.

"At first I tore up the letters he sent," she answered. "If I had known his address I would have sent them back. I hated thinking of him. One day in March last year I was near the *Announcer* office, and I went in and got them to put in the advertisement he wanted. I thought there was a whole week I could change my mind in if I liked. I didn't, and I waited, and he never came." Her tone was monotonous and dull, but one felt the strong emotion in it. In the same carefully restrained voice she added: "It was that week-end it happened."

"Perhaps Ronnie never saw the advertisement," Chris suggested.

"There was an answer in the *Announcer* next morning. It said: 'Thank God,' and there was his name, too—'Ron.' I always called him 'Ron,' " answered Cora, and in the same passionless voice she added: "I got everything ready. I thought we would start fresh. He never came."

"It may have been an accident. Why not?" Chris said. "There's nothing to show it was murder."

"Apparently his death was worth £20,000 to somebody," Bobby remarked.

"To a woman," Cora corrected him. "I think she knew he was going back to me. She wanted to stop him. She took that way. She knew about the insurance. She was passing as his wife. It was my advertisement that made it happen."

She lighted a fresh cigarette, puffing at it till it glowed.

"It's all more than a year ago," Bobby said musingly. "Makes it difficult. Hard enough to remember exactly what happened a fortnight ago, let alone fifteen months. It's a job to get at the truth when it's fresh. After a year's cold storage it's almost impossible. But there's something queer about that insurance. It's jolly certain no insurance company would have accepted Ronnie, with his heart in the state it was—not as a life risk. They might for accident. Besides, the woman who collected it wasn't his wife, and can't have had any insurable interest, and there can't have been any genuine deed of separation. There must have been some pretty tall forging going on. I think Cora ought to see her lawyers, and then, if they agree, they could put the whole thing before our people."

"I've arranged all that," Lord Hirlpool explained in a very satisfied tone. "I had a chat with the Home Secretary yesterday. He rang up the Commissioner while I was there, and you're to be seconded, or whatever you call it in the police, to look into the thing and find out what did really happen to poor Ronnie."

CHAPTER III

INQUIRY BEGINS

Bobby received this announcement with mixed feelings. On the one hand, it seemed to promise him an independence in investigation that, so often fretted by the red tape inherent in the working of every large-scale organization, he had come to think of as an ideal never likely to be realized in actual experience. On the other hand, he disliked above all things any appearance of privilege due to family influence—he knew only too well the jealousy and anger that always aroused. He reflected, too, that the grounds for suspecting murder were of the slightest, and that in any case the time-lag would make the inquiry one of extraordinary difficulty, while failure in it would be what failure always is, no matter how inevitable. For, if nothing succeeds like success, it is even more true that nothing fails like failure.

However, it would look worse still to try to back out, especially now all arrangements were made. He began to ask questions, to note down replies and details, and he understood now why Dick Norris had been asked to be present. As Ronnie's most intimate friend, Norris was the most likely person to know something of his movements after his disappearance. However, Norris had no information to give. Ronnie had simply walked out of the court after listening to a severe, ecclesiastically minded judge's denunciation of his conduct, and since then none of his former friends or acquaintances had heard anything of him.

Even the arrangements by which the whole of his capital had been put at his wife's sole disposition had been made beforehand.

"He must have gone straight to the lawyers," Cora said in her dull, expressionless voice, "the day before, immediately after Mrs. Stanley's evidence in the divorce case, when I told him I never wanted to see or hear of him again—and I never did, I never shall."

Lady Hirlpool had come back into the room. She was standing by the window, busy with her vanity case in an effort to repair the ravages certain recent events had made in her appearance. She said gently:

"We don't know anything for certain, Cora. Perhaps that poor man who died so dreadfully wasn't Ronnie at all."

Cora did not answer, but her slow gaze rested with a kind of blank despair upon the signet ring still lying on the table in front of the case of wax fruit, as if to emphasize artificially the dread reality the signet ring proclaimed.

"He walked sooner than any of the rest of you, before he was a year old even," Lady Hirlpool said, trying to polish her nails with her lipstick and then looking in astonishment at the result. "Ronnie . . . " She turned abruptly and fiercely upon Bobby. "You've got to find out," she told him, as nearly shouting as her thin old voice permitted.

"I'll try, granny," Bobby answered.

He went on asking questions. He learned little more, however. Lord Hirlpool had already told all he knew. Chris explained that, like Norris, he had heard nothing of or from Ronnie since the scandal, but then he had never been on very intimate terms with Ronnie. Ronnie, like many other people, had a strong dislike for weaknesses to which he was not prone himself, and he had expressed open disapproval of some of Chris's business methods and of those dexterous flirtations by which occasionally he supported them. Cora was able to produce a few newspaper cuttings from which Bobby learned such details as the names of the life and of the accident insurance companies concerned, and the address of the flat that had been the scene of the tragedy; a photograph of Ronnie just before his disappearance she allowed Bobby to take possession of; and finally the name and address of the business in the City mentioned at the inquest as that of which the dead man had been the principal.

"The E. & O.E. Development Syndicate," Bobby read out. "Bit of a rum name—Errors and Omissions Excepted. Might mean anything: being funny, warning, or sheer cynicism."

"The coroner remarked on it," observed Lord Hirlpool, who was glancing through the newspaper cuttings. "He said it appeared to be an outside stockbroker's business. He was trying to find out if there was any suggestion of financial trouble, and apparently a clerk produced the books to show there wasn't; quite fair profits had been made."

"Well, why not?" asked Norris, and added in not too pleasant a voice: "Ronnie knew a good thing all right when he saw it."

"He never had anything to do with the Stock Exchange except just once," Cora said. "He said he never would again. He used to say: 'Once a mouthful, twice shy.'"

"Still, when he found himself at a bit of a loose end, the fact that he had done so well with those gold-mine shares might make him think of trying again," Bobby remarked.

"Only I don't see where he got the capital from—unless he had more with him than £50."

"I am sure he hadn't," Cora said. "I got someone who understands accounts to go through his papers and things. He couldn't possibly have had more."

Bobby thought the possibility existed, though perhaps not the probability. But a man may always have sources of income he does not choose to put down in his accounts. It was not likely, perhaps, but it was a point that had to be remembered. Chris remarked:

"He may have got in touch with some pal who had coin to spare."

"Everyone who knew him has been questioned, apparently," Bobby pointed out. "What was the name of that clerk who gave evidence? I should like to hear what he has to say."

"His name's Albert Brown. Elderly man, lives in Earling," Lord Hirlpool said, referring to the newspaper cutting.

Bobby made a note of name and address in his pocket-book, and remarked:

"Jolly difficult when it's all so long ago. This chap may be dead by now or Lord knows where."

The fact that so long an interval of time had elapsed since the occurrence of the events he was to investigate made Bobby's mood somewhat gloomy as he returned to Scotland Yard for official confirmation of his uncle's statement that he was to be released from other duties in order to concentrate his energies on this affair. In criminal investigation a time-lag of a few minutes is often of such importance as to make the difference between success and failure, and here there was an interval, not of minutes, but of months.

At the Yard, Bobby found things even worse than he had feared. It was a special message that had come through from the living lips of the Home Secretary himself, instructing that he was to be detailed for this investigation, and Bobby knew that henceforth and forever he would be known as the "Home Sec's Own." He could only hope passionately that the next election would hurl this Government and all connected with it into outer darkness, and so return the Home Secretary to that obscurity from which office lifts the transitory politician. He made himself as humble and small as he could when, in preparation for the duty assigned him, he proceeded to hand over the various affairs he was dealing with at the moment to a very sniffy colleague, who went, indeed, so far as to ask when he expected to be promoted Assistant Commissioner. But for this insult his colleague preferred to offer abject and instant apology rather than accept Bobby's heated invitation to have it out then and there in the gymnasium with six-ounce gloves.

He was still in rather a depressed mood when late in the afternoon—for all this had taken time—he left the Yard to begin his task. A bus took him in a few minutes into the City, to the address given as that of the E. & O. E. Syndicate. He found another firm in occupation. Apparently the syndicate had vacated these offices soon after the Islington tragedy, and, as they had paid their rent and all other liabilities, no one had taken any great interest in their movements. Bobby discovered one tenant of a neighboring office who remembered vaguely Mr. Ronald Oliver, and thought the photograph of Ronnie Owen that Bobby showed was very like him. He thought, but was not sure, that there had been a staff of two, a man and a girl, but he had never noticed them much, and at this distance of time was quite unable to give any description of either of them, though he did seem to recollect that the girl was quite pretty. He thought, too, he had heard, or perhaps he had merely taken it for granted, that owing to the death of Mr. Ronald Oliver the business had been taken over by some other firm.

That was the sum total of the information patient inquiry, continued till the close of business hours, produced from such neighboring tenants as even remembered the existence of the E. & O. E. Syndicate.

By now the great evening homeward trek was in progress, so Bobby joined it, and, arriving at Ealing, was not much surprised to find the address given there as that of Mr. Albert Brown to be a lodging house, where no recollection remained either of Mr. Brown or of his sojourn there, except that it must have been brief. Deciding that it was too late now to do much more that evening, Bobby got something to eat and then returned home to his rooms, announced that he was going to bed as a precaution against interruption, and, in pyjamas and a dressing-gown, reclining in an armchair with his legs on another, a pipe between his teeth, gave himself up to meditation.

"Queer work somewhere," was the not very fruitful result of his musings when, somewhere about midnight, he gave it up and went to bed.

In the morning he took himself off to Islington, to the block of working-class flats where the tragedy had happened, and there the photograph he had with him of Ronnie

Owen was soon recognized as being that also of the self-styled Ronald Oliver whose dreadful end had naturally made a deep impression in the neighborhood, and caused him to be well enough remembered, even at such a distance of time.

"Very pleasant gentleman," was the general verdict. "A gentleman as was a gentleman." Occasionally was added, "No one's enemy but his own," and this Bobby soon found had reference to Ronnie's old weakness of over-indulgence in alcohol. But this was always passed over very lightly as something that might easily happen to anyone. Bobby, however, made a mental note of the fact that no one appeared to remember having ever seen Ronnie in such a state of helplessness as one would expect in a man capable of drowning himself in his own bath in boiling water. "One over the nine" or "jolly" or "a bit squiffy" were the expressions generally used, and one or two added that he had never been what you would call "really drunk." In fact, the good old rule that only those were drunk who stayed under the table, not those who "from the floor could rise to drink again," appeared still the guiding principle here.

Another point that seemed to be fully established, and that seemed to be of interest, was the strong evidence that on the fatal night Ronnie had returned alone and had no visitor later, so that he must have been alone when the accident happened—as, indeed, was indicated by his preparations for taking a bath before retiring to bed. The general impression seemed to be, indeed, that Ronnie had had few visitors at any time, though one woman Bobby talked to did remember that a gentleman had called once or twice. But her recollection did not go beyond a vague impression that he was a real gentleman—"quite the nob"—and an equally vague memory of an incident when he had dropped his eyeglasses on the stone floor of the corridor and broken them and seemed much annoyed.

Bobby reflected that this was but a slender clue. Probably a good many tens of thousands of people in London wore eyeglasses. He inquired about the charwoman Ronnie had employed, but not many of the residents employed such help, and no one knew her address or anything about her. At last, however, a stroke of luck came his way, for he found a woman who could give him Mrs. Oliver's Bournemouth address. It seemed Mrs. Oliver had asked her to send on any letters that might arrive. None had in fact been received, and none had therefore been sent on, but the notebook in which the address had been entered was there, and Bobby was quite welcome to copy it out. But, when asked for a personal description of Mrs. Oliver, the good woman who owned the notebook shook her head.

"It's more than a year ago," she pointed out. "I only saw her once or twice, and I don't remember a thing about her except that she had scarf, gloves, handbag, all in Princess Marina green to match, and toning with the silk trimming on her hat, which was one of those dinky close-fitters you wore all to one side that have gone out now—all very smart. She had a leopard-skin coat, very smart, too, must have cost a pretty penny, with a white silk blouse underneath, and tweed skirt, and reptile skin shoes, and her hair was in a roll at the back of the neck, not waved like most is. But there, it's more than a year ago, you can't expect me to remember much about her, can you? And her and him having been separated so long, you couldn't expect her to feel it the way you and me would. I'm sure I'm sorry I can't tell you anything about her, but the gospel truth is, if she walked into this room this minute I should never know who it was."

A slightly awestruck Bobby had been rapidly noting down the details given. Now he thanked her profusely, asked her to let it be known as widely as possible that anyone able to give him the address of Mr. Oliver's charwoman would be rewarded with a pound note, and then, having exhausted all apparent sources of information in that neighborhood, went off for luncheon to a restaurant he was careful to see was provided with a telephone. There he put through a call to the Bournemouth police, and was presently summoned from his meal to receive a reply to the effect that the address given was that of a large popular boarding house. That did not surprise him, and when, in response to his request, he was put through to the boarding house itself, he was equally not surprised by the information that a Mrs. Oliver had certainly stayed there during the March of the preceding year, but had not returned, nor was anything known of her. She had, of course, left her address—guests were always asked for their addresses—and they would look it up. When it came through, Bobby looked more thoughtful still, as he saw that it was that of the flat where Ronnie Owen had died so strangely and so horribly with an insurance on his life of £20,000 that strangers had drawn.

CHAPTER IV

THE BERRY, QUICK SYNDICATE

All this telephoning to and fro had taken time, so that it was late in the afternoon before Bobby was able to make his next call at the office of the insurance company with which the life of the self-styled Ronald Oliver had been insured.

Here, after he had explained his business and shown his credentials, he was admitted to an interview with the manager, who remembered the case very well and promised to have all the documents concerning it produced ready for Bobby's inspection by the next afternoon.

"Everything seemed quite in order," the manager said thoughtfully. "We made inquiries, of course; we gave it careful consideration; but in the end we saw no alternative to paying. Everything seemed in order."

"I suppose a marriage certificate was produced?" Bobby asked.

"Oh, certainly. Naturally that would be required. The deed of separation was shown us, too, to explain why so heavy an insurance had been thought necessary. I went through all the documents myself, and they all seemed quite in order. And yet . . . and yet . . . "

He lapsed into silence, and Bobby said:

"You weren't altogether satisfied?"

"There was nothing we could lay a finger on. And yet . . . "

Again he was silent. Bobby waited patiently, and in the

silence it seemed as though slowly there crept upon the room the shadow of dark and dreadful tragedy, till all the drab paraphernalia there of modern business grew significant with secret horror. The manager stirred uneasily, as though he, too, felt something of the sort. He said:

"We were all uncomfortable about it, distinctly uncomfortable . . . and yet we hardly knew why. There was nothing definite. The address seemed peculiar. A working-class block of flats is not the normal residence for a man carrying a total of £20,000 insurance. But there was an explanation. Mr. Oliver was paying a fairly heavy separation allowance to his wife, and she let out he was also paying off certain debts she had contracted, so he had heavy obligations to meet and had to economize in personal expenditure. The medical evidence was satisfactory; there was no suggestion that death had been caused in any other way. There was absolute proof Mr. Oliver was alone in the flat at the time. Definitely there was nothing we could lay a finger on . . . and yet. . . . "

"There is one thing I think can be established," Bobby said, "that the woman you paid the insurance to was not his wife."

"You mean, not legally?" the manager asked. "But the marriage certificate was produced, and there's no doubt she's the person to whom the policy was assigned and in whose favor the deed of separation was drawn up. A well-known firm of solicitors was employed."

"What I mean," Bobby explained, "is that I don't think Mr. Oliver—his real name was Owen—had ever seen or heard of the woman who passed herself off as his wife. I don't mean," he added, seeing that the manager was looking still more uncomfortable, and guessing he was beginning to suspect that all this meant a fresh claim might be made for money alleged to have been paid to the wrong person, "that if what I suspect turns out correct there'll be any idea of asking you to pay over again. If there were a legal claim—which I suppose is pretty doubtful—I'm quite sure the real Mrs. Owen wouldn't press it." Having emphasized this point—for he did not want to have the insurance company putting any obstacles in his way—Bobby went on: "Could you tell me what proof there was he was really alone in the flat at the time? Obviously, if that is certain, it must have been accident. You can hardly imagine anyone committing suicide like that."

"It was a point we took special notice of," the manager answered. "It happened that some people in the next flat were giving a party to celebrate the christening of their babies—twins they were. Quite a lively affair, apparently, and kept up till the small hours, with people going in and out all the time, and all knowing each other. They were quite emphatic that any stranger would have been noticed at once. And it happened that a perambulator had been bought for the babies—large size, as they were twins. There wasn't too much room in the flat, so the perambulator was put in the passage, blocking up the door of Mr. Oliver's flat, so that it had to be moved when he came. That is one reason why the fact that he was a little the worse for drink was noticed and why it was so clearly established he was alone. There was direct evidence, too, that the perambulator remained, blocking the way into Mr. Oliver's flat from noon till some time next morning, and that it was only moved that one time when he came home—alone. And it was clear anyone leaving the building after midnight would have been seen or heard. No stranger was noticed at any time. And yet . . . "

Bobby waited. He had a feeling there was more to come, and he watched the shadows that with an approaching storm were growing darker in the corners of the rooms. Hidden things, he thought, hidden things that needed light upon them. Abruptly the manager switched on the electricity. "The fact is," he said, "we know there was a similar case eighteen months earlier than this one."

"About three years ago?" Bobby asked gravely.

"Yes, about that. Not a risk we were carrying," explained the manager with some satisfaction. "It was the Priam people—small concern comparatively. Didn't at all like paying out £10,000 when only one premium had been paid. But it seemed a cast-iron claim. Then, too, unless there's a very strong case, it's generally wiser to pay and say nothing. Very likely, even if you succeed, you find the costs come to more than the claim would have done, and it's no advantage to a company to appear in the courts contesting claims. Besides, a good many people are nervous as it is about insuring themselves; no need to put it into their heads unnecessarily that they are going to be murdered. Naturally we should take action at once if we were sure, but we can't risk making a mistake."

"I quite see that," observed Bobby, feeling this meant that insurance companies preferred to pocket losses rather than risk scandals.

He asked one or two more questions, laid a little gentle emphasis on his special interest in the marriage certificate to be produced, and then went off to the office of the Prior

Insurance Company, an old-established and well-thought-of but comparatively small concern. Here, too, after explaining his errand, he was admitted to the presence of the manager, who, it appeared, remembered very well the case in question.

"It was just after I took over from my predecessor," said the Priam manager. "I remember it well enough; there was some grumbling at the next board meeting. But there was nothing we could do—nothing we could lay hold of. And yet . . . "

"And yet . . . ?" repeated Bobby questioningly.

"One of the board wanted us to refuse payment," the manager went on. "I had to advise against it. Not a shred of substantial evidence; and probably a full inquiry and fighting the case would have cost more than the claim, with no prospect of recovering costs even if we had won."

He went on to give details, promising at the same time that all the papers dealing with the case should be ready the next day for Bobby to examine. It appeared the victim had been a young Australian named Will Priestman. He had insured his life in his father's favor for £7,000, that being the sum advanced by his father to purchase a controlling share in a Japanese imports agency known as the Yen Developments Syndicate.

"Rather an odd name," commented Bobby, remembering the E. & O. E. Syndicate.

"It was a short-term policy," the manager continued; "ten years—to cover the risk of anything happening to young Priestman during that time and the business having to be sold again, probably at a loss. It was explained to us that at the end of the ten years the elder Priestman's loan would probably have been paid back. Young Priestman also carried a £3,000 insurance policy, as well as another £1,000 given by the proprietors of a popular diary to everyone who bought it and filled up a coupon and paid a small registration fee."

"Eleven thousand pounds in all," Bobby said.

The manager agreed. Then young Priestman had been found dead in his bath in the flat he occupied alone in the West End, where it had to be admitted he had been living somewhat riotously. But none of his disreputable associates appeared to have any interest in his death, and it was proved that none had been near the flat on the day of the tragedy. The weather had been exceptionally warm—a heat wave towards the middle of September—and the doctors suggested that possibly the young man had entered the bath while hot and perspiring, and that the shock of the cold water had brought on a fainting fit. No other cause of death was discovered, and a verdict of "Accidental Death" was returned, the jury adding an expression of sympathy with the elder Mr. Priestman, who, it was mentioned in the newspaper accounts, had shown great emotion in court.

"Quite a painful scene," the manager told Bobby.

Bobby asked if the manager could give any description of Mr. Priestman. He got no very clear reply. It was so long ago. The only interesting detail remembered was that Mr. Priestman had worn beard and moustache, and this fact had apparently tended to soothe suspicion as going to confirm his claim to be an Australian—the manager apparently thought that all Australians lived in the bush, far from civilization, and would have little time or opportunity for such refinements as shaving.

"There was nothing to lay hold of," he concluded.

"And yet . . . " said Bobby.

"Precisely," said the manager.

"Could you give me the address of the Yen Developments Syndicate?" Bobby asked.

"I can get it for you if you like," the other answered, "but I don't think you will find it any help. The business was wound up after young Priestman's death, and the father returned to Australia. I may say that, as we were a little troubled about the case, we—er—kept in touch with him without—er—his knowledge. There's no doubt about his having sailed for Australia a few weeks after his son's death."

Bobby thought to himself that keeping in touch with a person without that person's knowledge sounded much less crude than just saying watch had been kept upon him.

"Was anything said at the inquest about the financial position of the syndicate?" Bobby asked.

"It wasn't too satisfactory, but there was nothing to suggest young Priestman had been worrying about that. In fact, he had been neglecting it and enjoying himself. The elder Mr. Priestman admitted that £7,000 had been an excessive price to pay; and I gathered that most of the insurance money would have to go to clear off liabilities. He let us see the books, as well as the documents concerning the sale of the business. Everything seemed most satisfactory, quite straightforward. And yet . . . "

Bobby waited. The room was very quiet; again it was as though the silence of death itself brooded there on the big roll-top desk, the telephones, the files, all the common everyday appurtenances of everyday business. The manager said, half to himself:

"Yesterday one of the Universal people was in to see me about some business. He happened to mention a case they had about six months back. It was very similar. A youngish man drowned in his own bath. He carried £5,000 life and £15,000 accident, both with the Universal. At the inquest there was evidence he had complained of not sleeping well and that he had been taking veronal or some such drug. The Universal wasn't at all happy about it. But there's nothing you can do without proof, and they had to pay."

"I think I'll slip round and see them," Bobby said.

"I'll give them a ring to let them know you're coming," the manager volunteered. "For us a case is closed when the check has once been cleared. But if there's been any crooked work, the whole profession would be glad to see it cleared up."

Thanks to the friendly offices of the manager of the Priam, Bobby was admitted without delay to the presence of the chief of the Universal. He remembered the case well, and gave Bobby details very similar to those he had already listened to twice that day. The name of the dead man had been Samuel Sands. The insurance had been in favor of his partner, a Mr. Alfred Briggs, to compensate for the capital Mr. Briggs would have to refund to the Sands family, represented by a Mrs. Ellis, his sister. Everything had seemed quite in order; all necessary documents were produced at once. No suspicion whatever had been roused at the time that the affair had been anything but pure accident. It was of the essence of the insurance business to be prepared to meet such unexpected losses.

Bobby agreed, and secured the address of the business, of Mr. Alfred Briggs, and of Mrs. Ellis. The business was that of a metal merchant, and Bobby got permission to use the Universal office telephone to make a few inquiries. He was not altogether surprised to find that the metal merchant business had been closed down, the premises were vacant, and no one knew what had become of the late tenants, nor was he more astonished when he found that Mr. Briggs had been a resident of Ealing, but that the address given was that of a flat consisting of three rooms on the top floor of one of those large old-fashioned houses that, as it is difficult to find occupants for them, have now in all the London suburbs been turned into flats. The apartment had never been occupied, however, as Mr. Briggs was staying at an hotel until his wife arrived from the north, and when she did arrive she disliked the flat so much that Mr. Briggs had paid another week's rent in lieu of notice, surrendered the key, and vanished, whither no one knew.

"Looks very much like an accommodation address," Bobby remarked.

Mrs. Ellis had given her address at a small Hampstead hotel. But over the phone Bobby was informed that she had never occupied her room, which she had secured, not for herself, but for a friend expected from Australia. The friend had never arrived, the room had never been occupied, Mrs. Ellis had been very apologetic, had paid the bill without a murmur, had collected one or two letters that had come for her, and so had disappeared into the wide world, as hotel guests do, leaving no more behind than a vague memory and an entry in the hotel books. Mrs. Ellis had, of course, been asked for her address, and Bobby was given it. It sounded familiar, and, referring to his notebook, he assured himself it was that of the Islington flat in which the man he was now convinced was his cousin, Ronald Owen, had met his dreadful death.

"I suppose," Bobby said, returning from all this telephoning to the manager's office to thank him, "I suppose there's no one here who could give me any description of this Mr. Briggs or of Mrs. Ellis?"

The manager did not think so, but he would inquire. He had never seen Mr. Briggs, but he had had an interview with Mrs. Ellis, who had been the claimant for the benefits due under the accident policy. But he remembered nothing much about her.

"It's months ago, and one sees so many people," he said. "A nice little woman, tall and dark, I think, unless I'm confusing her with someone else; spoke with an Australian accent; very like the Cockney twang, you know. Nervous, I thought; very natural in the circumstances. I remember one thing—that the coat she was wearing seemed quite out of keeping with her rather shy, quiet manner. It was one of those flashy leopard-skin affairs."

"Was it, though?" Bobby exclaimed, with a sudden catch in his breath. "Do you know, I half expected that."

"There's something else," the manager went on, "you may care to know, as you seem interested."

"Oh, I am," agreed Bobby grimly.

"Naturally I come in contact with a good many in the insurance line, and the other day one of the Spread Wings representatives—very good concern, old established and progressive, a most energetic outside staff—told me he had just put through a £10,000 short-term policy and a £10,000 accident on the life of a Mr. Percy Lawrence in favor of a Mr. Andrew Berry. Lawrence has bought an outside stockbroking business—the Berry, Quick Syndicate—from Mr. Berry, and the insurance is to cover the risk of Lawrence's dying before the payment for the business is completed."

"What," Bobby asked, almost incredulously, "what did you say the syndicate was called?"

"The Berry, Quick—Mr. Quick was Mr. Berry's former partner, I think. Yes, the Berry, Quick Syndicate," he repeated, and only when he had thus repeated the name a second time did he seem to notice its significance.

In silence the two men looked at each other across the office table.

"Good God," the manager muttered then, "bury quick. That can't . . . it must . . . I mean, no one could, could they? Not play on words like that. Not possible."

Bobby made no comment. He got to his feet, a little pale, too. Even he could hardly believe the mocking, ghastly challenge in that name could be intentional. He said:

"I think I had better go round to the Spread Wings office and get the address of these people with the—funny name."

"Yes. Yes," agreed the manager. He added sadly: "Our check has been cleared, and for us the case is closed."

"But not closed, I think," Bobby remarked, as he took his leave, "for this Mr. Percy Lawrence, though I hope he is not in the habit of taking too many baths."

CHAPTER V

A FACTORY OF DEATH

All these inquiries had eaten up the day; and once again had come that blessed hour of relief when the City empties itself to suburb and country. But the address given him as that of the Berry, Quick Syndicate was not far from the office of the Spread Wings Insurance Company, and Bobby thought he would go and have a look at it, even though most likely the staff of the syndicate had departed.

A few minutes' walk took him to the building designated—one of those huge blocks of offices a simple-minded optimism caused to be erected in days when increase of business seemed nature's inevitable law, and only King Solomon's ignorance prevented him from adding purchasing demand as a fifth to his list of the four things that say not "It is enough." This particular building was more prosperous than most, though, for it was occupied to nearly half its capacity. A lift took Bobby to the eighth or ninth floor, where, at the end of a corridor he had begun to think interminable—he had ascended by the northeast battery of lifts instead of by the southwest by west lot—he found two doors, one marked, "Berry, Quick Syndicate—Please Enter," and the other, less hospitably, "Berry, Quick Syndicate—Mr. Percy Lawrence—Private." Both doors were locked, and Bobby's knock remained unanswered. He was still standing there, deep in thought, and had been for longer than he realized, when he heard an approaching step. It was that of a man who was evidently a caretaker or watchman employed in the building, and who was now engaged in testing the various doors of the different offices to see that none had been left unlocked. To Bobby this man said:

"Everyone on this floor gone home."

"I suppose so," agreed Bobby. "These Berry, Quick Syndicate people been here long?"

The caretaker put his head on one side and looked Bobby up and down very carefully.

"Police?" he asked.

"Why? What makes you ask that? Noticed anything wrong?"

"Not so as you would mention," the caretaker answered, "only I know we had a bit of trouble over their refs. If you ask me, we wouldn't never have took 'em only for being that hard up for rentals we would take Old Nick himself if he paid a half-year in advance. But they haven't hardly any post, nor any callers neither, except for canvassers and suchlike you might as well try to keep out as keep flies from a sweet shop—and the office can say what it likes."

"You don't think the syndicate does a great deal of business, then?"

"Well, there was something went wrong with the phones all along this side of the corridor—three suites vacant and the one the Berry, Quick Syndicate has—and never a complaint and nothing known about it for near a week. So there can't have been a call in or out all that time. It was the young lady in our private exchange told us that, her having thought all must be vacant along here."

"Certainly doesn't sound as if business were booming," agreed Bobby.

"It was what made me take notice of their post," explained the caretaker. "We have to keep an eye on new rentals in case there's any funny work going on. Why, we had a case once when a bloke took an office next to a nudist propaganda company, and bored a hole in the party wall to see what was going on—which was nothing, and less than anyone can see any day on Brighton Beach."

"Just as well to be careful," agreed Bobby. "Do you know what staff is employed?"

"There's Mr. Lawrence what's the boss and a young lady typist. Very quiet gentleman, Mr. Lawrence, and, if you ask me, bit too fond of crooking his elbow—not that I've ever seen him with more than he could carry comfortable. Looks it though, if you see what I mean! sort of dazed-like, lost look to him. Young lady very smart, like all of 'em are; goes with the typing some way. Lumme, my missis says you can study the fashions here all right, and see the latest hats at nine a.m. and six p.m. long before the swagger shops up West are on 'em, especial this young lady when she first come, with her leopard-skin coat you could see the eyes of all the other girls bulge at the sight of, and never came from any typing machine, as my missis said herself, and Miss Andrews—her at our private phone exchange—said so, too."

"I suppose leopard-skin coats are a bit expensive," Bobby agreed, giving no sign of how much this second reference to a leopard-skin coat interested him. "Well, there's my card. You see, you were right. I am from the police."

"Blooming sergeant, eh?" said the caretaker, reading the card with respect. "C.I.D. too. Lumme, I ain't seen a split since I got as near as maybe run in year before last when your chaps raided the 'Slap Up' Club when I was having a quiet drink after hours. I was in a cupboard under the stairs like winking," he added with satisfaction; "three hours there, and nearly smothered, too."

"Oh, yes, we always try to be tactful," agreed Bobby; "if we've got a good enough haul, that is. After all, three hours' stifling in a cupboard under the stairs does deserve some consideration."

The caretaker looked gloomy at this point of view, and then asked, nodding towards the syndicate offices:

"Them lot been up to anything? If there is, we'd like to know."

"Oh, no, it's only a case of making inquiries," Bobby explained. "There's some information they may be able to give us. Nothing to do with them, so far as we are aware, but there are things they may be able to tell us. But, of course, that doesn't mean they are concerned themselves."

"Of course it don't," agreed the caretaker, obviously meaning that of course it did.

"Be careful not to say anything to anyone," Bobby warned him sternly. "You understand all this is strictly confidential?"

"Not a word, you can trust me," declared the caretaker, his eyes bright and eager, his lips visibly twitching, so that Bobby knew there was about as much chance of his keeping what he had heard to himself as of a wide-mouthed jug keeping its contents to itself when held upside down. Still, one had to try. Bobby took a ten-shilling note out of his pocket and smoothed it slowly between his fingers, while the caretaker watched with interest.

"I shall hope," said Bobby thoughtfully, "to be satisfied

by this day next week that nothing has been said to anyone." Briskly he put the ten-shilling note back in his pocket, whither the eyes of the caretaker followed it longingly. "This day next week," he repeated.

"You can trust me," the caretaker affirmed, with a note of gentle reproach in his voice. "Anyone could. I never was one to talk. Just like an oyster I am, and always have been."

As Bobby's impression was the exact opposite, the ten-shilling note remained in his pocket, and he decided to try an additional curb.

"Very likely we're quite on the wrong track," he said, "and there are such things as actions for slander—or complaints to bosses about spreading gossip."

The caretaker looked very offended indeed.

"Such has never been with me," he said stiffly. "Gossip is what none could ever say of me, however spiteful or wanting to be nasty. Why, my missis, she says: 'Don't you never hear nothing spicy where you work?' and I says: 'My dear, if so be I did, mum would be the word, same as duty calls.' "

"Then that's all right," Bobby interrupted, "and I needn't worry. A careless word makes a lot of trouble sometimes, you know, even when it seems it couldn't possibly matter. Well, I must be off now. Elevator still working?"

"No, it ain't," retorted viciously the still-offended caretaker. "You might get it on the fifth," he added, relenting a little.

"Oh, well, if it's running that far, perhaps it'll come up here, too," observed Bobby cheerfully.

The caretaker took himself off, still grumbling his offended dignity. The elevator duly arrived in answer to a pressed button, and, as he sank earthwards, Bobby's thoughts were very busy. It was too late to do anything more that day, and he was still deep in thought as he made his way homeward. Short as was the time since he had begun this investigation, he had already learned much. Impossible, he thought, that such a sequence of tragedies as this that he had heard of, all of sudden deaths of heavily insured persons, all occurring in baths, could have an innocent explanation. The arm of coincidence is not so long as that, and he remembered the "Brides in the Bath" case he had read about. There were resemblances between that case and this, though this seemed upon a bigger and a bolder scale, and though this time apparently all the victims were men, while in the other affair all had been women. Easier, he supposed, to secure heavy insurances upon a man.

But it was going to be very difficult to secure proof. Each time the death had been certified as accidental by verdict of a coroner's jury. One case was nearly three years old, one fifteen months, one six months—and in much less than six months clues are lost, witnesses disappear, facts get covered up, details forgotten. For guilt there is no cloak like the lapse of time.

It was true, careful examination of the different documents the different companies had promised to place at his disposal might provide additional information it would be possible to follow up. Already there were interesting and significant facts jotted down in his notebook. For instance, this Mr. Percy Lawrence had recently taken out a heavy insurance on his own life. Did that mean he was the next destined victim? Or did it, as Bobby grimly surmised, mean that somewhere another "Lawrence" waited unsuspectingly a fate for which preparations were already being made? Already Bobby felt sure a good deal of impersonation had been practised in these cases. It was certain, for instance, someone else must have taken Ronnie's place for the insurance company's medical examination.

Though if in fact Mr. Percy Lawrence were meant himself to be the next in this long trail of death, and if that could be demonstrated to him, the investigation would become easier. He would presumably know his life had been insured, and for whose benefit.

The history and identity of the wearer of the leopard-skin coat would have to be investigated, too.

Then the machinery of the Yard would have to be set to work in an attempt to discover the identity of the different victims. Probably all of them had lived—and died—under false names, as had Bobby's unfortunate cousin, Ronnie. The lists of men who disappear every year would have to be gone through carefully, though it was likely enough that they were all men who, as Ronnie had done, had cut themselves off for one reason or another from their former friends and acquaintances, and for whom, therefore, no inquiry had been made. To this day no one had been able to identify the body of the victim in the Rouse case; no one could say whose was the headless body found in a trunk at Brighton.

One thing seemed certain. Each of these deaths had been most carefully arranged.

CHAPTER VI

THE PLAIN TYPIST

THAT EVENING Bobby spent pouring over the notes he had made during the day, trying to co-ordinate them, comparing every detail, asking himself, for instance, if there were significance or mere coincidence in the fact that in two of the tragedies the names of one witness called had had "A. B." for its initial letters. He noticed, too, how often the addresses mentioned were in Ealing, and how none of them seemed to be permanent but always of a lodging house or hotel of some sort or else of a vacated flat, while the address of the Islington flat had been given often. Then, too, there was the leopard-skin coat worn by the woman who had passed herself off as Ronnie's wife. Apparently a similar coat—or was it the same?—had been worn by the typist engaged by the Berry, Quick Syndicate that, according to the caretaker, did so little business it hardly needed a typist at all. No doubt, Bobby reflected, there were plenty of similar coats being worn by various women in London, but he was inclined to think this must be a fairly expensive one—probably, from the description, ocelot fur—or it would hardly have attracted such respectful attention from the sharp-eyed young City women whose comments had reached the ears of the caretaker.

But Bobby knew enough of the world to be well aware that some typists, like some chorus girls, seem to be able to afford expensive furs on salaries of forty or fifty shillings a week. It did not do to jump to conclusions, and very likely the fur coat meant nothing.

Again in the morning Bobby studied his notes, and one thing that seemed even more plain to him than before was the extraordinary difficulty caused by the lapse of time. What hope was there after so long an interval of obtaining, for example, any description of the personal appearance of those who had given evidence at these inquests, or been in any way concerned?

Always, Bobby told himself, time was the detective's greatest enemy; and, looking at the clock, was startled to observe that it was nearly the lunch-hour, so that he had spent the whole morning dreaming and musing over his notes when he ought to have been up and doing. Lapse of time the detective's greatest enemy indeed, and here he was allowing it to slip by unheeded. Feeling very guilty, he seized hat and stick and made off as fast as he could, though, in spite of his haste, it was after one when he reached the City. His own appetite was in good condition, and it is elementary that the well-lunched man is more likely to be communicative than the man still hungry. Bobby decided to wait, therefore, till lunch was over, and—for he still had enough to occupy his thoughts—he lingered for some time over his own coffee and cigarette. One computation he made was that the total involved in these different cases came to something like £70,000, a total that seemed bigger and more impressive to Bobby than it had done to the insurance company officials, more used to thinking in large sums. One of them had mentioned quite casually the previous afternoon that a client of theirs—a member of the House of Lords—was insured for £400,000.

And Bobby reflected that, with a profit of £70,000 in view—paid down in cash, too; none of your jewelry to be sold at a tenth of its value, none of your traceable securities to be dealt with only at risk and heavy discount—it was easy to understand the elaborate organization, the careful, long-distance planning, the trouble taken to provide all necessary documents, that these cases seemed to show.

But surely, Bobby thought, this Mr. Percy Lawrence, in charge, apparently, of the operations of the Berry, Quick Syndicate, would be only too ready, once he understood what apparent peril he himself stood in, to help to unravel what in Bobby's eyes was beginning to take on the semblance of a murder plot of an audacity and on a scale unparalleled. Lawrence would have to be handled with tact, since there was at least the possibility that he was implicated in the previous cases, in which event his own neck might be in danger. Nor are the officers of the Crown too eager to accept the evidence of an accomplice if doing so can possibly be avoided. But Bobby thought Lawrence much more likely to prove the new destined victim rather than a former accomplice, or why this heavy insurance on his life? There was, of course, the possibility that the insurance was merely a blind, and that Lawrence was in fact responsible for everything that had happened.

These different reflections, and the planning out in his mind of the best course to follow in the forthcoming conversation with Lawrence, occupied him so long that it was three o'clock before Bobby at last arrived before that door whereon was inscribed the name of the Berry, Quick Syndicate and the cordial invitation to "Please Enter."

Accepting, accordingly, the invitation, and without waiting for any reply to his knock, Bobby pushed open the door and went in. He found himself in a small, box-like compartment, formed by temporary partitions, and cut off by them from the larger office, of which plainly it had been meant to form a part. As the partitions did not reach to the ceiling by at least a foot, the kind of entrance-lobby or cubby-hole they made received over them plenty of air for ventilation but not enough light to save the necessity of keeping an electric bulb burning. On his right as Bobby entered was a large roll-top desk, with a slide extension for a typewriter, whereat was seated a woman whom at first he took to be middle-aged or more, till it dawned upon him she was young—not more than twenty-five or so. She was busy, not with her typewriting, but with some needlework. He noticed that it was not knitting—girls in City offices not infrequently indulge in knitting when work is slack—but something that looked as if it required much greater skill and attention, and he thought idly that it must be trying to the sight to do such work by this not very good artificial light.

He saw now, too, that his first mistaken impression of her age had been given him by her sallow and worn complexion, which indeed was in a dreadful condition, blotched, pimply, unhealthy-looking in the extreme. He thought vaguely that perhaps she suffered from some skin disease that made the use of cosmetics impossible for her, and then he told himself, as he looked at her more closely, that but for the unfortunate condition of her skin and for the unbecoming way in which her hair was done—drawn back tightly from her forehead, to be knotted in a kind of tight bun behind—but, in fact, for an almost defiant neglect of every feminine art and grace, she could easily have passed for an unusually pretty girl. Bobby had some slight artistic gift—he had a really good sense of form, though his feeling for color was defective—and he was able to appreciate the fine shape of the head, well set upon a slender neck, the regularity and harmony of the features, a grace and balance apparent even in her seated position. It struck him that a visit or two to a beauty parlor would turn very quickly this extremely plain duckling into a swan scarcely to be recognized as the same creature. He also became aware that she had slipped her needlework, wrapped in the tissue paper that protected it, into a drawer, and was now regarding him with a gaze passionate and strange in its fierce intensity of question. But no question came, though he waited for it. She put her hand—he saw it was a slender, well-shaped hand—before her face once or twice with an odd kind of movement, as though to brush away something hanging there. Once or twice she blinked, as if again her eyes could not endure the strength of inquiry and demand she put into them, but she still did not speak. At last Bobby said:

"I wanted to see Mr. Lawrence. He is your manager, I think. Is he disengaged?"

Even yet she did not answer, and more and more Bobby was aware how tremendously the whole force and content of her being was concentrated in her gaze directed upon him. Yet its meaning baffled him. He did not know whether it was hostile or no; whether it held menace, or passionate appeal, or what. Her whole body, too, had tightened itself there beneath his eyes, like a spring invisibly coiled back upon itself. He understood with certitude there was something she experienced and yet controlled with an almost dreadful energy, though what that could be he had no more idea than has the traveller in a strange land of what is meant by the trumpet peal he hears sounding from afar.

His first idea was that this emotion, whatever might be its cause, was too powerful, too powerfully felt, not to find relief in word or action. Knife-thrust or pistol-shot would hardly have surprised him, so much an outlet seemed needed and natural, or a cry of help wrung from uttermost despair. He was all prepared as he leaned forward. He put one hand on the roll-top desk. He said:

"Yes . . . yes."

In an instant she changed. The awful fire vanished from her eyes. They blinked mildly. Again she passed her hand before them with that odd action as of brushing away some web or veil that hung there. The tension and vitality went from her body; her whole personality seemed to shrink.

"Have you an appointment?" she asked. Her voice was low and pleasant and carried well; she had forgotten apparently to be careless with her voice, or more probably had never thought of it. "I am afraid Mr. Lawrence is engaged at the moment, but I am sure he will be very pleased to see you if you can wait. There is one other gentleman first, or, if you prefer to call again, I can make an appointment."

"Mr. Lawrence seems busy," Bobby remarked, still watching her closely, more bewildered than ever by this sudden and complete change in her, thinking, too, that these demands on Mr. Lawrence's time did not accord well with his previous information that the Berry, Quick Syndicate had so few callers and did so little business.

"Yes, very busy," she agreed, fumbling with a book

marked "Appointments" at her side. "So many of our clients insist on seeing Mr. Lawrence personally."

Bobby came to a sudden decision. Plainly, in her present mood, it was hopeless to think of getting the girl to talk. But she might change again, as quickly and as strangely as she had changed before. He said:

"Oh, if you don't mind, I'll wait. I rather wanted to see Mr. Lawrence personally, too."

"I don't think he will be long. May I have your name?" she asked, changing once again, this time to the brisk, efficient young woman of business.

He gave her his card—his private card, not his official one. She looked at it, put it down, and then spoke into an office phone at her side. She said:

"Mr. Lawrence will be delighted to see you, and won't keep you waiting long. He is so sorry he has to see another client first."

She got up from her typewriter as she spoke and opened a door in the partition just behind her into the inner apartment from which that partition cut off the little outer office in which she sat. As is often the case in the newer office buildings in London, the rooms were arranged so that their size and number could be easily altered by the arrangement of substantial partitions, strongly made and often doubled, with an air space between to prevent any possibility of sounds penetrating, but that can be swiftly put up and taken down without any risk of damaging the outer walls. The floor space rented to a business firm can, therefore, easily be arranged, after the American fashion, as one office in which the whole staff sits, or in as many separate divisions as may be preferred.

The apartment into which Bobby was now shown was large, well lit, and very comfortably furnished with easy chairs in the latest style, fitted with their own lighting, bookcases containing various works of reference, two writing-tables near the windows, and one large table in the middle of the room covered with newspapers, daily, weekly, illustrated, and financial. There was a box of cigarettes on this table, too, with the friendly exhortation above:

"Please help yourself and please us."

The day was fine and warm, sunshine streamed in at the open window, the whole air of the room, which indeed more resembled a drawing-room than a City office, was friendly, welcoming, confidence-creating. By the table stood a small, erect, brisk-looking man, elderly, very well dressed, dandified almost. His perfectly cut lounge suit whispered—too well bred, of course, to do more than whisper—Savile Row from every stitch; his gold mounted umbrella was a miracle of neat rolling; his hat and gloves were perfect; his spectacles were gold rimmed and seemed to regret there was no metal more precious to use; on one finger shone a ring whose value must have been in the three-figure order; in the cuffs of his silk shirt twinkled two diamond links; his shoes seemed as though never meant to tread the common earth. A little ostentatious, perhaps, the whole effect, and yet still within the bounds of taste and breeding. In age Bobby took him to be between forty and fifty, though very possibly some years younger. His eyes behind his glasses were bright and alert, and his every movement had a quality of swift unexpectedness that was at times even a little disconcerting, as though one could never be quite sure of his exact position. The only real sign he gave of advancing years was that his hair, dark and of unusually strong and vigorous growth, was beginning to show just a touch of gray at the temples; but, then, that is often the case with men at a comparatively early age. He was clean-shaven, a bluish tinge on the square, forward-thrusting chin suggesting that the growth of his beard, if permitted, would have been as strong and luxuriant as that of his hair. At the moment Bobby entered he was helping himself to a cigarette from the open box on the table, his hand flashing in and out with the quickness of gesture that seemed habitual to him. As he lighted the cigarette he gave Bobby a quick, all-embracing glance that seemed to take him in from top to toe, and then, as if satisfied that the newcomer was one whose existence could be recognized, he remarked:

"These City lads do themselves pretty well. I smoke this Regie brand myself, but they come a bit high, and I don't know that I should leave them about in my study for everyone who blew in to help himself as he liked."

CHAPTER VII

A DOCTOR OF PHILOSOPHY

Bobby glanced at the cigarettes and saw that they were in fact the somewhat expensive brand mentioned. The fact interested him, for, taken together with the comfortable, even luxurious, manner in which the room was furnished, it suggested that the Berry, Quick Syndicate was in no way short of capital. And yet according to the caretaker they did hardly any business and their references had not been of a nature to make the managers of the building very anxious to accept them as tenants. Indeed, had not tenants grown so scarce and rare a species, they would apparently have been politely refused accommodation. Facts to be remembered, Bobby thought, and, looking up, saw with surprise that his companion was now at one of the windows, enjoying the cigarette to which he had just helped himself and staring idly down at the busy street below.

He had moved so softly and so swiftly, with so strange a lightness of action, that Bobby had been quite unaware of it, and had thought him still standing by the table. Elderly he might be, certainly was, for age cannot wholly be disguised, but equally certainly he was still nimble as the nimblest of youths, and with no trace of that awkwardness that even nimble youths still show before they have acquired full control of their own limbs. Bobby wondered if he had been an athlete—a lightweight boxer perhaps—or it might be a dancing expert, and so had acquired that swift certainty of balance and of movement he seemed to possess.

All at once he began to laugh, a soft, rather musical laughter that gave the impression of being as entirely under control as were his bodily movements. He took off his glasses as if without them he could see better at a distance. He said:

"Jove, nearly got her." To explain his amusement, he added to Bobby: "Dear old lady scuttling across the road, and a car missed her by inches. Anyhow, the motor age is teaching the aged to leap."

"Yes," agreed Bobby, who knew too much about the statistics of the dead and injured on the roads, that Scotland Yard compiled each week, to regard any aspect of the subject as in any way amusing. "I think I'll have one of these," he added, helping himself to a cigarette.

"Why not?" said the other, and, when Bobby looked up again, he had left the window and was lolling in one of the armchairs. Once more he had shifted his position with such lightness and soft rapidity of action that Bobby had been aware of no movement, heard no sound. "After all, I suppose it's mugs like us who pay for them. But I beg your pardon. Very likely you aren't one of the great army of optimists who expect to make a fortune in the City."

"Well, I've just called to make a few inquiries," Bobby answered cautiously.

"So have I," the other observed. "Well, it's an amusement for an idle man, and generally I break even, though I'm a few hundreds down this last year or two. Must try to catch up soon." With that swift ease of movement that seemed characteristic of him, he flashed a visiting card from his pocket to the table in front of Bobby. "Introducing me," he said, with another of those soft, musical, yet controlled laughs of his.

The name on the card was Beale—Dr. Ambrose Beale—the address, The Thatched Cottage, The Hog's Back, Kent.

"Don't confuse our Hog's Back with the one near Guildford," Dr. Beale added. "Most people do. Ours is nothing like so well known, though we all think it much superior—our view is so much wider and there is the river in the distance."

"That's rather jolly," agreed Bobby, and added, chiefly for the sake of saying something: "I see you are a doctor."

Dr. Beale gave again that soft laugh of his.

"Doctor of philosophy, not of medicine," he explained, "though people who hear me called doctor often want me to prescribe them a few pills. But I never could see why doctors of medicine should have a monopoly. Music, laws, letters, philosophy, we are all doctors, too."

"Yes, of course," agreed Bobby, with the reverence due from laymen to one who had scaled the dizzy heights of doctordom. "I'm afraid it took me all my time to scrape through for a modest B.A."

"Ah, you're 'varsity," Dr. Beale said quickly, with a slight touch of surprise that was not, Bobby thought, too flattering. As if conscious of this, he added quickly: "I only meant you look more the athletic type. Examinations are a tricky business, though. A bit of luck and you might have got a double first. Now for a doctorate you only have to submit a thesis. Much fairer, in my opinion. Mine was on Spinoza's theory of monads—the monistic philosophy, you know."

"Oh, yes," agreed Bobby, still more respectfully, as he strove in a puzzled way to remember what in his university days he had learned of the different philosophies.

Dr. Beale helped himself to another cigarette.

"Sometimes people don't believe it," he remarked. "They seem to think a philosopher must be at least a hundred years old, with a beard at least a yard long, and that he ought to live in a tub. And I do draw the line at that, though if I'm not a hundred I'm getting on—sixty-five."

Bobby made polite sounds of incredulity, for, indeed it did seem to him hardly possible that a man of sixty-five should have retained the ease and swiftness of movement Dr. Beale displayed. He was, in fact, really surprised by the other's reference to his age; his whole appearance, his alert manner, his bright, quick glance, the extraordinary swiftness and lightness of his movements, all seemed to belong to a much younger personality. But, then, sixty is an age no one wishes to claim, neither young enough for adventure nor old enough for reverence, a dull, indeterminate age, indeed, to which no one would be likely to advance a false claim. So it was probably correct, however surprising, since, though time may have no bite upon the mind, the body remains its natural prey. Bobby said something polite about his companion looking much younger, and Beale gave that low laugh of his which had so much the manner of being so entirely under his control.

"Would you like to know why?" he asked. "Good wine and enough of it, good food and not too much of it. Over-eating is fatal—makes you fat." He paused to shudder at the thought, like any debutante detecting the approach of plumpness. "But you can't over-drink, because if you do you simply cease to drink and begin to swill. No drunkard can appreciate good wine. But dull food—ginger beer and cold mutton—that's fatal, too. Kills your interest in life.

Good food well cooked—it needn't be expensive—and good wine—it must be expensive, unfortunately. Make those your slogans and live to be a hundred." With his conjuring-trick air he flashed his watch from his pocket and back again. "Hope this Lawrence chap is not going to be much longer," he said. "I suppose they do a big business here, but I've another engagement as well. Generally I deal with my regular brokers—most respectable firm; their notion of a flutter is a wild plunge in Consols. So when I want a fling in gold mines I come here. My own man hardly knows gold mines exist. Generally I only risk two or three hundred, but this time I've a surprise for these people."

"Indeed," said Bobby.

"Twenty thousand," said Beale; and Bobby looked up quickly, wondering a little at the largeness of the sum, and guessing that perhaps it was a natural excitement over a prospective deal on so large a scale that was making his companion so talkative.

For the doctor of philosophy did not strike him as being of a type likely to chatter so freely in the general way.

"Twenty thousand," Beale repeated now, rolling the words on his tongue as if to get the full flavor of their meaning. "Gilt-edged securities yield too low. What does a capital of £20,000 bring in today? Five or six hundred if you're lucky. And if a woman's been used to spending a hundred a month—well, it can't be done, can it?"

"No," agreed Bobby, "only there's always the question of risk."

"Oh, I've drawn up a perfectly sound, safe list," declared the philosopher; and suddenly, Bobby hardly saw how, he was seated again in another of the armchairs with a bundle of papers on his knees. "Jolly good," he said complacently, "only, of course, my old stick of a broker can't understand. So I'm going to see what these people think of it. It's a lady I'm acting for. I'm her trustee. She's a widow, poor soul, and lost her only son very tragically some time ago."

"Indeed," murmured Bobby, beginning to be a little bored by such a stream of confidential reminiscence.

"Found dead in his bath," added Dr. Beale, and Bobby's heart nearly stopped with fear and wonder and excitement.

Dr. Beale was silent then. He was slowly turning over the papers on his knee, but less as if interested in them than as if oppressed by memory of this tragedy he had referred to. Bobby said presently, as indifferently as he could:

"Was that recently?"

"Oh, no, two or three years ago," Dr. Beale answered. "Three years to be exact. Very sad affair altogether. Most tragic. The poor woman's only son, and making a big name for himself in the City. A financial genius. She misses the liberal allowance he used to make her, too. It stopped with his death."

"Didn't he leave anything?" Bobby asked.

"Not a penny," Beale answered. "Liabilities, in fact. Very sad affair—it happened on the Continent, no one could explain how. He was found dead in his bath in a furnished villa he had taken for holidays. They thought he fainted and his head went under the water. He had a number of big schemes in hand, and he had probably been overworking. Of course, everything collapsed with his death. I can tell you I've been very careful ever since never to fill my bath too full."

"Wasn't he insured?" Bobby asked.

"Oh, heavily—£20,000, I believe, including £1,000 on a coupon from a diary they wouldn't pay because it happened out of England. His mother would have got that, I suppose, but all the rest went to the people who held the policies. I don't know why, but they tell me a life insurance policy with a good company is the most easily negotiated financial instrument there is."

"I suppose so," agreed Bobby. "Do you know what company it was?"

"Some American concern, I think. But I don't know much about it. All I'm sure of is that the mother didn't get a penny. I never understood why, but then I'm not instructed in business ways. Ask me anything about Hegel's philosophy of realism and I dare say I could talk about it for an hour or two. But ask me about business methods and I'm dumb."

Bobby thought that improbable, but he said nothing. His mind was in a whirl of doubt, confusion, even dread. Dr. Beale added:

"The poor fellow had had dealings with this firm—or, rather, with their predecessors: that's how I got in touch with them."

The door opened, and there entered the girl typist Bobby had seen before.

"Mr. Lawrence can see you now, sir," she said to Dr. Beale. To Bobby she added: "Mr. Lawrence says he's so sorry to have kept you waiting, but it's always a little difficult if no appointment's been made."

She was looking directly, even fiercely, at him as she spoke, and again Bobby was aware of that expression in her eyes he had seen before and that had then, as now, puzzled him so much. There was fear in it, but not the fear all officers of the law are familiar with in those whom at last the arm of the law has reached. There was hate, defiance, too, but a hate and a defiance different from that to which officers of the law are accustomed when their duty brings them into contact with those in whom hate and defiance are the general mood. There was desperation as well, and with that, again, Bobby, like all his colleagues, was only too sadly familiar. But it seemed as if there were in addition a kind of wild appeal and trust—almost hope—and that was less easy to understand. It was only for a second, or less than a second, that their eyes thus met; and then the girl was moving to the door of the inner office to open it for Dr. Beale to enter. With his characteristic light speed of movement Dr. Beale followed, and, as he vanished, Bobby heard a loud yet dull and curiously expressionless voice saying:

"I'm so sorry, doctor. So awfully good of you to have waited. It was Montague with me, and he's such a suspicious, cautious old beggar he would have been dead sure something was wrong if I had made even the least attempt to hurry him through the papers. It's rather a big thing—"

The girl closed the door then, shutting out the voices. She went back to her cubicle by the outer door without another glance at Bobby, though he was certain she was acutely aware of him. For a moment, indeed, he had the idea that she was going to stop and speak, and then he thought that he would speak to her himself. But he did not. The only thing he could be sure of was that she was in an intensely emotional and nervous state, and he felt it would probably be better to let that nervousness and emotion find their own vent.

Besides, he did not know in the least what to say or how to approach her. His mind was in a turmoil, and, warm as was the day, warm the sunshine streaming in by the open windows, he felt strangely cold, so that he found he was shivering slightly.

He heard a slight noise of movement behind him. Turning, he saw that the typist girl had opened her door again an inch or two and was looking at him through the crack.

"Did you want to speak to me?" he said.

She closed the door again, and almost at once he heard the clatter of her machine as she banged it to and fro at a feverish rate.

CHAPTER VIII

LINES OF APPROACH

BUT HE FOUND it difficult. The simplicity with which Dr. Beale had told his story had intensified a thousandfold the terrors it concealed. No doubt the doctor felt keenly the tragedy of a young and promising life abruptly cut short, but what did he know of the fresh light thrown by it upon what now appeared a conspiracy of murder as callous, wide-spread, and successful as any the whole dread history of crime could show?

It suddenly occurred to him that the very cigarette he was smoking might well have been bought with the proceeds and profits of what was beginning to show itself to him as a kind of murder factory. Perhaps that was why it was an expensive brand. Expense no object with death so easily transmuted into gold. With a strong effort he applied himself to clear his mind of all emotion and to consider dispassionately the facts so far established.

Of these, the first and most important was this series of deaths of men heavily insured, in each case but one the insurance on their lives being paid, not to their natural heirs, but to business associates, and in each case, too, the death occurring in a bath and arousing no open suspicion. Though, of course, it was likely enough, as Bobby knew well from his own experience, that many doubts and misgivings had been in fact aroused, even without sufficient justification being found to permit of open expression.

He noted the second fact, apparently well established, that there existed some sort or kind of connection between this series of deaths and the firm of outside brokers in whose waiting room on the eighth floor of a London office building he was now seated at his ease, smoking one of their admirable and expensive cigarettes. It was a connection, too, that explained the luck of his chance encounter with Dr. Beale, but for the fortunate coincidence of the meeting with whom nothing might ever have been heard of the further death that had apparently taken place somewhere on the Continent. A bit of luck, Bobby told himself gravely, that showed, he hoped, Providence was on his side, intending to help him.

For he realized well that the task before him had been rendered so difficult by the passage of time that to gather convincing evidence of what had happened so long ago would require for success every possible aid that diligence, luck, or brain could give. At any rate there was one quarter from which he thought it reasonable to suppose he could calculate on getting every help. The Mr. Lawrence apparently in charge here, and so ominously insured for that sum of £20,000 which seemed to run like a *leit-motiv* through all these different tales of death, could surely be relied upon to give all the information in his possession. Warning would have to be given him with tact and care, but, once he understood that he was almost certainly destined to be the next victim—or why this heavy insurance?—then evidently he should be willing to do all in his power to help, if only for the sake of his own threatened safety.

A big point in his favor Bobby felt this to be, one that promised real hope of success. For Lawrence must know how and why and by whom he had come to occupy his position.

Another thing, Bobby reflected, was plain enough—that something was already known here about his own identity. Only some degree of previous knowledge could explain the behavior of the typist girl. Not so would she have looked at any casual caller; only a degree of understanding of his identity and errand could account for the profound agitation she had displayed. But that implied also some previous knowledge of the ghastly realities this apparently commonplace business office concealed. Nor in that connection was it to be forgotten that both this girl and the woman who had passed as Ronnie's widow possessed a fur coat in what is often called "leopard skin"—one sufficiently smart and valuable to have drawn admiring comments from feminine beholders. Were they, wearers and coats, identical, then?

If so, must it be concluded that she was accomplice and decoy?

Bobby's looks grew grimmer still as he contemplated the probability. Yet there remained the enigma of her behavior, it was a little hard to reconcile with the temperament of either accomplice or decoy or even dupe. A dupe would not have been terrified, a decoy would surely have shown greater self-control, an accomplie an alarm less oddly mixed with other elements less easy to understand. Bobby told himself that she had looked at him as a drowning person might look at one holding out a lifebelt, but doubtful whether to lay hold of it might not to be to risk a worse fate still. And, even if in all this his imagination was running away with him, and her troubled looks no more than his own fancy, it was fairly certain she knew who he was.

But that could easily be accounted for, since it was likely enough the caretaker had been chattering. Bobby blamed himself for not having paid his visit earlier in the day. The affair seemed now to show itself in outline with the typist as accomplice and Lawrence as dupe and prospective victim, while behind must be concealed the personality of the prime mover and originator of the whole conspiracy.

Three lines of approach, then: Lawrence himself; Dr. Beale, who should prove a willing assistant, ready to help by telling all he knew about the death on the Continent; the girl typist, whose past would have to be investigated, a procedure likely to be fruitful, Bobby thought, and who might also, if handled with tact, be willing to tell what she knew about a business of which it was hardly possible she was quite ignorant and yet of which it was equally improbable she should turn out to be the principal.

He turned his thoughts to the consideration of another aspect of the case that he had not forgotten, though till now he had kept it in the back of his mind. Dick Norris had chanced to mention that he himself had recently taken out an insurance on his life—for £20,000. And Bobby was growing sensitive to any mention of any insurances of that amount. Moreover, he had recently shown signs of an unaccustomed affluence, even while complaining of an increasing difficulty in disposing of his golfing articles. He had moved, for instance, into a flat just off Park Lane, and, even if Park Lane no longer stands where it did, still flats in that neighborhood are not for the poor and struggling. Besides, it was known he had been speculating freely on the Stock Exchange of late.

It would be as well, Bobby decided, to have a chat with

Dick Norris. Probably Chris would know in which of the new buildings by Park Lane his flat was situated. It was only a chance, but he might have some useful information to give, and Bobby was aware of an odd curiosity and unease when he reflected on the amount of the insurance Norris had taken out. He wished it had been £10,000 or £30,000—anything but that perpetually recurring figure of £20,000.

Bobby glanced at the clock. The caretaker had asserted that the syndicate did little or no business, but they seemed busy enough this afternoon. He wondered if everyone had to wait as long for an interview as he had been obliged to do. First there had been some client or another calling on apparently important business that couldn't be hurried and needed much examining of documents. Then there was Dr. Beale, with his proposals for investing a clear £20,000—a small fortune, and, in these days, not so small either. Bobby fancied that few City firms in this time of depression would hope for a busier afternoon, or one providing better prospects. His own presence, of course, was in a sense accidental, a coincidence having nothing to do with these other transactions; but, still, he did help to keep the waiting room occupied and, of course, to the casual eye, would appear as yet another client.

Abruptly there broke upon his hearing a sound of voices from the neighboring room. He could not hear what was said, but plainly someone was in a temper, and expressing it in very loud tones. It was Dr. Beale, he thought. Something must have happened to annoy him. Bobby heard distinctly: "Insolence . . . " and then "Do you dare . . . ?"

Mingled with the louder tones was a quieter voice, trying

apparently to soothe the other. Bobby got to his feet, not quite sure what to do, ready for developments. The door opened, and Dr. Beale flashed out, and in the one movement pirouetted round to face the room he had just quitted.

"Most uncalled for . . . unheard-of impudence . . . a deliberate insult . . . " he shouted incoherently, stuttering with his indignation. Again he swung round, and his glance fell on Bobby. He said to him: "I never heard of such a thing . . . never; did you?"

Without waiting for the answer Bobby could not have given, since he had no idea what the question referred to, the angry philosopher had vanished, rather as if he had dropped through a trap door or dematerialized through the ceiling, though the echo of the slammed outer door and the quivering of the door itself showed that through it he had passed. Next moment he was back again, crossing the floor in a stride or two to the still open door of the inner office. "When I want to insure my life," he shouted into it, "I'll insure it for my own benefit, in my own way, not in yours."

Then he was gone, and the room seemed to settle once more into quiet, as does a still pool when the darting fish has left it. Bobby had a vision of the doctor transferring himself from this eighth floor to the ground level in a single bound, disdaining alike elevator and stairs. There was something almost terrifying in the extraordinary agility of his movements, as terrifying as those last words of his that seemed to suggest few clients entered here but that an insurance on their lives was suggested. A slow, dead level voice from behind said:

"I must apologize . . . "

Bobby turned. He had been gaping at the door through

which for the second time Dr. Beale had vanished. He now saw, standing in the doorway behind, a tall, strange-looking man, his hair quite gray, his eyes deep sunken beneath heavy swollen lids, his face deeply lined and utterly expressionless. The features were so regular, so well shaped, one had the idea that once he must have been extremely good-looking before he had grown so thin, so pallid, so expressionless. The breadth of his shoulders, the length of his limbs, suggested that he had possessed an unusually fine physique, but now he seemed as though borne down by a weight too great for him. Bobby noticed especially his hands, large and well shaped, with a mixture of strength and fineness, the hand of an artist and an athlete, but now so thin, almost transparent, the sunlight from in front seemed to penetrate them.

After he had uttered the three words he had already spoken, he appeared to forget both what he had meant to say and even the presence of Bobby. He stood there silently, looking straight in front from his dull, deep-sunken eyes, but not as if they saw anything there present; rather as if, forgetting all that, they were staring back into the past. Bobby's nerves were strong enough, but he felt curiously uncomfortable.

"Mr. Lawrence?" he asked, a little loudly.

The other started slightly, as if abruptly and unpleasantly recalled to the present. He made a little bow of acquiescence, and even to that common gesture he seemed to impart a dreary, chill intention.

"That is my name," he said. "You wished to see me? I am the manager of the syndicate. Will you please come in?"

He turned back into the room, and Bobby followed him. It was a comfortably furnished office apartment, like a thousand other City offices, with a Turkey carpet on the floor, chairs, writing table, a desk telephone, safe, deed-boxes, filing cabinets, and so on. Warm as was the day, an electric fire was turned full on, so that the atmosphere resembled that of a hothouse.

"Please sit down," he said, indicating an armchair.

In silence Bobby seated himself. There was stirring in his mind the strangest recollection possible—a memory of a day when he, a young constable new to the force, had been in the Central Criminal Court on some errand or another, and had listened to the stern words spoken by the grave presiding judge, banishing for five years from the world of living men one who stood before him in the dock. But that man the judge had addressed had been young, splendid in the glow of youth and strength, superb in physical perfection, and this man was gray and worn, his face lined, his tall form bent as though bowed by the passage of the years, his eyes—those of that other had been so bright and eager, ready to affront the sun itself—dull, deep-sunken, lifeless.

Bobby took his cigarette case from his pocket.

"May I smoke while we are talking?" he said. "Won't you take one?"

He put the case down, as he spoke, on the table before Lawrence. For the first time Lawrence lifted his dull gaze and looked full at Bobby. Then, with a gesture that almost seemed to say he understood, he took up the case between the tips of his fingers and pressed them hard upon it and handed it back to Bobby.

"No, thank you," he said. "I don't smoke."

CHAPTER IX

QUESTION AND ANSWER

A TRIFLE disconcerted, Bobby put back his cigarette case in his pocket. He felt that Lawrence had understood, and had quite deliberately impressed his fingerprints upon it, though whether in conscious innocence, in mockery, or in defiance, Bobby could not make up his mind.

For in the other's manner there seemed neither mockery nor defiance, and conscious innocence was a theory Bobby was not yet prepared to admit, since, for one thing, an innocence that is conscious can exist only where suspicion has been entertained, and in this case how could suspicion have been roused except by a knowledge incompatible with innocence?

Lawrence had taken his seat at his desk behind which burned the electric fire that was on this warm afternoon lifting the temperature in the room to what Bobby was inclined to think must be well over the hundred mark. But, though Bobby was perspiring freely, the lean, cadaverous Lawrence seemed quite unaffected. His worn features, so deeply lined, his dry and parchment-like skin that seemed so incongruous with his apparent youth, showed no sign of being affected by the heated atmosphere. Nor did he show any sign, either, of being still aware of Bobby's presence. He might have entirely forgotten him. Motionless he sat, his dull eyes fixed upon the wall opposite, but not as though they saw anything there. He gave the impression of being utterly withdrawn from the present, of being unaware of the future, of existing only in the past. There was something unnatural, terrifying even, in his entire withdrawal from his surroundings, almost as if he had ceased to be man, though not because he had either risen above or fallen below our common humanity, but more as if he had slipped, or been pushed, outside.

One thing at least seemed clear to Bobby: that if this place, this ordinary-looking office, were really, as he was coming to believe, a kind of twentieth-century murder den, the center of such a conspiracy of death as scarcely the criminal annals of any country could tell of, then its occupants were the strangest conceivable.

Was it possible to reconcile this dull, incurious personality that Lawrence showed with any plottings so deep and fierce as those concocted here must be? The little typist, too, with the suggestion that hung about her of a terrified bewilderment, of an appeal she dared not make, showed no sign of the qualities one would have expected in any of those associated in such a conspiracy. More and more Bobby became convinced that somewhere in the background must hide a stronger will, a more cunning mind, and that these two were only pawns. But then there was the question whether they were cognizant and willing pawns, or pawns in full meaning of the word. He said:

"I expect, Mr. Lawrence, you are wondering why I have asked to see you."

If Lawrence did entertain any such sentiment of wonder, he certainly hid it well. One might even have doubted if he had so much as heard what Bobby said, so unchanged remained his attitude, so unaltered his expression. Even when Bobby repeated his remark in a somewhat louder tone he still took no notice, still seemed utterly withdrawn into a far-off and gloomy past.

Bobby told himself that silence is a game two can play at. By experience he knew how powerfully silence and waiting work upon those whose conscience is bad, who have reason to fear the knowledge of others. Natural enough, since the instinct of fear is always to cry aloud. So Bobby, too, sat still and motionless, and the minutes passed and Lawrence gave no sign. He might have been sunk in a trance for all awareness of Bobby or of his surroundings that he showed, and yet it was not so, for when Bobby, finding perspiration caused by the heat of the room trickling down his cheeks, made a movement to wipe it away, Lawrence stirred and switched off his electric fire. Then at once he sank back into his previous abstraction.

Bobby began to find the situation growing rapidly absurd. Apparently they might sit there like two stuffed dummies forever, without Lawrence either speaking or moving. In the game of silence, Bobby felt he had to acknowledge himself badly beaten. Giving it up, he said crossly:

"There are a few questions I want to ask about your firm and your own position with it."

Again it might have been that Lawrence had not heard, only this time Bobby was well convinced he had.

"May I take it you will be willing to tell me what I want to know?" Bobby asked.

Lawrence responded by a slight negative shake of the head.

"You understand I have good reason for asking?" Bobby said. Fairly certain as he was that his identity was already known, he went on: "I am an officer of police. There is my personal card and that is my warrant card. If you refuse to answer questions, naturally certain conclusions will be drawn."

"Your conclusions are your affair, not mine," Lawrence answered slowly, dragging himself back as it were from what had seemed so like undirected, aimless contemplation of past and distant things.

"I think you may find they may become yours," Bobby answered. "Mr. Lawrence, are you sure you would not be glad of our help? I think perhaps you might be." But Lawrence took no notice, and Bobby had the feeling that he might as well have offered help to the rain driven by on the wind, or to that wind itself. He tried another way and said: "I think something happened to upset Dr. Beale just now, didn't it?"

"Yes. I meant to apologize for that. I began, I think, then I forgot," Lawrence answered in those dull, level, emotionless tones he seemed always to use. "I must apologize, too, for having kept you so long. We do not like to keep clients waiting, but it is a little difficult if no appointment has been made. One may be disengaged all day and then two or three clients will come in on top of each other, all wanting an immediate interview. I was sorry Dr. Beale took such offense, but I hardly think we are to blame."

"He seemed very much upset," remarked Bobby. "He seemed to think some suggestion made to him wasn't quite the thing."

"He didn't like what we suggested," agreed Lawrence. "We are outside brokers, which means, as I expect you know, that we are not bound by the Stock Exchange rules

—very excellent rules, no doubt, for their own purposes, but hampering business greatly. We are really a kind of private Stock Exchange of our own. We bring our clients into direct personal contact, avoiding all middlemen, so that very often they deal with each other direct on terms much better than the Stock Exchange can offer. They aim at safety; we are out for big profits. We consider that speculation and safety are contradictions, while speculation and big profits are complementary."

"Big losses, too," Bobby interposed, wondering at this sudden burst of speech, delivered in a tone that lacked all emphasis and significance, like that of a schoolboy reciting a proposition of Euclid he has learned by heart without understanding a word of it.

"It is our business to try to avoid losses for our clients," Lawrence countered. "Naturally they do occur at times; that has to be expected; it's inevitable. So we have to exercise great caution."

"Caution and speculation are contradictory, too, aren't they?" Bobby asked.

"I don't mean caution in speculating, though there's that, too," Lawrence answered. "I mean caution towards our clients, so as to be sure they understand what they are doing. We don't want to give them any chance of turning round and declaring they only intended to buy gilt-edged. Then we have to be sure as well that they have the money and that it is their own." For the first time his dry, hard voice, harsh as in a mechanical reproduction, became touched with what seemed human emotion as he went on: "We do not want the client who turns out to be the bank clerk using his employer's money—or the trustee using trust funds or anything like that, you understand," and now again his voice had gone back to its previous dull monotony.

"I think I remember," Bobby remarked, "Dr. Beale said something about trust funds while we were talking."

"Very probably," observed Lawrence. "It was a trust fund he wished to operate. He was very excited about it. He had a very carefully thought-out scheme. I had to tell him we could not possibly accept dealings in trust funds unless he gave us an indemnity. That was what annoyed him so. He seemed to think it insulting, a reflection on his honesty. Of course, that wasn't meant. We've no knowledge of the terms of the trust. It may give him full authority, as he said. It may not. We don't know; we can't know. We must protect ourselves."

"What indemnity did you suggest?" Bobby asked, a little catch in his voice, for already he felt he knew the answer.

"We suggested his taking out an insurance on his life in our favor for £20,000," Lawrence answered. "I expect you heard Dr. Beale say so."

There was a silence then, for Bobby made no comment and Lawrence seemed sunk once more in his former dim contemplation. Bobby got to his feet and went to the window. He had begun to perspire again, for he found the room still intolerably hot, so that breathing had become difficult.

"May I?" he asked, and, without waiting for the permission, he pushed the window up and leaned forward, glad to breathe the pure fresh air without.

He felt a little dizzy. He felt as if with those last words all the monstrous horrors he had before suspected had begun again to accumulate in this quiet office, to surround with an aura of terror and of dread unspeakable this dull, slow-spoken man with the lined face, the expressionless eyes, so set aside it seemed from all common humanity.

"You feel the room too hot still?" Lawrence asked. "I am sorry. Clients often complain. It seems that now I am always cold. Even in the sunshine I am cold."

Bobby was certain the temperature in the room was close on a hundred, and how Lawrence could bear it he could not imagine. Standing there by the window, grateful for the fresh breeze blowing in, the fresh breeze that blew across a thousand scenes of sport and traffic of every kind all through the land, that told him life was still sane and normal, he said:

"Mr. Lawrence, do you know I think I have seen you before?"

Lawrence made no answer, seemed to have fallen into his former state of not noticing what was said to him.

"Mr. Lawrence," Bobby said, "does your firm often suggest to clients that they should insure their lives in your favor for £20,000?"

"It happens when it happens," Lawrence answered.

"And then . . . do they die, and does your firm collect the money?"

Lawrence looked at him now. After a moment or two he answered with the one word:

"Sometimes."

Bobby came back from the window to the chair he had occupied before. Lawrence said:

"A life insurance policy is the most easily negotiated financial instrument you can have."

"So I am told," Bobby agreed. He leaned forward. "Mr.

Lawrence," he asked, "has your life been recently insured for £20,000?"

"If you know that, as I suppose you do, why ask?" Lawrence retorted, unmoved as ever.

"We know a good deal," Bobby muttered.

"Then you need ask fewer questions," answered Lawrence.

"I'll ask one more," Bobby said slowly. "What is the name of your principal?"

Silently Lawrence handed him a sheet of notepaper. It bore the name and address of the syndicate, and across the top left-hand corner the words:

"Percy Lawrence. Manager and Sole Proprietor."

Bobby took it, read it, laid it down again.

"I am asking for the actual facts," he said; "for the names of the people behind you, the people finding the money."

Lawrence made no answer. He seemed sunk again in his mood of gloomy contemplation of the past, in which it appeared as if he lived so much and so entirely he had difficulty in drawing himself back again to the present. One felt that in that past there were memories from which he could not free himself, memories more real by far than the events that passed around him. Bobby got to his feet. He felt baffled. He told himself he must take time for reflection and for obtaining advice. Besides, it was possible that another day he might find this strange enigma of a man in another mood. But he made one more effort.

"Mr. Lawrence," he said, speaking deliberately and slowly, with all the emphasis he could command, "an insurance of £20,000 is a considerable fact. Is there anyone who has a real interest in your life to that extent?"

This time Lawrence, though with a palpable effort, drew himself sufficiently back to awareness of the present to be able to answer.

"Apparently," he said, "since the premium has been paid."

"Insurance," Bobby told him in the same grave tones, "is very literally an affair of life and death. Suppose I told you I had reason to believe your own life is in danger?"

Lawrence turned his slow, dull, far-off gaze on Bobby. He remained quite unmoved. He said nothing, made no comment, only continued staring fixedly at his visitor, but not somehow very much as if he saw him.

"Don't you believe it?" Bobby asked.

"Life," Lawrence muttered, "life is for men and women, not for things."

CHAPTER X

A BARGAIN

It was in a very puzzled, slightly disconcerted mood that Bobby left the office of the Berry, Quick Syndicate.

He did not in the least know what to make of his visit. He knew still less what to make of the personality of Lawrence, with his manner of indifference to his surroundings, his air of being plunged in a perpetual aimless contemplation of the past, as though for neither present nor future had he any care. It was, Bobby thought, as if something had happened to him that had squeezed from him every drop of vitality, so that he was left a mere automaton—and yet not that either, for automata do not suffer, and about Lawrence there hung, so to say, a kind of suggestion or aura of continued torment. Bobby even entertained for a moment the idea that it might be the memory of these past murders, if he were in fact responsible for them either wholly or in part, that was troubling him. But that was not an idea that seemed to fit either psychologically or the facts, since the operations of the firm appeared to be continuing in full activity.

There was the little typist girl, too, and her behavior, not easy to account for, with the suggestion in it that she recognized in Bobby both potential enemy to be dreaded and potential savior to whom appeal might perhaps be made for help. Nor did Bobby feel any too satisfied with the way in which he had conducted the interview.

One thing alone seemed clear: that if from this quiet-looking business office in a modern London building a highly efficient murder machinery was being operated, then both Lawrence and the girl were as queer and unexpected inmates of it as could be well imagined.

Again Bobby told himself there must be a very different and probably far more formidable personality hidden behind those two. He wondered, also, what Dr. Beale would say if he knew the nature of the danger from which apparently his fit of temper had saved him. Bobby had been careful to slip Dr. Beale's card into his pocket. As soon as possible he would pay him a visit and obtain full details of the additional tragedy he had spoken of. It was a line of inquiry that Bobby thought might well prove useful, even decisive.

On the ground floor, when the elevator deposited him there, he sought out at once the row of telephone booths in the entrance hall and thence called up Scotland Yard. With as brief explanation as possible, and promising to make a full report in person later on, he asked that two plainclothes men might be sent to follow home both Lawrence and the typist.

"They knew at once who I was," he explained. "That means they'll realize inquiries are being made, and more than likely they'll do a bolt. I got fingerprints of Lawrence. I'm nearly sure I've seen him before, I think in the dock at the Old Bailey, but I can't quite place him and I may be wrong. If snaps could be taken both of him and of the girl, it might be useful. The whole thing looks to me as if it might turn out a pretty sensational sort of affair. Already I've had a hint of another death of the same sort—on the Continent this time."

The Yard listened, uttered various expressions of incredulity and contempt, warned him not to let his imagination run away with him as he was only too apt to do, rebuked him severely for allowing his identity to become known, and expressed the opinion that this carelessness might compromise the whole investigation—it was the firm belief of headquarters that no member of the police force could ever be so recognized by any member of the public save by the police officer's grave fault—promised reluctantly that the measures asked for should be carried out, and finally reminded him very sternly that his full report, together with complete and satisfactory explanation and justification of this sudden demand for the services of two men from the most notoriously starved, under-staffed, and neglected department in the public service, would be awaited with interest.

"Some of you youngsters," growled the discontented voice over the line, "seem to think there's nothing for us to do but run about after any mare's nest they've run their silly heads into. Besides," added the voice, with more than a touch of venom, "aren't you supposed to be on some private stunt of your own?"

Hanging a humbled head, Bobby replaced the receiver—he knew better than to attempt any reply to a senior in a bad temper at having to tell off for unexpected duty two men no doubt badly wanted for other work—and then took a bus to the West End, alighting near the small antique shop in an unobtrusive by-street where his cousin, Chris Owen, conducted his business.

The shop itself was a tiny little place, though there were extensive storerooms on the top floor of the building. The window contained little of real value or interest, the chief object in it being an old meat-dish on which was piled a huddle of odds and ends marked magnificently: "Your choice at five shillings each for all in this heap," though, indeed, there was hardly any one article worth as much, and most would have been dear at half a crown. But Chris depended very little on chance trade, and, in fact, carried out here but few of his bigger deals. The shop was useful as an address, even though the counter trade barely paid the rent, and, of course, storerooms conveniently to hand were a necessity, but what Chris depended on were sales and purchases made privately. The collector known to be interested in color prints would be fairly certain sooner or later to meet Chris on the golf links or dining in a restaurant, or possibly at the theatre and cinema first nights Chris made a point of attending, and there be tactfully informed that a wonderful portfolio could be seen at Chris's flat—not for sale, of course; the owner did not wish to part, but open to the inspection of anyone really interested. And if that interest ran to a check drawn and signed then and there, Chris would generally take the responsibility of accepting it. Or the man furnishing his house anew would be apt to hear that some fine Chippendale chairs were in Chris Owen's storeroom, and could be seen as a favor.

It was not, therefore, very often that Chris was at this shop of his, but this time Bobby was in luck, for he found his cousin there in the tiny room behind, and found him, too, in a very good humor. He was handling lovingly a small piece of Chelsea china—a shepherd and shepherdess by a gate with flowers growing over it.

"Bought that piece," Chris told Bobby proudly, "for a ten-shilling note. Just sold it to Lady Endbury for a hundred guineas."

He held it up against the light and looked at it lovingly, for he had a real appreciation of form and color and could at a glance, almost instinctively indeed, tell good stuff from bad, just as a cricketer can tell from the way the new man handles his bat or swings his bowling arm whether he is good class or not.

"Seems a good profit," Bobby commented.

"If you ask me," declared Chris, shaking his head at himself in grave reproach, "I've let the thing go too cheap. I believe it would fetch fifty at Christie's any day. Still, it doesn't do to hang out for top prices all the time—got to let your clients have a bit for themselves."

"So long as it's not too big a bit," suggested Bobby drily.

"No, of course," agreed Chris, and then, scenting perhaps a note of irony—or even perhaps of envy—in Bobby's voice, he added: "It's not so often it works out like that; generally it's the other way round. You buy for a hundred on a rising market and then the fashion changes, bottom drops out of your market, and you're glad to sell for ten bob. Why, not so long ago I had a firm commission from an American banker to buy Adam fireplaces from old houses they were pulling down here. I got some jolly fine specimens, paid six hundred cash and my own costs of removal and cartage, cabled America at once, got back word my client was in jail charged with fraud and embezzlement, and there's my Adam fireplaes on my hands. Best offer I've had since the slump set in was from a man who said he would cart them away at his own expense if I liked and would promise to do him a good turn some day."

"Hard luck," agreed Bobby.

"Nearly did me in; it was as near as that," said Chris reminiscently. "Only thing that saved me was that two thousand poor old Ronnie gave me after he had his lucky stroke with the gold mine. You remember?"

"Was that a gift? I thought it was a loan," Bobby asked.

Chris looked at him sharply and suspiciously.

"Mrs. Ronnie been talking to you about it?" he demanded. "It was a loan in a sense. What Ronnie said was: 'Pay it back if and when you can, but not till then.' Lord knows, Mrs. Ronnie should have it tomorrow if I had it to give her. But it's God's truth, I couldn't raise two thousand just now if I sold up. Mind you, the book value is a lot more—five or ten times as much—but book value and cash returns from a forced sale—"

With a sweeping gesture he indicated how enormous was the distance, as from equator to pole, that separated book value from cash returns, and Bobby nodded thoughtfully.

"I can understand that," he agreed, still thoughtful, for an unpleasant idea was creeping into his mind.

"The truth is," declared Chris, "I'm over-bought. So is nearly everyone else in the antique business. The slump caught us all; it came like a skid when the surface changes without your knowing it; one moment bowling along a straight, clear road and the next in the ditch and lucky if you're still alive."

Again Bobby nodded. It was, he remembered, an odd repercussion of that same slump when men had left their offices on Saturday, well off and prosperous, to return bankrupt on Monday morning, that had brought about the disclosure of the scandal in which Ronnie had been so unhappily involved.

"What I came for," he said presently, "was to ask you for Dick Norris's address. He was Ronnie's closest friend. Someone must surely have known where he was and what he was doing. If only I could find that out, I might be able to get a clue to who these people were who drew his life insurance money."

"Ronnie kept out of everyone's way on purpose," Chris answered. "It was all rather hard luck on him. He never meant it the way it turned out, and when it did he felt it a lot. He played the fool, but he was fooled as well, and afterwards the one thing he wanted was to cut himself off entirely from everyone who had known him before. I'm sure of that. You can ask Norris, but you'll find he'll tell you just the same."

"Ronnie had hardly any money with him when he disappeared," Bobby remarked. "Yet he must have got hold of some somehow. The evidence at the inquest showed he was in business for himself—unless that was faked, too. Anyhow, he had to have money to live on."

"Well, I don't know anything about that," Chris said.

"He never asked you for any of that two thousand, I suppose?"

"He did not," Chris snapped. "What's more, I don't believe he would have if he had been starving. Ronnie always stuck to what he said; never budged an inch from it. That's Norris's address, but you can save yourself the trouble. He won't be able to help you, either. Ronnie deliberately cut himself off from everyone who knew him."

CHAPTER XI

THE NEW BATHROOM

THIS LAST sentence hung oddly in Bobby's mind as, leaving the little antique shop, he walked briskly on to the address Chris had mentioned. Had those others, too, he wondered, who had met their deaths in a manner so strangely similar, also deliberately cut themselves off, like Ronnie, from all their friends? If that were so, it was easier to understand why there had been comparatively little investigation into the circumstances of their deaths, if there had been no friend or relative to press for further inquiry. But, then, that seemed to suggest they had all been carefully sought out and chosen, and again Bobby was aware that his blood ran chill at this suggestion that continually seemed to force itself upon him—of a carefully prepared, widely spread organization of death, working in a strange and dreadful secrecy. But, then, how was it possible to find over and over again men who had deliberately made themselves alone in the world, and for whom, therefore, no inquiry—at any rate no immediate inquiry—was likely? One could hardly advertise openly for such unfortunates, and it would be difficult to pick them out from those likely to answer any ordinary advertisement—or even to make certain any of them would be among the applicants. There was, of course, the Thames Embankment, that goal of the lost, home of the homeless, refuge of the solitary. Possibly cautious search and inquiry along there for such lost creatures might have been successful.

Wider and wider still, darker and darker yet, the whole thing seemed to show itself to Bobby's eyes.

He turned out of the street he had been following into that behind Park Lane, where stood the block of flats to which he had been directed, and for a moment or two stood watching it with awestruck admiration, so vast it seemed, so high it reached to the heavens above, so far it stretched on either hand, so plainly had the architect derived his inspiration from the workhouse of the Victorian era.

Extremes meet, Bobby thought, as he reflected how entirely at home Oliver Twist would have felt in this grim and bleak abode of twentieth-century luxury and wealth, where a room twelve feet square, with a bath and a cupboard called a kitchen attached thereto, was labelled "Mansion Flat *de luxe*," and rented at the kind of figure more familiar to astronomers than to ordinary mortals.

Dick Norris's flat was, however, of a more spacious kind, though, the supply of adjectives being finite, it was entered like the others in the books of the letting office as "Mansion Flat *de luxe*." It possessed no less than three rooms, not counting a bathroom and a kitchen, both of reasonable size, or even the cupboard for hats and coats in the lobby, a cupboard almost as large itself as some of the rooms elsewhere in the building. The apartment was fitted up, too, with every contrivance—useful or not—ingenuity could imagine, from provision of a television set to an automatic victrola contrivance in the bedroom guaranteed to play the Réveillé at any desired hour of the morning until turned off by pressure of a button that could not be reached from the bed.

Norris had furnished and decorated the flat in the most completely modern day-after-tomorrow style the youngest futuristic heart could have desired. In the decoration not a curve was to be seen—Hogarth being quite out of date. All the furniture was in chromium and red leather.

On his arrival, and on his giving the number of the flat he required, Bobby found himself treated with great deference by porters arrayed as never was Solomon at the height of his glory, for deference to the visitors to certain of the more expensive flats was strictly exacted by the management and duly considered in the rent. An equally deferential elevator attendant wafted Bobby heavenward, and as soon as he stepped out of the elevator he saw Norris himself standing in a doorway nearly opposite, apparently saying goodbye to a stocky little man in whom Bobby thought he recognized a prominent amateur golfer.

Norris nodded a greeting to Bobby, and, stepping aside from the doorway, told him to go in and sit down. The amateur golfer, shaking hands with Norris, said:

"Well, so long. Sorry you can't manage it."

"Only wish I could," said Norris, waiting to see him enter the elevator, and then turning back into the flat, where Bobby was standing looking round with wonder, admiration, and a general feeling that he had never seen anything in all his life so strongly reminiscent of a dentist's operating-room. There ought, he felt, to be a drill and a case of shining little instruments—picks and pincers and so on—but these were missing, and on the table, instead of illustrated papers months out of date, were scattered two or three financial papers, the prospectuses of some new companies, what seemed a typed draft, corrected in blue pencil, of a circular headed "London, Brighton & South Coast Syndicate," and a letter with the printed heading of that Berry, Quick Syndicate from whose offices he had just come and beginning in capital letters: "WE RECOMMEND—"

No doubt the Berry, Quick Syndicate, like other businesses of its type, distributed its recommendations wholesale and at random—bait flung upon the waters in the hope some fat fish would bite, and no waters more likely to hold a better catch than these blocks of flats. Before Bobby had time to notice more, Norris came back into the room, and, as if he did not much want Bobby to see them, swept all these papers and documents from the table into a drawer. He said:

"That was Pips who was just going—you know, P. I. Phipps, high up in the Open last year; means to pull it off some day. He wanted me to join in a freak foursome competition he's getting up, but I can't manage it. I may be off to China any day almost."

"China?" repeated Bobby, surprised. "Why? Anything special?"

"Silver," explained Norris mysteriously. "Not in your line, of course, but there's a big game on in silver. The U.S. trying to buy cheap, and the rest of us trying to buy cheaper to dump it on them at as fat an increase as they'll stand for. Big money in it."

"I see," said Bobby, who had, in fact, noticed various headlines in the papers about the silver situation. "I suppose that explains—"

He glanced round as he spoke at surroundings very different from those in which he had last seen Norris, when he had had occasion to call at the rooms Norris had formerly occupied in a square, half offices, half lodginghouses, where Bloomsbury tails off towards Islington.

"Not a bad little place, is it?" Norris asked, with a gleam of satisfaction showing for once in those generally expressionless light blue eyes of his. "You know, I was half expecting you. About that notion of Cora's that Ronnie was done in, I suppose? But how did you know where I was? I've only been here a week or two."

"Chris told me," Bobby explained, and Norris grumbled:

"Oh, did he? I never told him I had moved even. Do you know how he knew?"

"No. How?"

"He's on the board of the company running the show here—gets twenty guineas for doing a doze at the directors' meeting once a month. If I had known in time I would have gone somewhere else. But I heard he had been recommending the place—not to me; didn't think I had the money. Chris knows a good thing all right though, I'll say that much for him, and of course I didn't know that he had a reason for plugging it. So I came round to have a look, and liked it and signed the lease before I tumbled to why Chris was talking the way he was."

"You've got it fixed up all the very latest," observed Bobby, his tone full of insincere admiration, for there still haunted him painful memories of the last dentist's apartment he had visited, so that he almost expected to hear Norris inviting him to be seated and uttering the usual perjury about not going to hurt.

"Well, anyhow," agreed Norris, "I haven't got any of that junk off the dust-heap Chris palms off on suckers."

"No," agreed Bobby. "He'll be able to drop that sort of

thing, though, if he's getting on boards of shows like this. Wonder how he managed to get the job."

"Big stockholder," Norris explained. "He's taken up sixty thousand in five percent debentures in three instalments of twenty thousand each in the last three years."

"Oh, he has, has he, though?" Bobby muttered, and, because he feared that something of the discomposure he felt might show itself in his expression, he stooped as if to pick up something he made pretense of having dropped. Fortunately, Norris did not seem to have noticed anything, or, if he had, his brown, tanned face and those cold, light-blue eyes of his gave no sign, and in his voice sounded nothing but envy, as he added:

"Pretty good to have come out of a lot of moldy old rubbish."

"I never thought you could make such a pile out of antiques," agreed Bobby, wondering in spite of himself if it had come out of antiques; telling himself, too, that it was absurd to let the mere mention of the sum of £20,000 affect him so unpleasantly, like a nervous shock; his nerves must be getting out of order, he thought. "Better than golf—better even than silver," he added, trying to make his voice sound as natural as he could, "though it looks as if silver did you pretty well, too."

"Oh, it's not only silver," Norris explained. "I've brought off one or two other little things just lately. You can, if you get inside information. Now you're here, come and have a look round; the bathroom's a regular box of tricks."

Bobby was taken round accordingly, shown the television screen—there was no television programme on at the moment, unfortunately—the working of the air-conditioning plant—it was out of order temporarily—the lighting scheme governed by so many switches you had to make the tour of the room to turn them all on and then generally found you had forgotten several; and finally the bathroom, a very pearl and nonpareil of bathrooms, the bathroom of a hundred dreams that were perhaps not very far removed from nightmares, at any rate for the simpler souls never likely, however, to have to use it. The bath itself was almost big enough to swim in, the walls were lined with glass decorated with mermaids and water nymphs not always behaving with a strict propriety, and with various fishes in whom, somehow, the artist had managed to express a certain shocked consciousness of that fact. In addition there was provided every conceivable fitting; a sunray apparatus at the head of the bath, a heating-lamp at its foot, and so on in an endless catalogue.

Even Norris's curiously unchanging, light-blue eyes glowed with enthusiasm as, like a child with a new toy, he showed off all the complicated wonders the twentieth century has added to the simple act of washing; but Bobby paid but scant attention, for somehow it was as though he had a vision of that wide and ample bath with a dead man lying in it. He said abruptly:

"Might be a bit awkward if either of those things fell into the water."

"What things?" Norris asked. "Oh, the sunray lamp and the heater, you mean? That's all right, they fit into slots; quite secure, you see; screwed down as well."

He showed how they were held in place, and Bobby said:

"Yes, I know, but accidents happen, and you can't be too careful of electricity in a bathroom. There've been one or two cases of people electrocuted, you know." He added: "Didn't you say the other day you had insured yourself for —for £20,000?"

It was odd, but he had a certain difficulty, or hesitation rather, in pronouncing that figure, as if something warned him against uttering it, or at least wished him to understand there was menace there. But Norris only laughed lightly.

"You are thinking of Ronnie?" he asked. "If he was done in, he got no more than he deserved after the way he let Cora down, the swine."

"Sounded as though she meant to take him back," Bobby remarked.

"Good thing she didn't get the chance," Norris said. "It would only have been the same thing over again." He paused, and added slowly: "It saved her."

Then, almost as if he thought he had said too much, he led the way quickly into the adjoining room, and, opening a drawer and bending over it, produced a box of cigars.

"Have one?" he said, pushing the box carelessly across the table; but the idea in Bobby's mind was that he had done all this to hide how he had looked.

"No, thanks," Bobby answered the invitation. "You think Ronnie was murdered, then?"

"I don't think anything about it one way or the other," Norris retorted sharply. "So long as Cora knows the chap's dead and done for, that's all that matters. Oh, yes," he added, staring hard at Bobby, who had looked up at him suddenly, "I'm still keen on Cora. I'm trying to get her to come on this China trip with me. Do her good. A change, that's what she wants. What's the good of brooding over things now the truth's out?"

"It must have been a bad shock for her," Bobby said. "She'll want a little time to get over it."

"Why?" demanded Norris. "She ought to be jolly glad to know she's rid of the bounder after the way he treated her. I can tell you she felt it pretty badly. At the time she would have killed him herself if she had had the chance. She told me so, and she meant it, too."

"Did she?" murmured Bobby, a little startled to hear this.

"You would have thought so if you had heard the way she said it," declared Norris. "I was there with her when she first understood what it all meant."

Bobby was inclined to suspect this meant it was Norris himself who had first told her what was happening; he even wondered whether it was through Norris's instrumentality that the scandal had finally become public. Norris continued in the same somewhat excited manner:

"Now she knows he's been dead a couple of years she won't go on brooding about the past. I could have told her at the time he was dead, but she wouldn't listen to me, though I knew all right."

"How was it you knew?" Bobby asked.

CHAPTER XII

LAWRENCE'S RECORD

IF NORRIS's remark about Cora had startled Bobby, Bobby's question in return more than startled Norris. He looked thoroughly disturbed; even those generally unchanging light-blue eyes of his showed now something almost like alarm. His voice was shaken as he said:

"I didn't mean that. I mean I didn't mean I knew, only it stood to reason, didn't it? Cora puts in that silly fool advertisement; he answers it quick enough, trust him, and that's all. Plain enough something happened to stop him coming back to her, and what else could it be when he never gave another sign? Everyone knew his heart was rotten and he was liable to pass out any day."

Bobby did not answer. Uncomfortable thoughts were crowding into his mind. Norris had spoken with deep feeling, and evidently still cherished his old passion for Cora. Any reconciliation between her and Ronnie would have put an end to all such hopes. When that reconciliation appeared likely to take place, the prospect of it had been put an end to forever by Ronnie's strange and sudden death. And now Norris declared he had had previous knowledge of Ronnie's death, this death timed so precisely to avoid the ruin of his hopes.

Bobby's silence—and silence can be as significant as speech—began to affect Norris. His eyes were still troubled, his skin a little pale beneath the sun-tan, his feet uneasy, and it is often in movements of the foot that inner nervousness betrays itself. In a harsh and angry voice he broke out suddenly:

"Look here, Owen, did you come just to pull this C.I.D. stuff on me?"

"No," Bobby answered. "Or, rather, I suppose—yes. What I really wanted was to ask if you could suggest the name of anyone likely to have known anything of Ronnie between the time he disappeared and the time he answered Cora's advertisement. He was in London all the while, it seems, in business in the City; he knew plenty of people; there seems a good chance he may have been seen by someone. Any scrap of information might be a big help. What we want is to get some idea of who were his associates and what he was doing during that time."

"Nothing I can tell you," Norris answered. He seemed to have recovered his self-possession now, though his voice was still sullen. "I never heard a thing about Ronnie after he cleared out, and didn't want to either—or anyone else, I should think, after what the judge had to say about him in his summing-up that day in court. If you ask me, he showed his sense in getting out before he got kicked out. Anyhow, I never heard anything more of him, and I never heard of anyone who did."

Bobby asked one or two more questions that Norris answered in the same sullen and resentful manner. He made no attempt to deny the fact that he still regarded Ronnie's death as a fortunate circumstance, leaving his own path free; or that at the time it had been a great shock to him to learn from Cora herself that she was once more in touch with her husband, and even expecting his return. But it was equally plain that he either actually knew nothing that could help the investigation, or that, if he did, he had no intention of telling it.

"The bounder's dead; why not leave it at that?" he demanded. "I told you just now, I was certain something had happened when Cora never heard any more. If he hadn't meant it, he wouldn't have answered her advertisement at all, let alone putting in that sloppy 'Thank God' I expected he reckoned was just the way to fetch a soft-hearted, sentimental woman. And, of course, he was only too jolly glad of the chance. If Cora had taken him back again, everyone else would have had to accept him, and he would have been back at once in his old position. What I guessed was that he had gone an extra burst in the excitement, and it had been too much for him, with his heart in the state it was. Pretty near the truth of what did happen, too, don't you think?"

"I see what you mean," Bobby answered cautiously, a noncommittal reply that set the other scowling afresh.

"Plain enough," Norris insisted. "He came home carrying a stiff load, thought he would have a bath to sober up on, filled it, thought another little drink wouldn't do him any harm, and that and the steam and the heat altogether were too much for him. That's all there is to it. The bath was full of boiling water when they found him, but that could happen easily enough. Most likely he put in cold water first to save steam in the room, and then turned on the geyser to warm it up. Take it from me, that's the way it happened."

"I suppose it might be that," agreed Bobby. "There's the insurance, though, collected by the woman who passed as his wife and wasn't."

"Well, hang it," Norris argued, "if he had taken out an insurance, someone was going to collect it. A woman got it, didn't she? Most likely he had been living with her, and she had talked him into making provision for her if anything happened to him. I don't see much in that."

It was a theory Bobby, too, might have been willing to accept—even though it seemed to agree little with Ronnie's evident anxiety to return to Cora and win her forgiveness—but for those other deaths, here and on the Continent, so strangely resembling each other, forming such a series of coincidences as seemed beyond all natural explanation.

However, there was nothing more to learn from Norris, and Bobby took his departure, receiving no invitation to come again. It was late now, for time soon slips by in these journeys and inquiries, but Bobby made his way back to Scotland Yard knowing some of his colleagues would still be on duty there. Arrived, he first took his carefully preserved cigarette case to the fingerprint department and then went to report to the officer in charge, Inspector Ferris, who greeted him with a worried frown.

"Nice cheery nest of eggs you've tumbled on in this Berry, Quick Syndicate," he said. "We told off Jones to take care of Lawrence, and he's rung up to say he's fairly sure he's recognized Lawrence, just as you said. Didn't you report something about having got his fingerprints?"

Bobby was just beginning to explain that he had left them with the fingerprint department when there came a knock at the door, and there appeared a messenger with a report from it. For the system is so complete it takes no more than a minute or two either to identify those prints already registered or else be sure they are not there.

Ferris, too accustomed to this promptitude and accuracy even to notice it, took the report and glanced through it rapidly.

"That's right," he said, "it's what Jones said. The prints on the cigarette case are identical with those of a man named Percy Lawrence, a bank clerk, sent up for five years for embezzlement, awarded twelve strokes of the cat for an aggravated assault on a warder shortly after reception, sentenced to an additional two years for attempted murder of another convict, served the full five years without remission of a day, but given a free pardon for the additional two years partly because he stopped a runaway horse that was heading straight for a group of wives and children of the warders and partly because fresh evidence showed that the other convict he nearly murdered had not only asked for it, but it was a pity he hadn't got it. Probably the affair with the runaway horse made some of the warders go into the other business more carefully. They couldn't let him off the cat, though, because he had already had it. Well, they say the worst of prison is its soul-destroying monotony, but Lawrence seems to have had a lively enough time."

"He wasn't released till he had served his full time, then?" Bobby asked. "He wasn't on ticket of leave at all?"

"No; full term served," agreed Ferris, "for the first sentence and a free pardon for the second. We had no more to do with him, and apparently he never came under notice again until now. Embezzlement, attempted murder, aggravated assault—lively sort of record. I don't wonder he's described as 'reckless and sullen, desperate character, dangerous.'"

Bobby did not answer. He was trying to reconcile the

picture thus presented in the official records with the quiet-voiced, slow-spoken, dull-eyed personality he had interviewed that afternoon, withdrawn from the world, as it were, and lost apparently in gloomy contemplation of the past. He found it difficult; he almost wondered if, in spite of the evidence of the fingerprints, two different men were not concerned. But that was not possible. Fingerprints are conclusive. Or was it that prison had so broken the spirit of this once "dangerous" and "reckless" man as to have reduced him to the automaton he seemed today? But, then, there was that background of dark horror against which his figure seemed to be outlined afresh.

"Jones," continued Ferris, "followed him to a house in a street off the Edgware Road. Lawrence went in with a key as if he lived there, and Jones phoned us he would wait for further instructions. It's time he rang up now—that's him most likely," he added, as the phone bell rang.

It was in fact a call Jones had put through from a Bayswater phone booth, and Ferris looked discontented as he listened.

"He's given Jones the slip," he explained to Bobby. "Says Lawrence came out after about an hour and went off west towards Notting Hill, walking very fast. Jones thinks he knew he was being followed. He walked slap across a traffic-stream lights had just released, as if he were trying to get himself killed or daring Jones to follow. Jones says the motorists are still most likely using language about it. Anyhow, he got away with it, and Jones says he didn't want to commit suicide by attempting to follow. Instead he went back to the house Lawrence had left. It's a lodging house and Lawrence has had rooms there for two years.

Jones got the landlady talking. She describes Lawrence as a very quiet gentleman, never complains, gives no trouble; the nicest lodger she ever had, in fact. She'd jump a bit if she knew his little record, though. It seems he is out every evening from eight to eleven, when he comes in and goes straight to bed. So what we've to do next is to find out what's his little game, and where he spends those three hours every night."

"I can't understand," Bobby said, "why he put his fingerprints on my cigarette case the way he did. I feel certain he understood and did it on purpose."

"Thought you had recognized him, and wanted to show he didn't care," suggested Ferris. "Just the sort of defiance his record suggests. 'What are you going to do about it?' sort of thing. We shall have to be careful he's not armed if we have to pick him up, or there'll be a vacancy or two in the force most likely."

"Is there anything in about the girl typist?" Bobby asked.

"Oh, yes," Ferris answered. "We told Tommy Ryan to look after her. He knew her at once. Name of Alice, surname to taste; just at present, apparently, it's Yates; better known as Slimmy Alice to distinguish her from Fatty Alice, another of the same sort but dead now—they don't last long. Slimmy generally described herself as a film actress when run in. Probably her film acting amounts to her having tried to get Connie's to put her name down, and being refused because they spotted her at once for what she is."

"I never thought of her as being one of that kind," Bobby said.

"Oh, some of them look as if butter wouldn't melt in their mouths," Ferris answered. "They're the worst. Slimmy Alice has been sent up once or twice for short terms—soliciting and so on. About eighteen months ago she had to appear as a witness against her bully, who had been beating her up and got run in for it. Of course, she swore as black and blue as she was herself that he had nothing to do with it. Our man had made it all up out of his own head for fun and to pass the time. So they had to let him off."

"Was it Lawrence?" Bobby asked.

"No, a fellow named Watson—Sandy Watson, fine boxer once before he went to the bad; tough as they make 'em. Most likely he had a hand in kicking that man to death down Shadwell way last year, but we couldn't prove it. He's dropped Slimmy Alice now and taken on another girl with more pep and go to her—does well out of her, too, they say. Nothing been heard of Slimmy lately. But it's Notting Hill where she has a room now, and it seems she goes out every evening but is always back in good time. We'll have to check up on that, too, to find out what they're both up to."

"Lawrence seemed to me so sort of dead and lost," Bobby said, "it doesn't seem as if he could be up to anything much. Just as if he—he—"

Ferris was frankly amused.

"Put on," he said. "Put on to put you off. When you've been as long at this job as I have, you'll know the more that sort look as if they weren't up to anything, the more sure it is they are. Never trust appearances, my boy."

CHAPTER XIII

A CONFERENCE

THAT EVENING, by the time Bobby had finished writing out his report he had a goodly pile of manuscript completed; and, as it was long past post time, and as it was necessary the report should be in the hands of authority first thing in the morning, and as he knew a good deal better than to make a request for a messenger that would at that time of night probably have been refused and certainly have been highly unpopular, he had to convey it to the Yard in person.

Altogether it was well on in the small hours before he got to bed; and then it was in a mood of considerable depression that he retired, for his duty had compelled him to point out that his cousin, Chris Owen, cousin to himself and to the dead Ronnie Owen, had recently invested three several sums of £20,000 in a commercial concern, even though there did not appear the slightest reason for identifying those sums with the amounts paid by the insurance companies in the different cases under consideration. So, too, he had felt it necessary to mention that Norris had shown a somewhat odd early knowledge of Ronnie's death that also seemed to have happened very conveniently for his hopes of marriage with the widow, though Bobby had been careful to add that all this seemed too vague to be regarded as ground for suspicion. It was with considerable relief that later on in his report he had been able to draw emphatic attention to the past history of Percy Lawrence and of his girl associate, Alice Yates. Nor had he forgotten to remark on the coincidence that the unidentified woman who had claimed to be Ronnie's wife, and Alice Yates, both possessed a coat described as "leopard skin," but more likely, in fact, ocelot fur as the fur appeared to have been of good quality.

Early next morning he reported at the Yard, and presently was informed that his proposed plan of operations had been approved. One or two alterations and additions were indicated, one or two details were severely criticised, but all that chiefly because it would never do to let juniors think too well of their own ideas. Youngsters must be kept in their place. But the help Bobby asked for was duly promised, and at any rate it was clear his report was being taken very seriously indeed, and that there was no inclination to regard it as a discovery of a mare's nest. But he got a severe rap over the knuckles for not having pointed out that the exhumation of Ronnie's body was necessary, both for the purposes of establishing identity, if that were still possible, and also to ascertain if any other cause of death than drowning could be found. An order to carry out this gruesome task would be applied for, he was told, and probably the same procedure would have, later on, to be adopted with regard to the bodies of the other victims.

The rest of the day, therefore, Bobby spent calling at the offices of the insurance companies concerned, examining the papers there ready for him, securing permission to have them copied, and collating the information so obtained. Not that that amounted to much more than was already known, though Bobby's conviction was strengthened that the witness describing himself as a clerk who appeared in two of the cases, each time giving a name with the initials "A. B.," and an address that was not permanent, and of whom it was mentioned once or twice in reports of both inquests that he wore beard and moustache, was certainly the same man; either, Bobby supposed, an accomplice, or possibly the chief conspirator himself. Bobby remembered, too, that Mr. Priestman, the supposed father of the victim in the third case, had also been described as heavily bearded, so possibly he again was identical with these witnesses who had such a trick of vanishing from their given addresses.

Other inquiries were already on foot for obtaining fuller accounts of the inquests held, though these, as it turned out, did not yield any further points of interest. Inquiries were also being made in the City to discover what was known of the Berry, Quick Syndicate; of its director, Mr. Percy Lawrence; and of the various other concerns whereof the names had been mentioned.

All this took time, and documents steadily accumulated, till by the end of the week the dossier of the case was beginning to resemble a small library. The authorities were grateful, though, that since as yet nothing about the case had appeared in the Press, they were spared that avalanche of letters of every sort and kind that in such sensational affairs is apt to descend upon them.

On the Sunday—for Scotland Yard can take scant heed of high days, holidays, and feasts—a special conference was held, presided over by the Assistant Commissioner himself, attended by half a dozen dignitaries, and, for part of the time, by Bobby, who, ordered to be in attendance, was called in presently and questioned and cross-questioned at length. It was a relief to him to find that not much importance seemed to be attached to the coincidence of the successive investments of £20,000 each made by Chris with the amounts paid out by the insurance companies. But a good many questions were asked about Norris's early rivalry with Ronnie for Cora's affections, and about the strength of his continuing passion for her, whereof the realization had been made possible, as it seemed, by Ronnie's death occurring just when the prospect of a reconciliation between husband and wife would have rendered futile all such hopes. Heads were nodded, too, over Norris's apparent admission that he had had early knowledge of the tragedy, though it was agreed that in the circumstances that knowledge might be, as he claimed, no more than a reasonable inference from probabilities. Bobby had mentioned, too, in his report, having noticed on Norris's table what looked like correspondence with the Berry, Quick Syndicate as well as the draft prospectus of some concern calling itself the London, Brighton & South Coast Syndicate. From the questions that were asked him, and the remarks made, Bobby soon divined that very careful attention was being paid to what might be called the City end of the inquiry.

Efforts were evidently being made to discover everything possible about the present dealings of the Berry, Quick people, and about the past operations of the other concerns that had been mentioned. But not much success had been achieved. Nobody seemed to know anything much about the Berry, Quick Syndicate, either for it or against it, and as for the London, Brighton & South Coast Syndicate, no trace of it whatever could be found. One stockholder had carried out some orders for the Berry, Quick people, but they had been for comparatively small amounts, with no unusual features about them. In these hard times he had been glad to accept the commissions, and there had been no occasion to ask any questions. As for the other concerns, the E. & O.E. Syndicate, the Yen Developments Syndicate, the Sands Metal Company, they had vanished, and left neither trace nor track behind.

"Only there is this," pointed out the senior officer who had been conducting this part of the inquiry; "you come across all kinds of funny little odd coincidences. There's the names, for instance. The E. & O.E. Syndicate—whoever heard of a business calling itself that? The next two aren't so bad, but now we've the Berry, Quick Syndicate; nice name, bury 'em quick, for what looks as if it might turn out a gang of murderers. There seems a sort of infernal, devilish insolence about the whole affair that 'Berry, Quick' is typical of. Then in each report of the inquest there's always a principal witness whose initials are always 'A. B.,' and who always lives at Ealing and can never be traced because his address is always an hotel or lodgings or a small flat never really occupied—accommodation addresses, the whole of them, if you ask me. Then there's an extraordinary resemblance in the figures given. There's always proof produced that income tax has been paid on profits of about £400—enough to show there was no financial trouble to suggest suicide and not enough to make the payment heavy. Other figures mentioned, and even the names of clients, seem similar, and, if you ask me, what I say is, it looks as if the books had been very carefully and elaborately faked, with sham entries to show a business that very likely didn't exist at all."

"Can that be proved?" asked the Assistant Commissioner.

"No, not without obtaining the actual books and going through them carefully," answered the other. "Even then, with the lapse of time it might be difficult. Even if I could show a client's name and address were faked, it wouldn't go for much. People who deal with bucket shops sometimes use false names and addresses—don't want their business associates or their families, perhaps, to know what they are doing. It's all suspicion; no proof, unless we can get more information or all the books to compare. A peep at the Berry, Quick books might be useful," he added, looking "search warrant" at the Assistant Commissioner as plainly as words could have expressed it.

But the Assistant Commissioner shook his head resolutely.

"Can't do that at this stage," he said. "It's not nearly like far enough advanced yet. If any more deaths in baths occur, we may be able to do something—too late for the poor devil concerned, whoever he may turn out to be. Or if we could identify these other two on whom insurance was paid—William Priestman and Samuel Sands, if those were really their names. We're working in the dark till we know who they were and how they got mixed up in it. Then there's this other case said to have happened on the Continent. We haven't yet traced what insurance company was concerned in that, have we?"

"No, sir, not yet," answered the same man. "None of those we've inquired of seem to know of it."

"May have been a foreign company," observed the Assistant Commissioner. "However, probably this Dr. Beale will be able to give us full information. He's not been seen yet?"

"No, sir," answered Bobby. "I rang up to ask for an interview, but I was told he was away on business in Sweden and would be back early this coming week."

"We ought to see our way more clearly after you've heard what he has to say," remarked the Assistant Commissioner. "Meanwhile, I don't see that it is much good proceeding with any attempt to exhume the bodies of Priestman and Sands, though I expect we shall come to it. No one to identify them if we do, for one thing. Different, though, if the doctors find any cause of death other than drowning in Ronald Owen's case. But you can never tell with doctors. They'll shy at the simplest thing, and swear up hill and down dale to what anyone would have thought was the merest guess. If they do find any other cause of death beyond drowning, that'll be clear proof murder was done. If not, what with the coroner's verdict and the time lapse, it rather looks to me as if we should have to drop it —for the time, anyhow."

One of the others present referred to the threats Cora was said by Norris to have made against her husband when she first knew the truth. Bobby had been careful to say in his report that these alleged threats rested on Norris's statement alone, and now he was instructed to make further inquiries to see if Norris's story could be substantiated.

"I never heard anything of the sort before," Bobby said.

"Most likely only talk," agreed the Assistant Commissioner. "All women talk."

"Sometimes they act, too," observed someone else, and Bobby ventured to point out that apparently Cora had had no knowledge of where her husband was living and no communication with him save through the advertisements in the *Daily Announcer.*

"So far as we know, that is," observed the other; "but put it this way. We know the advertisement was seen and answered. They were in touch again. Suppose he let her know by another letter, or by ringing her up or somehow, what his address was, and suppose she, in an impulsive sort of way—the way women are—felt she couldn't wait any longer and rushed off to find him, and kiss and make it up then and there. Now we know, too, there was another woman in his life, the one who was at the inquest as Mrs. Oliver. Well, suppose the real Mrs. Owen found out that, while he was thanking God for getting her back again, he had all the time another woman in her place. Perhaps she actually went to the Islington flat and found her there. You can imagine things happening."

"No evidence she had any knowledge of the Islington address or was ever near the place," the Assistant Commissioner remarked, but was plainly disturbed by the suggestion.

"Is this Mrs. Ronald Owen the passionate, revengeful type?" someone else asked Bobby, and Bobby, uncomfortably remembering Cora's smouldering eyes and dark and brooding personality, had to take refuge in declaring that he had seen so little of her, and knew so little of her character, that he did not feel justified in replying.

But they were all evidently aware of his hesitation, and the Assistant Commissioner offered suddenly to take him off the case and assign him to other duties, if he so desired. Bobby answered, however, with all his native instinct of persistence, that he would prefer to continue. He said aloud:

"If I may say so, sir, any suggestion that this was an isolated act of passion or revenge by a jealous woman ignores the connection with other cases that seems fairly well established."

The Assistant Commissioner agreed that that was so, someone else pointed out that such connection was purely a matter of surmise and might not exist in fact, and there followed a good deal of somewhat desultory talk about Percy Lawrence, his record of such singular recklessness and violence, and about Alice Yates, known as Slimmy Alice, as an accomplice, and as possibly identical with the unknown woman who had passed as Ronnie Owen's wife.

"It seems Lawrence has insured his own life for this same figure of £20,000 that keeps continually turning up," the Assistant Commissioner remarked. "Is that a blind, or does it mean he is intended to be the next? If it's like that, there's someone else behind the whole affair. And, judging from Lawrence's record, he is the sort of man who might be jolly useful at first and then turn nasty and have to be got rid of when he got to know too much."

Bobby wondered silently if this remark indicated a line of inquiry it might be wise to follow up, and then another of those present said abruptly:

"Owen, did you say this Mr. Dick Norris told you he was insured for the same amount?"

"Yes, sir, that is so," Bobby answered; and the members of the conference all looked blankly at each other, as if asking what that could mean, and one of them mentioned in an abstracted sort of way that apparently Mr. Norris was in touch with the Berry, Quick Syndicate, if it was right that a letter of theirs had been seen by Bobby in Norris's Park Lane flat.

After that there was a good deal of desultory talk, and Bobby was told he could go for the present, but was to remain available for further instructions if any were thought necessary. So he retired to the canteen for a cup of tea, and over it he began to wonder again how the unknown, whose figure seemed to loom in such dark terror behind all this series of deaths—and who might perhaps be Lawrence himself, but who might also be someone of whom as yet they had no knowledge—managed to get in touch with his victims. They appeared to be carefully selected, but Bobby did not quite see what method of choice could be used. He was still trying to solve the problem when he was joined by Inspector Ferris, who had been acting as secretary to the recent conference.

"They've broken up and all gone home," he explained. "Want some part of Sunday for themselves. It'll take me pretty near to midnight to get it all down."

Bobby expressed polite and respectful sympathy, and Ferris, who had ordered tea for himself, went on:

"Worrying case. You're up against it all right when you have to tackle things so long after they've all happened. Witnesses lost, memories gone, everything dispersed. You're to have another try at the Islington address to see if something useful can't be picked up. It must have made a bit of a stir among the neighbors; some of them may be able to remember something to help. After that, tackle this Dr. Beale—doctor of philosophy, isn't he? What's that mean?"

"Oh," answered Bobby, "it means he's made philosophy

his special subject, and, after taking his degree at the university, he wrote something original—either in the way of theory or research—and put it in, and it was thought good enough to give him his doctorate on. It just means he's good at it, that's all; a recognized authority."

"I suppose you've studied it, too?" Ferris suggested. "It means proving that everything isn't what it looks like, so it's all just the same and nothing to worry about?"

"Well, I suppose it's a bit like that," agreed Bobby, "but I never went in for it much. Beale talked about Hegel's realism, and a chap called Spinoza, and monads, I think it was, unless I've got it mixed somehow. I just know their names—Hegel's and Spinoza's, I mean—but that's about all. I'll try to look it up a bit before I go to see Beale."

"Good idea," applauded Ferris. "You can often get a man to talk by showing you know something about whatever he's interested in. I remember once getting a lot of useful information out of a fellow by letting him see I was nearly as well up in shove-ha'penny as he was himself. Did you know there were fresh reports in about Lawrence and his girl friend, Alice What's-her-name?"

"Anything important?" Bobby asked eagerly.

"Dashed queer, anyhow," answered Ferris. "The girl's given us the slip. Paid up at her Notting Hill lodgings. Paid a week in advance instead of notice and went off, and that's all we know."

"Looks as if she had taken alarm; knew she was being watched and decided to clear," observed Bobby.

"That's right," agreed Ferris. "The funny thing is, and her with her record, her landlady's so sorry to lose such a nice, quiet, steady, respectable young lady, so different from the flighty girls most are today, and never even used so much as a dab of powder on her nose."

"Is that what the landlady said?" asked Bobby.

"Pretty near word for word what she told Higson," Ferris answered. "Anyway, she's done a bunk—back to her old trade, most likely. We are instructing the men round Leicester Square way to look out for her again."

Bobby said nothing, but somehow he did not think that idea probable. Why, he did not know, but the impression was strong in his mind that Alice Yates had done with all that, even if it was possible she had adopted an even grimmer trade in its place.

"If it's like that," Ferris continued, "we shall soon pick her up again, and then perhaps she'll be willing to talk. Or, again, she may simply have changed her lodgings, and means to turn up at the office tomorrow same as before."

"Doesn't seem likely," commented Bobby. "I should say it looks more as if she had made up her mind to go while the going was good, and we shall hear nothing more of her."

"Dare say you're right," agreed Ferris, "and I shouldn't wonder if Lawrence hasn't done the same. Tomorrow most likely we shall find the office closed, and Lawrence leaving the country right under our noses and us not able to say a word. The report about him's queer, too. You remember, first report was he made a practice of going out for about three hours every night—eight to eleven regular—then home and to bed like clockwork. Well, now it seems all he did every night, without fail, rain, hail, or snow, fog or clear, was to walk to Kew, round by Acton, and back home—about twelve or fifteen miles heel-and-toe walking, and never a stop all the way. What's that for, if anything?"

Bobby was puzzled, and said so.

Ferris suggested an explanation himself.

"Knew he was being followed, and thought he would give our chaps a bit of a chase," he said, "only it seems like it's been going on for some time. Man on beat out Acton way got to know him quite well, and wondered what his hurry was. He had been noticed other places, too—taximen in Bayswater thought he was training for a London to Brighton record. Our men say they've lost pounds following him, and they mean to put in for a special allowance for boots worn out. Here's another odd bit, too. Slimmy Alice's lodgings were in Notting Hill, you know, and every night about eight, and about eleven, she used to go out for a quarter of an hour or so—never longer. She walked as far as the Bayswater Road Lawrence always went along, coming and going. They never took any notice of each other. They mightn't ever have seen each other before. But there she always was as he passed by."

"They never spoke?"

"Not so much as a word or a look. After he passed, she always went straight back home—the last time straight to bed. And he always went straight on, same heel-and-toe business, back to his room off the Edgware Road and straight to bed, too—as innocent as you please. Something behind it all right," opined Ferris, "only what?"

CHAPTER XIV

THE COFFEE STALL

IT WAS a warm, fine evening, not yet very late, and Bobby, leaving Scotland Yard, turned to the left and, deep in troubled thought, walked slowly along the Thames Embankment.

Why had the girl Alice Yates disappeared, and what significance, if any, had her departure from her lodgings?

Had she taken alarm and gone back to her old, sad trade, as Ferris believed? But Bobby's vivid memory of her manner towards him, of the strange way in which she had regarded him, was still fresh in his mind, and did not seem to him to accord well with the easy explanation Ferris had put forward. Her eyes had shown fear indeed, but not the fear that seeks escape in easy flight; rather, indeed, the fear that so keys itself up to meet threatening danger it is transmuted into a higher courage. In her manner, too, there had been a profound appeal, but not the kind of appeal Ferris had in mind. Bobby still remembered the impression she had made on him of something in her profound and elementary, as of a peculiar, purposed gravity.

But, then, how to reconcile that with her presence in the office of the Berry, Quick Syndicate, about which were gathering clouds of such dark suspicion, or even with her present disappearance?

Then, too, what could be the meaning of this odd tale of Lawrence's apparently purposeless walks, fifteen miles or so every night in three hours?

No wonder the man looked lean, but what could be his object?

Again Bobby rejected as totally inadequate the simple explanation that Lawrence was merely amusing himself by inflicting long, aimless walks on the police officers he knew to be watching him. The grim, absorbed, indifferent personality of Lawrence suggested no childish pleasantries of that kind. Connected with these walks of his, too, whatever their purpose, was the incidental puzzle of Alice Yates's nightly excursions, twice every evening, coincident with Lawrence's passage, going and coming, along the Bayswater Road. Apparently no signal or sign of recognition had been detected passing between them, but, then, that signal might simply be a mutual awareness, unacknowledged, each of the other's presence. Or, again, it might be that the girl was charged with the mission of reporting that Lawrence passed that way at certain hours.

Only what significance could that fact have, and who could want to be informed of it, and why?

An insoluble puzzle, Bobby found it, and was inclined to think no answer was possible till more pieces were at hand to fit into the jigsaw. Instead, he turned his mind to that aspect of the problem which had been mentioned at the conference as crucial—the establishing of the identity of the other victims. Dr. Ambrose Beale, on his return, would be able most likely to give full information about one, though the fact that in that case the death had apparently taken place on the Continent would again hamper the investigation. But how to find out anything about the others?

Even about the death of Ronnie nothing might ever have been known but for the accident of the signet ring having been sent to Lord Hirlpool. No one had connected with him the newspaper paragraphs concerning the fatal accident to a Ronald Oliver, so completely had Ronnie cut himself off from his wife and friends and former life. Only too probably the other victims, if victims they were, had done the same thing and also deliberately cut themselves entirely adrift.

Leaning against the parapet with his back to the river, Bobby watched how, in the darkness of the night that now had fallen, there drifted by a shadowy procession of the lost, of the outcast, of the disinherited, of those who had fallen or been thrown from their places in a society that knew them no more—men and women shuffling by like ghosts of their own past, like phantoms of the dead waiting only a signal to return to the graves they had deserted.

There came into Bobby's mind the conviction that it would be possible to find here those for whom no inquiry would ever be made—as no inquiry had ever been made, apparently, for two at least of the victims of these accidents in baths, as no inquiry would have been made into Ronnie's death but for his signet ring having come into a relative's possession.

Perhaps in the gloom of some other night another had leaned as he was doing upon the parapet, back to the river, and watched that shadowy line of the lost trailing aimlessly by, and watched them with the appraising eye of the butcher searching out the fattest sheep for the slaughterhouse.

Bobby had strong nerves enough, and the night was warm and calm, but he felt himself shivering now with a cold that seemed to penetrate to his bones.

A short distance farther on was a coffee stall with a little group of men clustered near, some of them customers, some looking longingly in the hope that a cup of coffee or a bun might come their way, or even a stray cigarette that means almost as much.

With that chill still in his bones, the thought of a cup of hot coffee seemed attractive to Bobby, and then, as he walked towards the stall, he thought suddenly that here was the very spot where such a dark messenger of death as his imagination pictured, chooser of the slain like the Valkyr of ancient legend, might first begin to search.

Bobby knew the coffee-stall keeper well. His name was Young—George Young—though he was more generally known as "Cripples"; so much so, indeed, that only a few were aware of his actual name, and he himself would often sign receipts or notes with the word "Cripples," as though it were his proper title. He owed it to the fact that he had but one eye—he had lost the other in a fight with a customer who had wished to be served without payment—one arm—he had lost the other in the accident in a Durham coal-mine that had driven him from his occupation of collier to that of coffee-stall keeper, the compensation he had received providing the capital necessary for a start—and one leg—the other having been amputated after a young gentleman returning from a cocktail party in a sports car had charged him and his coffee stall at sixty m.p.h. It was an accident for which the victim had received no compensation, as the young gentleman was under twenty-one, had forgotten to renew his accident insurance policy, and had a father unable to accept further financial responsibility since he was faced with the necessity of buying a new sports car to make up for that the coffee stall had ruined beyond repair.

However, an unusually severe magistrate had fined the young gentleman £5 and warned him sternly about what might happen another time, and Cripples's own savings had proved just sufficient to start him in business again, so the incident had ended well enough.

The appearance of Bobby, who was himself fairly well known, whose tall form and disciplined bearing would in any case have borne their own warning with them, caused a certain ebbing movement among a few of the stall's customers, and Cripples's one eye was alight with suspicion as he handed Bobby the cup of coffee and ham sandwich asked for. Bobby was well aware that questioning Cripples was a process calling for much tact and patience if it were not to come up against the blank wall of his famous "Well, I don't just rightly remember"; and for the present, as he directed his attention to working his way through his sandwich—a formidable affair of a slice of cold bacon, "ham" being a purely courtesy term, inserted between the two halves of an enormously thick and long roll—he contented himself with complimenting Cripples on the dexterity with which he made his one arm do the work of two.

"Why not try an artificial arm, though?" he asked. "They fix up wonderful contraptions nowadays."

"Did once," Cripples answered briefly. "It hurt like fun, and I get along all right. Lucky," he added, "it was left arm and right leg—keeps you from being lopsided like."

"Yes, I suppose there's that," agreed Bobby, still manfully facing up to his ham sandwich.

"I don't deny as, taking it all round, I've had my share

of luck," Cripples admitted gratefully, and hopped away to the other end of the stall to serve a new customer.

"How's business?" Bobby asked him when he returned.

In reply, Cripples admitted cautiously that it was not so bad but that it might be worse, and not so good but that it might be better.

"Want anything more?" he asked, noticing that the ham sandwich was beginning to show signs of admitting defeat and adding a broad hint that the presence of a "busy" never tended to improve business. "Makes the boys nervous like," he explained.

"They needn't be," Bobby assured him. "I'm not looking for anyone who could be here, only for someone I know isn't and can't be."

Cripples did not ask for any explanation. He had noticed that the explanations of police officers tended to be unsatisfactory. Bobby finished his coffee and asked for another cup.

"I thought it was going to be fatal, judging from the first taste," he remarked, "but as I've survived that one, I'll risk another."

"Best cup of coffee on the Embankment," declared Cripples with emphasis. "Why, when it's closing time at the Savoy, up the street there, all the toffs come down here for a taste of the genu-ine. Line up for it, they do."

"So I've heard," agreed Bobby, shamelessly confirming this quite untrue claim. "I had a cousin, Ronnie Owen. He made a pile on the Stock Exchange, and used to go to the Savoy and then come down here sometimes and treat the other chaps. Remember him? It's some time ago—two or three years back."

Cripples did not remember the name, and asked what he looked like.

"A bit like me," Bobby said. "Now he's lost his money and is a down and out himself. If you ever see him, tell him I've been asking for him. He knows where to find me. He might," said Bobby carelessly, "go by the name of Priestman —William Priestman."

"There was a chap of that name," admitted Cripples, "as used to hang around—funny sort of chap, too. He near did murder once before the whole crowd here and not a soul dared say a word."

"How was that?" Bobby asked.

CHAPTER XV

THE NEW LODGER

"It was a rum go," Cripples explained reminiscently, "as rum as any ever I saw. Started when a girl asked for a coffee and a doorstep and I saw she had the jumps. What I thought was you fellows were after her, but it wasn't that, it was her bully she was trying to give the slip to, and up he comes and took her arm and started to twist it just to show she wasn't going to give him the go-by so easy. So she let out a squeal and he twisted some more."

"Didn't anyone interfere?" Bobby asked.

"Well," explained Cripples, "she was his girl, and it don't do to come between a bully and the girl he's running—like as not she'll round on you as well as him. One man did try, she squealed so pitiful like, and got laid out with a straight one on the point of the jaw, the bully being an old boxing bloke and handy still with the fists. So the rest of 'em kept quiet, and he gave her arm another twist just to show, and she did a faint, and no wonder neither. She come to when he shoved a lighted cigarette against her arm, and said it would have been her face, only that being bad for business. Some of 'em shouted out to him to stop, and he did it again, just to show 'em; three times he did it on her arm above the wrist, and her whimperings and crying and asking him please not to; and then this chap I'm telling you about—Priestman I found out his name was afterwards —came up—a tall bloke, and his toes through his boots and his coat that way you wondered how it hung together; a proper scarecrow even for along here, which ain't no Bond Street nor Sunday parade neither. But none of us noticed that; for he pushed right through them that was looking on, and he never said a word, but just stood there, and he put out one hand towards the bully and the girl."

"What happened?" Bobby asked as Cripples paused in his narrative.

"That's the rummy part of it," answered the coffee-stall keeper slowly. "Somehow he seemed to grow tall as he stood there till he was like a tower, and all about him we could feel a fury blowing like the wind, and I heard a man say: 'My God, he'll kill him'; and the rummy thing about that was we all knew what he meant. It was the other fellow who was going to kill the bully, not the bully him, as would have been natural like and only to be expected. The bully felt it, too, for he doubled up his fists and we thought he was going to hit out, but someway it seemed he didn't dare, for when he saw how the other looked, and his eyes, and how there was that wind of anger round him only waiting to be loosed, then he seemed to wilt like, and there was no more spunk in him. He gave a sort of a whimper, and he said: 'I ain't nothing to do with you,' and the other said to him: 'Kneel down'; and s'elp he, true as I stand here, the bully done it, and, what's more, none of us was a bit surprised; sort of knew, all of us, he couldn't help, him being up against something so much stronger than him as a steam roller's stronger than the mud it goes over. Then the other chap said to the girl: 'Stand up,' and she done it, too, and there they was, her standing up and her bully kneeling there in the gutter before her.

"I've seen some queer things along by here, but never

none like that; him on his knees, and her standing up looking at the other chap with her face all lit and the tears on it still, and a look on it the way you see on a woman's face in church sometimes, like it was God she was seeing. So then he said to the bully: 'Get out,' and, believe it or not, that fellow just ran—ran, he did; ran so I don't suppose he stopped till he was a mile away or more. Then the new-come chap says to the girl: 'Better find someone else to go whoring with,' and with that up comes a copper. 'What's all this about? Move on there,' he says, and that was the end, no one wanting to tell what had happened, which anyway the copper wouldn't have believed, as no one would who hadn't seen for themselves. But we all knew someway that fellow in rags would have killed the bully if he had said a word, broke him in two and chucked the halves over the rail into the river there as easy as I could a doll from a Christmas-tree. Like ice on fire he was, all cold and still outside, and yet, you knew, all aflame within."

"Ever seen any of them again?" Bobby asked.

"Not the bully. Take a team of horses to get him here any more," answered Cripples confidently. "Dreams of it still, most like, and sweats when he does. Nor the girl, this being out of the beat for the likes of her, except when finished. She was only this way trying to dodge her bully, as no girl ever does, except for luck like hers, them sort being worth money. If you ask me," said Cripples suddenly, "it was the eye done it. Some of 'em said afterwards it was just like you read of at the circus, when a bloke goes in among the lions and tigers and such-like, and there's not one of them dares touch him. But it was a brave thing to see, and, eye or no eye, I don't know how he done it."

"I suppose there's more in us than any of us know," Bobby said slowly. "A man with a hungry tiger after him would probably beat most of the running records."

"Reckon I could myself like that," agreed Cripples with a grin. "Only where's it come from, and why can't you always?"

But those were questions too difficult for Bobby. He made no effort to answer them, and the coffee-stall keeper went on:

"I suppose it was a bit like that with this bloke I've been telling you about; you just felt somehow he was tremendous, bigger than he was himself—if you see what I mean."

"Have you ever seen him again?" Bobby asked once more.

"Just once, and that's another funny thing about it," Cripples answered, "for then he was so different like you couldn't never have told he was the same if you hadn't known it was—sort of shrunk he was, and gone little like, and all humped up and slouching like the rest of 'em you see looking out for cigarette-ends along by here, because there isn't anywhere else for them to go. You know the sort?"

Bobby nodded an agreement as he looked out from the tiny circle of warmth and light around the coffee stall into the dark shadows of the night, where formless shapes drifted slowly by without hope or purpose.

"It was the next day," Cripples resumed, "after what I told you about happened. I had just been serving a customer, and I turned round and he was there, as different as you like but the same in spite of that. He put down three-pence, and he says, and his voice had gone all flat and slow: 'A coffee and the best value for two-pence you've got.' So I gave him a ham sandwich same as you've just had, which has more eating in it, so to say, than most, though a steak and kidney runs it close. He ate it the way you eat when you've had nothing for a day or two—you can always tell—and then he said: 'If anyone asks for Priestman—William Priestman—say he says, 'All right.' "

"Did anyone ask?" Bobby inquired.

"No, but a customer told me he saw someone speak to him as he went away, and most likely it was Mr. Smith."

"Who is he?"

"There's no one knows," Cripples answered, "but every so often you hear of him asking questions along the Embankment, trying to find someone suitable for a job he has. If he comes across a fellow what's real up against it, no friends, no home, nowhere to go, and he seems likely to suit, then Mr. Smith will give him a chance. That's what I call real, sensible charity. And if you don't seem likely to suit, half a crown for you after he's finished asking you questions. Particular he is to get just the man he wants."

"I suppose," Bobby said slowly, "he has his reasons."

"Wants to be sure he gets the right sort, and he generally does, because no one that goes with him ever comes back again."

"Yes, that sounds as if he chose well," Bobby agreed.

"We all reckoned he must have heard about this chap Priestman and thought he was the sort likely to turn out suitable. He must have told him to leave a message with me, and then he happened to meet Priestman himself and so they fixed it up, and all I say is, Priestman deserved his luck."

"He deserved luck," agreed Bobby gravely, staring thoughtfully out where the dark river flowed and wondering to himself what that luck had been. "I should like to meet this Mr. Smith," he said.

"Ah, that you'll never do," Cripples answered, "for no one ever has. Some has seen him like a shadow going by and some has heard him speak a word, and some has known he was standing there behind them, but when they've turned he's been away again, off into the dark. There's some he touches on the shoulder and draws aside to ask his questions of, but even they don't see him, for he always has his hat pulled down and his coat-collar turned up."

Bobby asked some more questions, but could learn nothing further. No other description was to be had. Mr. Smith seemed only to be known as a shadow that passed by, as a low, hoarse, whispering voice from between down-drawn hat and up-turned collar. If the answers he received were not those he wanted, a half-crown would be slipped into your hand and in a moment he would be away, nor was it ever any use to try to follow, so sudden was he in the darkness, so swift and agile in his movements. But if he thought you suitable, then side by side you and he went away together, and for you, said Cripples and his friends, it was farewell forever to dark night on the Embankment and the river flowing by.

"Feeling cold?" Cripples asked suddenly.

"No. Why?" Bobby asked.

"I thought I saw you shivering, that's all," explained the other.

"It was only at my thoughts," Bobby answered.

"It's the draught comes under the bridge," Cripples suggested. "Catches you just where you are standing. Try another coffee—the best in London and no extract neither, like some use. All fresh ground every morning."

Bobby declined the offered coffee with thanks, but bought a packet of cigarettes instead, just for the sake of giving business. He asked carelessly:

"Would you know this Priestman if you saw him again?"

"No one who was there that night would ever forget the way he looked," Cripples answered. "I could tell him among a thousand twenty years from now, and so could all the rest of them."

"It's a long time ago, though," Bobby remarked.

"Not so long that I don't remember it same as yesterday—and always shall," answered Cripples.

Bobby said it was as queer a yarn as he had ever heard, but it was a good thing it had ended with Priestman getting a job, and he agreed with Cripples that this unknown Mr. Smith must be indeed a true philanthropist. Then he wished Cripples a good night and strolled back along the Embankment to Westminster, nor was there any figure of those who passed him by, half seen in the darkness, or whom he noticed huddled on the seats or watching by the parapet above the flowing river, but he asked himself if that might be this Mr. Smith in whose company it seemed friendless men left the Embankment to be so well provided for that they never returned there. He noticed presently a Salvation Army worker, and paused to talk to him. The Salvation Army man, too, had heard stories of a mysterious Mr. Smith who sometimes came looking for men suited to take work he had to offer, and who preferred them young, and, if possible, educated, and utterly without friends or resources.

"You can see his idea," the Salvation Army man said to Bobby. "If they're young, he thinks there's still a chance they'll make good. If they're educated, it seems to him worse they've come down so low. And if they've no friends left, then they need help all the more."

"I think perhaps he may have another reason for the choice he makes," Bobby said.

The other asked what that was, and Bobby answered that he would rather not say, as he was not sure and might be wrong.

"Have you ever seen this Mr. Smith?" he asked.

But the Salvation Army man shook his head. He had seen a shadow, he said, passing quickly and silently by. He had seen an empty seat, and been told Mr. Smith had been seated there the moment before. He had heard quick, light footsteps retreating into the night, and known that they were his, but that was all, except that once he had been told by a youngster, an exultant youngster, that Mr. Smith had promised him a good job, and for earnest had left him a ten-shilling note to go on with.

"A good long time ago that was—a year at least, maybe two or more," the Salvation Army man said. "I remember it well, though; young fellow was so pleased. Sands, his name was—Sammy Sands. Great luck for him, of course, and he's never been near the Embankment since. What's up?"

"Nothing. Why?"

"I thought you gave a sort of jump, that's all," answered the Salvation Army man.

"I was only thinking luck's a funny thing," Bobby explained.

"We don't call it luck; we call it Providence," answered the other gravely, and Bobby said:

"Better call it neither, perhaps, but take it as it comes."

The other shook his head disapprovingly, and added:

"I would give quite a lot to meet Mr. Smith. I feel we might be useful to each other."

It was fairly evident that he saw Mr. Smith as a possible contributor of large sums to Salvation Army funds, though that was a hope Bobby thought had small chance of fulfilment.

"I should like to meet him myself," he said. "A most interesting man, I'm sure."

Then he said good night and walked on, and from Westminster took a bus home, where, when he entered, he was met by his landlady, who, as he noticed at once, was looking very cheerful. She told him his supper was waiting for him, and added beamingly, unable to keep such good news to herself, that she had at last, after all this time, secured a rental for the top back bedroom that had been empty so long, as it was small, dark, inconvenient, and had for sole outlook a blank wall not much more than three yards away.

"Such a nice, quiet, respectable young lady, too," beamed the landlady; "so different from most of the girls nowadays."

"Jolly good. A real bit of luck," agreed Bobby, thinking privately it was better luck for the landlady than for the prospective tenant of so cheerless a room.

However, it would be cheap, and it had a roof, and those are two major considerations.

"Out all day working in the City," the landlady continued. "As smart and neat as you could wish, and no make-up, and a wonder, that is, when even the girls at school dab their faces all over. But she's got not even so much as a pinch of powder on the end of her nose."

It was this last phrase that struck Bobby's attention. He remembered having heard the same thing said of another girl concerning whom again he himself had noticed the same fact. The idea seemed incredible, but he said quickly:

"Did you say what her name was?"

"Yates," the landlady answered. "Miss Alice Yates."

CHAPTER XVI

A BIT OF CHINA

It was in a very puzzled mood that Bobby ate his supper that night—from his young and healthy appetite all memory of the formidable ham sandwich dealt with on the Embankment had entirely faded. But what this new development could mean, or why Miss Yates had left her former lodgings in order to transfer herself to his, was a problem to which he entirely failed to imagine any answer.

It even broke from his mind the haunting picture that had formed itself there of a shadow going to and fro upon the Embankment seeking those of whom when found nothing more, it seemed, was ever heard.

The odd, dramatic tale Cripples had told at such length Bobby had already decided was not likely to have importance for the investigation he was engaged on. There was, of course, the coincidence of the name given being the same as that of one of the victims so strangely dead in their baths, but the affair on the Embankment had happened long after the death of the Priestman of the Yen Developments Syndicate, so that the outcast of the Embankment could not possibly be identified with the young man said to have lived extravagantly, and well supplied with ready cash, in a West End flat.

Probably a mere coincidence of name, Bobby thought, and so he noted it down in the diary or history of the case he was keeping, though he was careful to add a note to the effect that coincidences in this affair seemed altogether too frequent.

Then he dismissed it from his mind, and began instead to jot down on bits of paper every possible reason he could think of that might explain Miss Yates's abrupt appearance. Was it possible, for example, that she wished to keep a watch on his activities? But surely if that were her object she would hardly proclaim it so openly. All the same he took the precaution of placing every scrap of document he had concerning the case in an attaché case for removing to headquarters next morning. When he went up to bed he took the attaché case with him, and he also took certain other precautions that would insure his being aware of it, if any attempt were made to examine the contents of his desk.

Nothing happened, however, and in the morning he met the new lodger in the hall. She was standing there, drawing on her gloves, preparing to go out. Her umbrella and a small attaché case were on a chair near. She was dressed simply and neatly, like any other of the innumerable body of City workers, typists, cashiers, secretaries, who take their share each day in guiding and directing the great machine of modern business. Only lines of experience about her pale lips, a depth of knowledge in the reddened and watery eyes she generally kept hidden behind heavy, slightly swollen lids, seemed in any way to differentiate her from the rest.

Pointedly, of deliberate purpose, Bobby stood watching her. He noticed that she still showed no sign of the use of any cosmetic—not even, to quote the expression twice used by approving landladies, "so much as a dab of powder on the end of her nose." Yet surely, with that unfortunate complexion of hers, the use of such things would be for her entirely justifiable. It was almost as if she had deliberately, defiantly, of set purpose, put aside any and every aid to feminine attractiveness. Was it a disguise, he wondered? That could hardly be, he thought, and the fine moulding of the head, the harmony of the well-shaped features, the grace and distinction of her bearing remained to insure prompt recognition.

She closed her eyes for a moment, and then, when she opened them again, fixed a direct gaze upon him, as if now she saw him more clearly, more intently, and had wished to do so. He became conscious that there had crept back into her attitude that suggestion of hidden force, of a coiled intensity of purpose, that had impressed him when he had seen her before in the office of the Berry, Quick Syndicate. He felt somehow quite certain that she had in her mind some settled purpose, and that while she lived nothing would turn her aside from her effort to attain it.

Apparently her scrutiny of him satisfied her. She turned her eyes away; with that gesture he had noticed before, and that seemed characteristic of her, she put up her hand as if to brush aside something hanging there before her eyes, and was moving towards the door to depart, when Bobby said:

"Oh, excuse me, I think we have met before."

She gave him one quick glance, full at him, full again of a purpose and significance to which he had no clue. Then she veiled her eyes once more, and, in her low, husky voice, she said quietly:

"You are making a mistake."

She let herself out by the front door and was gone, and Bobby went into his own room.

"Clean beats me," he reflected, and, when he arrived at Scotland Yard and reported this new development, he was at first hardly believed.

"Are you sure it's the same girl?" Ferris asked.

Bobby answered patiently that the fact was as certain as any fact could be.

"Well, what's the big idea?" demanded Ferris.

Bobby replied with continued patience that he had devoted most of his time trying to find a reasonable answer to the question, but had not so far succeeded.

"Going to try to vamp you?" suggested Ferris.

Bobby thought that unlikely, but undertook to report any vamping, as, if, and when, it developed.

"I suppose she knew it was the same place where you lodged?" Ferris wondered.

Bobby thought it quite impossible her appearance could be a mere matter of chance.

"Beats me what she's up to," Ferris declared. "Got a bathroom you use, I suppose?"

Bobby admitted that that was so.

"Then," said Ferris decidedly, "all I can say is, if I were you, I should be jolly careful to keep the door locked."

Bobby promised accordingly, and thought, privately, the case must be getting on the nerves of others besides himself when a man like Ferris could solemnly offer such a warning.

"You know," Ferris admitted, "what gets me is this yarn of yours of some fellow prowling up and down the Embankment and no one ever seeing him, just a shadow like, and . . . and . . . "

Ferris did not finish his sentence, and Bobby agreed that it "got" him, too.

"Only, you know, sir," he pointed out, "we have no proof of what really happens. Both Cripples and the Salvation Army man took it for granted that those who go off with Mr. Smith, as he calls himself, don't come back, simply because they've been given good jobs."

"It may be that," agreed Ferris, but neither he nor Bobby believed it for one moment.

From the Yard, Bobby went on alone to Islington, in the hope of being able to obtain more details of his cousin's life there and of the circumstances surrounding his death.

He did not seem at first likely to meet with much success. Memory of the actual tragedy was strong enough, but with the lapse of time details had become blurred or forgotten and others had been invented. Most of what he was told was hearsay, some of it wildly inaccurate. But it was clear that no suspicion of foul play had been entertained. It was only of a tragic and unusual accident that the memory remained in the neighborhood. Many of those who had been living in the building at the time had moved away, and of only one or two of these could Bobby get the present address. He felt he had lost his time and wasted his efforts when finally he called at the office of the landlord's agents. Nor had they much more to tell him. It was no part of their business to keep track of tenants who moved away. They remembered the tragedy, of course—not a thing anyone was likely to forget; an accident, they were glad to say, unparalleled in their experience. Of course it could never have happened to anyone not far gone in drink. There had been some difficulty in renting the flat afterwards. People hadn't fancied it somehow, though what had happened made no real difference. It was that idea of the boiling water pouring on the dead body hour after hour, for so long a time, that turned people off. At last the agents had been obliged both to lower the rent and redecorate the whole flat, as well as put in a new bath, before tenants could be obtained.

"Perfectly good bath, too," said one of the agents. "We used it somewhere else where they didn't know. Quite all right really."

"Yes, of course," agreed Bobby.

"Funny thing about that, though," said the agent, growing confidential. "We put it in some new converted flats, quite near, and the very first tenant was a Mrs. Charles, who had had the flat under the poor chap you're asking about and been friendly with him—took in his milk and that sort of thing. Of course, she never knew about the bath being the same."

"Well, there wouldn't have been any sense in telling her," agreed Bobby amiably, and, on giving his word not to betray the secret of the bath, was given her address.

Fortunately she was at home, and Bobby explained that he was a cousin of Mr. Oliver's and had only recently heard of the terrible accident that had ended his life. He was anxious now to know exactly how it had happened. Mrs. Charles was quite willing to talk. She told again what a nice man Mr. Oliver had been—always the gentleman, no matter how much he had had to drink; and, even if he could hardly stand, would lift his hat when he saw you.

"Always a pleasant word," said Mrs. Charles, "though

keeping himself to himself; and such a surprise to know he was married, and him living in such a poor way, but making sure he provided for her—as is more than most men would have done."

"There was a heavy insurance on his life, wasn't there?" Bobby asked.

"Twenty thousand pounds," said Mrs. Charles, in an awed voice. "Poor gentleman, he meant she shouldn't suffer. I've always thought perhaps he had a feeling something might happen to him, what with cars and suchlike and the streets safe for none, let alone when having had a drop too much. It was living alone done it, and, the pity of it was, it happened just when him and her was likely to make it up again."

"Were they?" said Bobby. "I didn't know—what makes you think that?"

"She had just given him a ring—ever such a nice one," Mrs. Charles explained. "He showed it me. I saw it on his finger, and I said how lovely it was—three little fishes cut on it; ever so pretty."

"Three fishes?" Bobby repeated; for three dolphins formed the ancestral crest of his family, and were carved, as he knew, upon the signet ring that had provided the first hint of Ronnie's fate.

"That's right," said Mrs. Charles. "That was the first time I knew he was married."

"Did you—did you see her—his wife, I mean?"

"No, he had been to meet her at Charing Cross station, under the clock, but she wouldn't have given him a ring like that if she hadn't meant it was going to be all right again. I always say it was because of that he took too much the day the accident happened, being excited and such. When he showed me the ring, he said it was the first time he had seen his wife for ever so long, but it was going to be all right now. And the funny thing is," said Mrs. Charles, "when she came she had forgotten all about it, and didn't know what I meant when I said how happy it must make her feel to think they had as good as made it up and him wearing the ring she gave him as a sign."

Bobby was thinking deeply and unhappily. The story seemed to suggest very strongly that in point of fact Cora had been in touch with her husband more intimately than through the advertisement which was all she had spoken of. He remembered it had always been said that after the crash Ronnie had gone away leaving all his possessions behind. Vague, disquieting possibilities seemed to be floating in his mind. He tried to dismiss them as merely fancful, but they remained. He said:

"She never came here, to his flat—his wife, I mean?"

"Not that I knew of," Mrs. Charles answered. "All he said was he had met her and she gave him the ring and it was going to be all right; poor soul, it wasn't to be, and all because of a drop too much—that might happen to anyone," said Mrs. Charles tolerantly.

"He hadn't many visitors, had he?" Bobby asked.

"I never remember but one," Mrs. Charles answered. "But I do remember him, on account of his giving me a ten-shilling note for a bit of old china I had standing on the mantelpiece—took a fancy to it soon after I was married and bought it for sixpence, and this gentleman took a fancy to it, too, only he gave me ten shillings."

"What was it like?" Bobby asked slowly, making his

voice as flat and dull as he could, though now he was aware of a kind of terror in his thoughts.

"Two figures of a boy and girl by a gate, with bits of crockery like flowers growing all over it," answered Mrs. Charles. "Many a good laugh I've had to myself to think of buying it for sixpence same as I did and then selling it for ten shillings."

"Should you know it again, if you saw it?" Bobby asked.

"Anywhere," Mrs. Charles answered. "There was a bit of the gatepost chipped, behind, which when the gentleman saw it nearly stopped him from buying it. But then he said perhaps it didn't matter, and he took it just the same."

"And the ring you told me about," Bobby asked. "Should you know that again, too?"

"I should so," answered Mrs. Charles tranquilly. "Trust me. Why?"

But Bobby did not answer or explain as he went moodily away.

CHAPTER XVII

POISON

IT WAS INDEED in a troubled and thoughtful mood that Bobby went slowly back to Scotland Yard.

Assuming that Mrs. Charles's statements could be trusted —and it would be easy enough to test their truth—there seemed to be now clear evidence of closer communication between Cora and her husband immediately before his tragic end than she had admitted.

Did that mean, then, that there must be taken seriously the suggestion, already put forward once or twice, that, becoming convinced of Ronnie's treachery and deception, as she would naturally hold his connection with another woman to be, she had in her anger and disillusion taken a terrible revenge?

It was a conclusion Bobby was reluctant to accept. Nor did he see how to relate it with the equally strange, and possibly also suspicious, fact that Chris must have known of Ronnie's existence and where he was living. Impossible to suppose that Chris's appearance in the Islington block of flats had not been a result of Ronnie's residence there.

But this knowledge that both Cora and Chris seemed to have had, was it independently acquired or communicated from one to the other? Their silence, too, was that independent or mutually agreed on? And silence is a thing that wears an ugly aspect where murder is concerned.

Bobby told himself firmly that there must be some explanation, though he could think of none, and there came into his mind a strange and disturbing memory of the woman who had appeared at the inquest as Ronnie's wife, and in that capacity had received the insurance money though by means of forged documents.

Was it possible those documents had been forged and presented less to obtain wrongfully money not lawfully due than to provide cover against any possible future investigation? Grimly Bobby faced the possibility that the explanation might just possibly lie there—that Cora was guilty and the money had been Chris's reward for helping her?

And then, was it possible that Chris, finding so large a sum so easily earned, had continued the series with victims picked up on the Embankment?

More grimly still, he told himself that whatever the consequences, however involved members of his own family might be, he would neither rest nor pause till he had dragged out the truth.

He remembered that the self-styled Mrs. Oliver had been described as tall, dark, slim. So far that description fitted in well enough with Cora, even though the Islington pawnbroker had apparently declared definitely that Cora was not the woman who had sold him the signet ring. But that declaration had been made to Cora herself, and was it possible she had been at pains to obtain it? An ugly possibility! A different hat, a new way of doing the hair, a difference in "make-up"—all that could easily render casual identification difficult. Nor, after so long a time had elapsed, was there much hope of getting any more positive result. Nor, again, would there be any reasonable chance now of being able to obtain satisfactory evidence of Cora's movements during the relevant time, though Bobby was aware she had certainly been in London during those days. Then there was that disturbing matter of the leopard-skin coat. One had been mentioned in connection both with the typist, Alice Yates, and with the unknown, self-styled Mrs. Oliver, and it was certain Cora had at one time possessed one.

But then, again, there was the fact that, according to Mrs. Charles, the woman she had talked to had betrayed ignorance of the gift of the signet ring. If that were so, it seemed good evidence that another, not Cora, was concerned.

Bobby's head was beginning to turn. He told himself it was no good losing his way in a haze of conjecture. More facts must be patiently collected, sifted, related; after all, that was what detective work was, not brilliant deduction, not imaginatively accurate conjecture, but just the patient digging up of fact after fact and the fitting of them together till at last the pattern of truth was complete.

Then his mind went racing off again to Alice Yates, who, according to the evidence of the porter at the building where she worked, was one of the possessors of a leopard-skin coat, and whose action in choosing to become his fellow-lodger was so hard to understand. What had induced her to come and live in the same house with him, and how, indeed, did she know what his address was? And behind all these confused, dark, troubled thoughts of his remained always a clear picture of the story Cripples had told him with its background of that fatal haunting figure on the Embankment, slipping to and fro in the dark evening between the lights cast by the tall electric standards.

When at last he reached the Yard he went first to find Inspector Ferris, who was acting in this case as a kind of "registry"—that is, his duty was to receive all the different reports coming in and all information received from the different officers engaged, following up the various lines of inquiry suggested, so as to make sure that no item was overlooked, and to see that all concerned were kept informed of all relevant developments.

"Getting to know things," Ferris said cheerfully. "Though heaven alone knows what they all mean. But we've got the address of the London, Brighton & South Coast Syndicate."

"Oh, it does exist, then?" exclaimed Bobby, who had been inclined to suspect it would turn out to be purely imaginary.

He knew, of course, that instructions had been issued to every constable in the London district to keep a lookout for any business of that name. Name-plates were to be looked at, porters at blocks of business offices questioned, the usual routine in fact gone through; and now word had been received that one constable, chatting to a postman, had learned that letters so addressed had been delivered to a small flat on the first floor of a house in a street behind Green Dragon Square, off Holborn.

"The postman noticed the name," explained Ferris, "because his father was employed by the old London, Brighton & South Coast Railway. There are only very few letters, he says, so apparently it is not a concern that does much business. There's a sweets, news, and tobacco shop on the ground floor. The man who keeps it is the tenant of the whole house but lets off most of it. The Syndicate has been in occupation about six months. The landlord thinks they are A1 tenants. They pay regularly—it's a monthly rent—and there's hardly ever anyone there, so there's no trouble or wear and tear or anything. Besides, they paid all the cost of redecorating—and of the new bathroom they wanted put in."

"The—what?" exclaimed Bobby, startled in spite of himself.

Ferris did not answer for a moment or two, and in the silence he and Bobby looked strangely at each other.

"Gave me a bit of a turn, too, when I heard that," Ferris went on presently. "Bath, geyser, all complete, been put in in the back room."

They were both silent again, occupied with their own heavy thoughts. Ferris said:

"Well, there it is, whatever it means, and none of us like the look of it, but what are we to do till we know more? Nothing wrong about putting in a bath—nothing we can take action on there."

"No, sir, I suppose not," agreed Bobby, and their eyes met, and there was a deadly fear in that mutual glance.

"Oh, well," Ferris said briskly, "no use getting the jim-jams. The landlord was shown a photograph of Mr. Percy Lawrence—recognized him at once. If you ask me, fellows like him, with a record like his, oughtn't to be let out at all. You don't let a wolf loose from the Zoo, do you, just because, having been behind the bars, it hasn't had a chance to bite?"

"He has seemed to lead such a quiet, regular life lately,"

observed Bobby. "Office all day, that long walk at night, and that's all."

"Seemed?" scoffed Ferris. "It's him made all the arrangements, pays all the rent, and so on. Only there's something else. While Peters—it was him went round to make the inquiries—while he was talking in the shop, another man dropped in and toddled upstairs, and let himself into the L.B. & S.C.S. flat with a key. Who do you think it was? Luckily Peters had seen him before and knew him at once. Your Park Lane friend, Mr. Norris."

"Dick Norris?" Bobby echoed, utterly bewildered. "Why . . . why . . . ?"

"That's right," said Ferris. "Very much why . . . it's what we all said. Why? Some connection . . . only what? Where does it fit?"

It was a question to which Bobby had no answer.

"If you ask me," Ferris went on, "Mr. Percy Lawrence means Mr. Norris to take a bath there some night—and then there'll be another inquest and another fat insurance to draw. Or it might be the other way round. This Norris bird may have started with the Islington case to clear the way to his girl, found it easy money, and made up his mind to go on. Lawrence would be the sort he would pick on—no awkward inquiries. They've got the front room fitted up in first-class style as an office, only comfortable, not strict business, managing director's private-room style. The second room is a kind of bed-sitting-room with a small electric cooking-stove in one corner. It's the third room right at the back, quite small, where the bath's been fixed up; special water supply. Landlord's quite bucked about it; thinks when the Syndicate goes, the fitted bathroom will make letting much easier, and a higher rent, too."

"Yes, I suppose so," agreed Bobby, thinking to himself that the suggestion Ferris had just put forward about Norris was exactly the idea that he had had about Chris.

"Or what about this?" Ferris went on. "Remember that queer old bird you met at the Berry, Quick office—Beale wasn't his name—Dr. Beale? Well, what about him for the next bath?"

"I suppose there is that," agreed Bobby thoughtfully.

"It looks like it, if you ask me," Ferris declared. "We know they're in touch with him; we know he has a pile of money—£20,000—seems to be always that same figure—they're trying to get hold of. We know there's already been talk about getting him insured. If you ask me, they will get that insurance policy issued somehow or another. Then the old boy will be asked to stay in town a night or two. The yarn will be he has to be on the spot because there's a big chance coming along—one that will mean big profits if he likes to take it on after he has the facts. That's what he'll be told, and there's this Green Dragon Square flat all ready for him—bath and all. That's how I see it."

"I've thought of that, too," Bobby confessed.

"Or very likely," Ferris swept on, "no insurance this time—and none of that £20,000 capital either, all lost, and papers signed by Dr. Beale to show just how, and no Dr. Beale left to question papers or signature either. And if any questions asked, Detective-Sergeant Owen to be called as a witness to prove Beale himself said he wanted the money invested on a scheme of his own. It looks a cinch to me—and so, I bet, it does to them."

"Who are 'them'?" Bobby asked, though more to himself than to the inspector.

"Ah," said Ferris, and left it at that. He went on: "The A.C. is all lit up about this idea of some bird prowling about the Embankment, like the one in the Bible seeking whom to devour—only that was a lion, wasn't it? He's got half a dozen special observers hanging about, trying to get track of your Mr. Smith. Of course," admitted Ferris, "it is an odd yarn."

"I don't see yet where the Embankment business fits in with the rest of it," Bobby said, still half to himself.

"No, and it's going to be a tough job to get the evidence," agreed Ferris. "We're up against it, if you ask me. We know murder's being planned—but we've no evidence. We know Beale is likely to be the next—but we don't know how to stop it. We may warn him, but we can't be too definite, and like enough the bait they'll dangle before him will be big enough to shut his eyes tight. You are to see him tomorrow, aren't you? Isn't that when he said he would be back?"

"Yes, I think so," Bobby said.

"You are getting full instructions," Ferris went on, "to be careful and all that, and not drop any warning hints at present. He would go off and repeat them at once, and, if our birds get to know we're on them, we shan't stand a chance. There's a report in about him from the locals—well-known gentleman, very popular and respected; been a resident three or four years; lives very quietly, but in very good style; has a local reputation for his dinners and wines, especially his wines. Married; no children; Mrs. Beale bit of an invalid—doesn't go out much, and never without her husband. Staff: man, who is the gardener and chauffeur when required—but Beale generally drives himself—and wife, housekeeper. Local help as required. Beale understood to be writing a book on philosophy, and sometimes stays a night or two in London, busy on research. You can check up on all that, but, if you ask me," said Ferris, "a philosopher is easy mark for such as these seem to be."

"I don't quite see why a philosopher should want to do research work," observed Bobby, "unless it's a history of philosophy—even then the facts are all there, it's only the theories that are different."

"Give me facts," said Ferris, with emphasis. "There's one in about Alice Yates, by the way. Reported gone back to her old trade. Seems she was seen round by Piccadilly somewhere, talking to some of her old pals."

"I'll check up on that," Bobby said doubtfully, "but I think there must be a mistake—according to what her landladies say, she's never out in the evenings."

"Well, look into it," said Ferris; and Bobby promised, and then went on to tell of the results his own inquiries had achieved that afternoon.

Ferris listened with interest, and with a touch of annoyance as well.

"The more facts we get," he complained, "the less they seem to hang together. The signet ring is an exhibit, isn't it? Mrs. Charles will have to have a chance to pick it out. We'll have to get hold of the bit of crockery or china Lady What's-her-name bought and see if she can pick that out as well. If she does, it's going to look bad for Mrs. Ronnie, with the report that came in this afternoon—you knew the exhumation had taken place?"

"Yes, has anything been found?" Bobby asked quickly.

"Poison," Ferris answered. "Death was caused by that, and they think the patient must have been dead before being put in the bath. That and the boiling-water dodge were just to prevent too close an examination of the body. If you find a man dead in a bath in boiling water, you don't worry about looking round for any other reason—that one seems good enough. But now they've found poison, the other two bodies, Priestman's and Sands's, are to be exhumed, too."

"Has it been said what poison was used?" Bobby asked.

"Some Latin name as long as my arm," Ferris answered. "Stuff only a doctor would be likely to know about or be able to get hold of. And there's no doctor we know of in this case—none at all. Even Dr. Beale isn't a real doctor, is he?"

"Well, I suppose he's real enough," Bobby answered, "but he's a doctor of philosophy, nothing to do with medicine."

"What about Mrs. Ronnie?" Ferris asked. "She has no relations who are doctors, has she?"

"Her father," Bobby answered. "He's dead now. He wanted her to take up medicine, and she began studying, but, after a year or two at one of the London hospitals, she gave it up when he died."

Ferris whistled softly.

"She'll know something about it, then," he said. "She'll have had opportunities for getting poisons—and poison's a woman's weapon. Looks as if we were getting warm at last."

CHAPTER XVIII

DR. BEALE'S RETICENCE

When Bobby received his instructions next morning, he found, as Inspector Ferris had told him would be the case, that he was very strictly enjoined to be careful of what he said to Dr. Beale. On no account was Dr. Beale to be informed of the wide scope the inquiry seemed to be taking; no hint was to be dropped of the sensational developments that were now in view. It was evidently felt that philosophers were unaccountable creatures, to be handled with care, and that anything told to any of the species would be innocently babbled to the next comer.

Dr. Beale had not, in fact, impressed Bobby as being quite so innocent in mind, quite so ignorant of the ways of the world, as these instructions seemed to assume. Still, one can never be too careful, and, since it was a fact that Beale was in actual communication with Lawrence, there was no doubt a real risk that anything said to one might soon reach the other. And the difficulties presented by the time lapse, by the verdicts recorded at the several inquests, and so on, were quite sufficient already, without adding to them unnecessarily through allowing further warnings to reach suspected persons already probably alarmed and disturbed by Bobby's earlier visit.

It was with an unusual degree of excitement and sense of anticipation that Bobby left town that morning by train for his destination. He felt the information Dr. Beale would have to give might be, almost certainly would be, of the highest importance. If in this tragedy that had happened abroad there could be traced the hand of one or more of those to whom suspicion already pointed, then certainty would be reached, whether formal proof could be secured or no. At any rate, the horrid cloud resting on those who were innocent would be cleared away, and that in itself would be a great step forward.

Through the pleasant country town where he alighted, Bobby made his way to the address given. He found the house to be a comfortable, old-fashioned dwelling, standing back by itself in a large, well-kept garden. The whole place had an air of comfort and well-being, suggesting a substantial income liberally spent.

The front door of the house was open, and, before Bobby had time to knock, there came into the hall from one of the rooms a thin, tall woman, middle-aged, fair hair and fair complexion, plainly and even carelessly dressed. Bobby had but a glimpse of her; for, at the first sight of his tall form standing there upon the threshold, she gave a little frightened squeal and bolted like a startled rabbit, so that all his memory of her was of a pale, scared face, two large pale eyes full of fear, and a scuttle of disappearing skirts. Almost at once appeared another woman, a servant seemingly, a stout and comfortable-looking person with a stolid, capable, and somewhat stupid air, as if she could do very well what she could do but nothing else. Advancing firmly towards Bobby, and without waiting for him to speak, she said, in the loud, toneless voice of the deaf, that they wanted nothing today, thank you.

Bobby produced his card.

"Is Dr. Beale in?" he asked; and, when she cupped her

ear in her hand and leaned forward, he repeated the question more loudly and succeeded in making her hear. He added, still shouting into her ear: "Please say I should appreciate a few words with him. I am afraid I startled the lady I saw just now—Mrs. Beale, was it?"

"She's been ill," the woman answered, studying him and the card with interest. "Any little thing upsets her."

Bobby thought that that must be indeed the case if the mere sight of a stranger at the door could send her into panic-stricken flight. At a house so prosperous and well kept as this, surely callers must be frequent, but then, of course, chronic invalids—those who "enjoy bad health"—are often morbidly sensitive.

Without further comment, Bobby was ushered into a large, pleasant room on the ground floor, comfortably furnished with magnificent armchairs like those that had so impressed him in the office of the Berry, Quick Syndicate, fitted with the same self-lighting arrangement. In the middle of the apartment stood a lordly walnut writing-table, with an inkstand in onyx, a silver-mounted blotting-pad, and all around the walls were book-laden shelves. Bobby glanced at their titles. He knew the names of many of the authors. Hegel, Hume, Whitehead, Descartes, Berkeley; a whole shelf devoted to Kant. With the names of other writers he was less familiar, but the titles of their books sounded formidable: *The Philosophy of the Unconscious, Pleasure and Conation, Cognition and the World Structure, A Theory of Necessity.*

Much impressed, Bobby took down several while he waited, and regarded the clean unsoiled expanse of the printed pages with suitable reverence. Odd, he reflected, that all these apparently virginal pages were in fact fecund with ideas that might in time affect the life of every man, and he told himself that the woman—housekeeper or servant—who had admitted him must be both capable and tactful to succeed in keeping so neat and trim and clean the working room of a philosopher. A contrast, he thought smilingly, to the chambers of the Reader in Philosophy at his old college, where every chair had borne its pile of books, every corner been occupied by other piles, and no book ever there for more than twenty-four hours before being reduced to ruin by leaves turned back, bent covers, margins covered with scribbled comment, till even the hardest hearted must have wept to see so innocent a thing so harshly used.

He was still looking at the shelves of books when he heard the door open and turned quickly, though not so quickly but that Dr. Beale, with his strange swift ease of movement, was already in the center of the room, standing by the writing table.

"From Scotland Yard, I see," he said, glancing at Bobby's card he had in his hand; and then: "But I've seen you before, haven't I?"

"At the office of Messrs. Berry, Quick," Bobby answered. "In fact, that is why I have ventured to call."

"Oh, yes," Beale answered. "I remember. Dear me . . . but do sit down. Scotland Yard? Most intriguing; one hears so much of your wonderful organization. Most useful, most necessary, and yet so aloof, so alien, from ordinary, everyday life. No wonder Mrs. Beale was a little startled."

"I am exceedingly sorry," Bobby said, "but surely Mrs. Beale had no idea—"

"No, no, of course not," the doctor interrupted, "but we have so few visitors. I'm afraid," he went on, laughing pleasantly, "I lead a very secluded life. If one wishes to do serious work, there is hardly time for much society. Then, too, people seem to think philosophy's a dangerous trade, and are inclined to fight a little shy of any who follow it." He laughed again, and transferred himself with one of his flashing movements to a cabinet standing against the wall. "A glass of sherry, or do you prefer a whisky and soda?" he asked.

"Oh, please, neither, if you'll excuse me," Bobby said. "I'm sure you'll understand, but the fact is I'm on duty, and the regulations are very strict—red tape, of course, but there they are."

"Oh, in that case I mustn't tempt you," Beale said, and flashed back to his place at the writing table. He added abruptly: "I don't mean we are hermits, you know, but we do have few visitors, and then Mrs. Beale"—he paused, and said with great gravity: "Mrs. Beale is a genius."

"Oh, indeed," murmured Bobby, slightly taken aback.

"A genius," repeated her husband, his eyes raised admiringly heavenwards. "You ought to taste the dinners she prepares. It is only in the kitchen that she really lives. There she comes to life—a genius. But perhaps you are not interested in cookery?"

"Well, sir, I always enjoy a good dinner," Bobby said.

Dr. Beale shook a reproachful head at him.

"You mean you have a good appetite," he said. "The young often think a good appetite is enough. It is not. What is required is study, understanding, sympathy—sympathy, above all. Out of the kitchen you would take

Mrs. Beale for a most ordinary personality. In it, she is inspired, she—creates."

"Indeed," murmured Bobby, still somewhat at a loss.

"You aren't interested," Beale said quickly. "At my age, you will be. Your wine, your dinner—what else counts in life? But Mrs. Beale is not strong, an invalid, almost, and her strength must be spared, just as mine must be for my work. So you see we have little time for society. One cannot work out the difficult mathematical problems involved in present-day speculations, when it seems nature is merely a problem in algebra, if one fritters away one's time socially." He held up, as he spoke, the silver-mounted blotting-pad to show in reverse upon it row after row of figures in neat columns. "Blotting-pads reveal secrets to detectives, I've heard," he said, laughing amiably at Bobby's wide-open eyes and expression of intent interest, "and this betrays the time I've had to spend working out the equations one has to deal with in the new theories."

"Yes, sir," said Bobby, not attempting to hide how much he was impressed. "I was never any good at figures myself," he sighed.

Dr. Beale laughed again.

"A special gift," he said. "But I'm afraid we are wandering from the point. You had something you wanted to see me about?"

"Owing to complaints received," Bobby answered, in his most official tones, "inquiries are being made about certain outside brokers' offices. As it was known you have had dealings with the Berry, Quick Syndicate, my instructions are to ask if you are satisfied they are a genuine concern?"

"Do you mean complaints have been received about them?" the doctor asked quickly.

"General inquiries are being made, and their name has come up," Bobby answered. "We don't seem able to get much information about them. It was thought that possibly you could tell us something."

"Very little, I'm afraid," answered Beale, looking very anxious and disturbed, "but I certainly won't have any more dealings with them for the present. In fact the last time I was there—the time I met you—I was a good deal annoyed by a certain suggestion they made—uncalled for and unreasonable, I thought. They wanted me to insure my life in order to protect them if I failed to meet any liability incurred. I was most annoyed."

"You didn't do as they asked?" Bobby inquired.

"Certainly not. Afterwards I had a long letter of apology and explanation. It seems they've been badly let down some time—that's their affair."

"You were contemplating investing a large sum through them?" Bobby remarked.

"Twenty thousand pounds," agreed Beale.

"Was the transaction completed?"

"No, and it won't be—not if there's any doubt about them," Beale replied with energy. "It's a trust fund; if it were lost, I might find myself responsible. I suppose I could pay it, but I shouldn't want to. Make a big hole in my capital."

Apparently disturbed at the mere thought, he jumped up and began to pace the length of the room, or rather to flash from one end of it to the other, talking excitedly as he did so, and making it quite clear how disturbed he was by the mere thought that possibly he might have been dealing with untrustworthy people. Two or three times he asked Bobby to promise to let him know of any developments affecting the syndicate, and Bobby undertook to do so, subject, of course, to his duty.

"I understand," Bobby said, "you came in contact with them through a friend who was killed accidentally on the Continent. Could you give me the details? I was instructed to ask for them—indeed it's one reason why I came."

"But why? What for?" demanded Dr. Beale, standing still for once and looking very surprised.

Bobby said it was thought that a fuller knowledge of the tragedy mentioned by Dr. Beale might lead to a fuller knowledge of the people with whom the young man had been connected. Dr. Beale did not seem satisfied, and asked a good many questions that Bobby, mindful of his instructions, was careful not to answer. He pressed instead for a reply to his own, but Dr. Beale proved unexpectedly reticent.

"I should have to ask the permission of the lady whose son it was," he declared. "It would be most painful for her if it had to be all raked up again. She is travelling at present, so it would be two or three weeks before I heard from her, even if I wrote at once. The fact is," the doctor declared, with a sudden burst of candor, when Bobby still persisted, "the boy was not alone when it happened. He had gone away with—well, with a married woman whose husband has a very important official post. If the facts got out, there would be a most unpleasant scandal—best avoided, I think, for all concerned. It would be terrible for the lady concerned—drive her to suicide, perhaps. No, no, nothing must be said; nothing must come out."

In vain Bobby urged that nothing would come out, that Scotland Yard's discretion was absolute. Dr. Beale remained unshaken. He simply would not take the responsibility of giving even the merest scrap of information.

"You are asking me to let off a bomb that might destroy the lives of quite a number of people," he declared, and from that position he could not be moved, though he promised to think it over very carefully.

As for any suggestion that foul play might have occurred, though he expressed himself as very startled and upset by the idea, none the less he firmly denied the possibility. Certainly the young man's death had meant a payment of £20,000 to his associates, but then Dr. Beale had been told that had hardly covered the loss his death meant to them. The doctor would not even say in what Continental country the incident had occurred—he even hinted that perhaps it had been in America or the East—and so, having learned no more than he had known before, Bobby was forced to return to town with no more consolation than a promise that, if the doctor on further consideration saw any possibility of acceding to the request made him, he would at once communicate with Scotland Yard.

CHAPTER XIX

APPROACHING BLINDNESS

Bobby left Dr. Beale's house to return to the town in a very disappointed and worried mood. Headquarters had, he knew, been building a good deal on the information it expected Dr. Beale would be able to supply, and would not be pleased to hear of this blank refusal. The mind of headquarters might acquit Bobby of any responsibility in the matter of this refusal, but the heart of headquarters—if that is not a contradiction in terms—would continue to associate together the thought of Sergeant Bobby Owen and the thought of failure, so far removed always are the human intellect and human emotion. Bobby frowned at the prospect he found the more distasteful because he saw no hope that Dr. Beale's attitude would change. Only too well do all connected with criminal investigation know how the fear of scandal will close the mouths of those who know and dread that they themselves or their friends may be implicated.

Even if the restraint laid upon him was removed, and Dr. Beale was told plainly the nature of the foul play suspected, it was little likely that he would become any more communicative. To guard the feelings and the reputation of the living would still almost certainly seem more important than avenging the dead.

"It's checkmate there all right," Bobby told himself. "No willing help will ever come from that quarter."

Of course, there was the chance that independent inquiry

on the Continent might have useful results, but a continent is a wide field, there was again the time-lag to consider, and Continental conditions were still disturbed. No doubt the effort would be made, but Bobby felt success was unlikely, and in any case there would be more delay in a case in which delay had already caused difficulties threatening to prove insuperable.

Still deep in thought, going over in a mind a little slow perhaps, but tenacious to a degree, every detail of his interview with the philosopher, Bobby went on to the local police station. There he made himself known, and, producing his copy of the report concerning Dr. Beale, asked for a few further details on one or two points.

He learned nothing of any interest. Dr. Beale was known locally as a learned recluse, with a taste for good living. There was even wondering gossip in the town concerning the sums Dr. Beale would spend on out-of-season or rare delicacies, and those to whom from time to time had been accorded the rare privilege of dining with him would speak ever after of the experience in terms of awestruck reverence.

"They say," added the station sergeant, who, in the absence of a superior officer, was talking to Bobby, "that it's his old woman does it all, except the washing up, and that she's a wonder at the job. I'll bet a good deal," added the sergeant jealously, "she couldn't give my old woman a yard in a mile—especial if it's suet dumpling. My old woman's are that light you could use 'em for refilling an eiderdown quilt."

Bobby expressed a proper admiration, agreed that, taking it all round, a suet dumpling was the true test of a cook, and asked about the domestic staff. It seemed there were just the two, a Mr. and Mrs. Price. The sergeant knew nothing about them except that Mrs. Price was deaf and Mr. Price slightly addicted to drink. The police on the beat had once or twice known him in hilarious mood, and once had found him sleeping it off on a summer night in the garden of the Beale residence. Curiously enough, he was not known, except as a casual customer, at any of the neighboring public houses, and the theory was that occasionally he got hold of some of his employer's rare wines and found them too potent for him. However, as Dr. Beale never complained, and seemed content to continue to employ him, it was no business of anyone else.

Bobby agreed that it wasn't, though it seemed a pity that rare and precious wines should be wasted on a man who could put them to no better use than to get drunk on them, as if they were so many cocktails, and asked about Dr. Beale's reputation for learning. But that, it seemed, the station sergeant considered, shaking his head gravely, was better accepted as it stood. Philosophy meant deep water, best kept away from. On one occasion Dr. Beale had been persuaded to deliver a lecture to the local literary society. No one had understood a word of it; and the doctor had been so disappointed at the lack of appreciation and understanding, and by the fact that no member of the audience had asked a single intelligent question, that now it was impossible to get him to say a word about his subject. Talk to him of metaphysics and he would reply in terms of *soufflés* and sauces.

Bobby, though philosophy had never been any pet of his, was sufficiently interested to ask if he could anywhere get hold of a report of this discourse no one had understood. The station sergeant, when he had recovered from the shock of so unnatural and even morbid a request, promised to inquire. A report of the proceedings had no doubt appeared in the local paper, since most of the local big-wigs had been present, but it was more doubtful if much had been said about so complicated an address, so involved probably no one had even understood it well enough to prepare a synopsis. But the station sergeant promised to ask the honorary secretary, and, if any report had been made, to procure it for Bobby.

From the police station Bobby went on to the railway station, where he found he had missed the London train by two minutes and would have to wait an hour for the next. As a consequence, it was late before he got back to the Yard, where Ferris told him another conference was being held.

"You haven't seen the *Evening Announcer,* have you?" asked Ferris. "They've got hold of it somehow. Someone's been talking—that Mrs. Charles, perhaps, you saw at Islington, or Mrs. Ronnie Owen, or someone." Ferris paused to make a few lurid comments on the enterprise of the press. "It's not much as yet," he conceded; "just a hint or two to let us know they're on the track, and will spill the beans if we don't promise them the full inside story as soon as we're ready. Blackmail, I call it."

"Have we told them anything?" Bobby asked anxiously.

"They're talking it over at the Press Bureau meeting," Ferris answered. "Most likely we shall have to promise the whole story if only they'll be good for the time." Ferris snorted his disgust. "If you ask me," he said, "we ought to be able to suppress any paper we don't like."

Bobby agreed warmly that that would certainly be a provision of the ideal republic, papers being as big a nuisance as ever poets could be, and Ferris went on to tell him that both the china figure and the signet ring had been identified by Mrs. Clarke.

"Picked out the ring at once from a tray full of others," Ferris said, "and showed where the chip at the back of the china piece had been mended so you couldn't see it unless you looked pretty hard. So that's that, and what are you to make of it?"

Bobby said he didn't know.

"Proof," declared Ferris, "that Mr. Chris Owen knew all about where his cousin was, or what was he doing there? And then all those investments he's been making. He'll have to account for them all right."

"Perhaps he can," suggested Bobby gloomily.

"Perhaps—and perhaps not," said Ferris. "But they're taking seriously the theory that he saw how to put out of the way a man he knew was living under a false name and there wouldn't be any inquiry about—and then found the job so easy, and such big money in it, he went on with other poor friendless devils he picked up on the Embankment."

"But then where would Percy Lawrence come in?" Bobby asked.

"Accomplice. You would need accomplices in such a complicated business," answered Ferris. "Most likely Lawrence was picked up on the Embankment, too, perhaps meant first for another victim and then, when his record came out—well, he would be just the sort wanted to help, an ex-convict with a record like his. That part's plain enough. The Assistant Commissioner has a whole crowd down on the Embankment all the time now, on the lookout, and half of them have brought in dud reports already."

"Who are on the job?" Bobby asked.

"Oh, occasionals," Ferris answered. "Women, some of 'em."

Bobby nodded approval, for naturally the average C.I.D. man, large in size, upright in bearing, firm-footed, as well nourished, as is likely to result from a healthy appetite regularly satisfied, was not likely to pass unnoticed or unsuspected among those underfed and undersized laggards in life's race.

His chat with Ferris concluded, Bobby retired to make out his report of his day's activity, bringing it back to Ferris when completed that it might be added to the growing pile of documents in the case. After that he had to wait till he learned that the conference had reached an inconclusive end and that he had permission to return home. Thither, accordingly, he betook himself, highly pleased at being relieved from duty in such good time and to have before him the prospect of a quiet evening for a rest and a chance to think things over.

After supper it was not the maid, but the landlady herself, who appeared—an unusual honor—to clear away. But Bobby soon realized there was something she wanted to talk about, and as she folded up the tablecloth she began.

"It's wonderful comforting to be all rented," she said, "but I don't know that I'm easy in my mind about Miss Yates, though she does seem to be such a nice young lady."

"Why? How's that?" Bobby asked, sitting up quickly, with more interest than he always showed in his good landlady's gossip.

"She's going blind," said the landlady.

Bobby stared.

"What?" he exclaimed. "Blind . . . going blind . . . but . . . "

He subsided into silence, completely bewildered by this unexpected and startling announcement.

"A young lady like her," said the landlady, "and seems she knows it, too, but goes on just the same in spite of all."

"Knows she is going blind?" repeated Bobby, still more bewildered.

"They told her plain at the hospital when she went," the landlady assured him, "what she had to do and to come again, but she won't go near there now, and acts just the same, plain as they put it to her. 'Your eyes will be gone in two or three months or less,' they said, and might as well have never said a word for all the heed she takes."

"But surely . . . " began Bobby, his tone quite incredulous, for the story seemed to him beyond belief.

"I spoke to her myself," the landlady said, "not being able to believe it, either. All she said was, never even looking up: 'What must be, must be,' and what I say is, it ought to be stopped. Goodness knows, there ought to be some way of stopping her, so there ought."

"I don't understand," Bobby protested. "What's she doing . . . or not doing . . . ?"

The landlady was quite willing to explain as long as Bobby, by exception, was willing to listen. It appeared that from the start she had been a trifle worried about the new lodger. Bobby guessed, though this was not plainly stated, that the good lady could not quite understand why so eminently eligible a lodger, quiet, pleasant, anxious to avoid "giving trouble," out all day (quality No. 1 in a lodger), in good work, should be willing to rent a room so generally inconvenient and undesirable as the landlady knew in her heart this one to be. Moreover, it had been taken promptly, at the first figure mentioned, with no attempt to bargain; with, indeed, every appearance of satisfaction and even eagerness. To the landlady it had seemed too good to be true, and as her experience of life had led her to mistrust all—and more especially lodgers—that seemed too good to be true, she had gone to visit Miss Yates's former landlady in order to find out more about her.

The information she obtained regarding Miss Yates's own personality had been eminently satisfactory—quiet and amiable, never out late, paying regularly, giving no trouble.

"You don't often find young ladies like her nowadays," was the final verdict, delivered with heartfelt conviction.

But she displayed a feverish intensity of industry that had worried both present and former landladies with its suggestion of an inevitable breakdown certain to involve the girl herself, and therefore themselves as well, in difficulties.

"She sits up to all hours," Bobby's landlady told him, "and up again first thing in the morning, as I've noticed myself—it's one or later when she goes to bed, and up again at five or thereabouts when you hear her alarm going off. Ten hours' office work and coming and going, and then ten hours' steady work in her own room, except week-ends, when it's all afternoon Saturdays, and Sundays all day. It isn't natural or right, and I don't like it, any more than the other lady did where she's come from. I never heard of anything like it."

Nor had Bobby, nor did he know what to make of such a story.

"It's why she left where she was," the landlady said. "The other lady told her straight out, and quite right, too, that she didn't ought, and she said she couldn't stand being annoyed, and off she went, and sorry the other lady said she was to lose her but glad not to feel responsible any more, not knowing what might happen next."

"What work does she do?" asked Bobby.

"Sewing for the big West-End shops. Mr. Owen, what do you think she gets for it?"

Bobby had no idea.

"Threepence an hour," said the landlady. "The other lady went and asked, and that's what she found out—ten hours' work five days a week, and more on Saturday, and twice as much on Sundays, and, when all's said and done, not so much more than a pound a week."

Bobby was silent, contemplating with amazement and unbelief this picture of toil almost superhuman for a pittance so small. And by a girl believed to have followed the undisciplined and lawless life of the streets. The thing was incredible, impossible, beyond belief.

Nothing, Bobby told himself, could bring about a change so miraculous, transcending all knowledge or experience. In the streets they live at the mercy of every chance, drifting helplessly here and there as whim and accident may send, incapable of foresight or of energy, lacking will-power to carry out one course of action for one consecutive half hour. But this tale was of a discipline so strong, so persistent, so unvarying and bitter, medieval monk or hermit might well have shrunk from its endurance.

The inconsistency was too great, Bobby thought. How relate that strength, that virtue, to the frailty of the light-minded woman of the street, careless of all restraint and order?

He told himself there must be a mistake somewhere, and then he recognized there could not be. Impossible to doubt the truth of the landlady's story, and the identity of Alice Yates with Slimmy Alice of the Soho streets had been fully established.

"That's why she's going blind," the landlady said, "and good reason too."

"She knows?" Bobby asked.

"She's been told plain enough. Anyone can see how red and swollen her eyes are, and the way she blinks and puts up her hand to clear her sight—spiders' webs she says she sees and has to brush away."

"Couldn't she wear glasses?"

"She won't. She says she sees better without, and glasses would make no difference, they told her at the hospital, so long as she goes on the way she does."

Bobby sat still and silent. He closed his eyes for a moment, as if to realize what blindness meant, and then quickly opened them again, ridiculously afraid that if he did not he might never be able to. There were two pictures before his mind: that of a woman lightly profaning the deep mystery of sex by offering it for sale in the market place, that of a woman leading a life of such dull, fantastic toil with so rigid a determination as she knew must involve the loss of what is to many more than life itself.

He did not understand how it was possible to reconcile them.

CHAPTER XX

A DISCOVERY

Bobby was generally a sound sleeper. But tonight he found himself restless, his mind a tumult of many thoughts. The routine of his daily work had made him familiar enough with the discovery of the vice that masked itself as virtue, of the crime that sheltered behind the appearance of the most strict respectability. But how interpret this disclosure of what appeared so dull and drab and secret a heroism in one about whom such dark suspicions clustered, whose past was known to be of a kind to exclude her from decent society? What meaning could be given to a tale of toil so hidden, to all appearance so purposeless, and yet witnessing to a resolve and strength of will approaching the superhuman?

His sitting room was on the ground floor, and next morning, while eating his breakfast, he kept his door half open and listened intently till presently he heard upon the stairs a step so light he nearly missed it, and was only just in time to see Alice passing through the hall on her way to her office.

"Oh, good morning," he said, holding out his hand in greeting, and as instinctively she took it, he turned hers a little round to the light and saw there three tiny scars upon the wrist.

"It was you, then," he said.

"What was?" she asked, making that gesture he had

noticed previously of moving her hand before her eyes, as if to clear away something floating there before them.

"I heard a story the other night," he answered, "a story of a girl whose wrist was burned by a lighted cigarette on the Embankment near a coffee stall."

She made no answer, but she fixed those red and swollen eyes of hers upon him as though all her life were burning there, burning itself away. For a longer or a shorter time they stood so, and he was aware of an impulse to put up his hands, as if to defend himself against an actual blow, so much did the fierceness in her eyes resemble one. She took her glance from him, and he was relieved, and without speaking a word she moved on towards the door. He said:

"Won't you tell me? I believe I might help you if you would tell me."

She seemed to hesitate. She paused. Without looking back, she said over her shoulder in that low, husky voice of hers:

"Tell you what?"

"Why you don't care that you are going blind," he answered.

He had an impression that she trembled a little. It passed, and she walked on. The door closed softly behind her, and Bobby was alone in the hall. He went back to his unfinished breakfast and found that he had no more appetite.

"That was pretty brutal of me," he thought, and he tried to excuse himself with the usual metaphor of the surgeon's knife, and found it sufficiently unconvincing.

But when later on he arrived at Scotland Yard and reported his landlady's story, he found little interest taken in it.

"A bit of sewing's always a way women can earn a bit extra, and lots of them seem to like the job, too," observed Ferris cheerfully. "Nothing more to it."

"But it looks, sir," Bobby protested, "as if she were deliberately sacrificing her sight."

Ferris remained quite unconvinced.

"Not her," he said confidently. "No one would do that—not likely, not much. She'll stop her sewing long before there's any real danger of that happening. Mustn't pay too much attention to landladies' gossip." He added thoughtfully: "Very likely she's been told to keep busy so as to keep her off the streets and giving the show away."

"But wasn't there a report," Bobby objected, "that she had been seen hanging about Leicester Square or somewhere up that way?"

"So there was," admitted Ferris, "once or twice—mixing up again with her old pals apparently."

"Well, then," Bobby muttered, faced again with this absolute contradiction between the wanton and lawless life of the street and the bitter, unrelenting toil of the needle.

"Or maybe, if you ask me," Ferris added, "it's just a plan to give her an excuse for keeping an eye on you. Being careful to remember to keep the door locked when you're having a bath?"

Bobby said he always did that, and, besides, everyone knew a detective-sergeant was far too small game to be worth powder and shot.

"An inspector now," he said abstractedly, "an inspector might be worth going gunning for"; and Ferris changed the subject with some haste.

It seemed he had to tell of an important discovery just

made, one so interesting, significant, and important, indeed, that before it this incomprehensible yarn of a girl sacrificing her sight by working all hours of the day and night lost all meaning.

"You remember," Ferris said, "the A.C. had the Embankment lousy with occasionals on the lookout for your shadow Mr. Smith. A washout, of course; bound to be. I could have told him that at once. If the shadow man was even half as smart as your story made out, he would fall to it at once what was on and just fade away till the A.C. took his occasionals off again—putting salt on a bird's tail idea, if you ask me. I suppose the A.C. saw that at last and had another idea—a real brainstorm this time," admitted Ferris reluctantly, for a thing like that one does not care to say about an Assistant Commissioner, whose rank should alone be a safe protection against such doubtful things as brainstorms—as it generally is, if their subordinates can be believed. "What he did," said Ferris with reluctant approval, "was to have 'em all trailed."

"All?" repeated Bobby, a little uncomfortably.

"The whole blessed lot," Ferris told him, "whose names have been mentioned—every one of 'em. Mr. Chris Owen, who bought bits of china where one death happened, and what was he doing there? Mrs. Ronnie Owen, widow, who found hubby had been carrying on with another woman while making up to her again, and known to have owned a leopard-skin coat same as worn by woman at the inquest. Also your Alice Yates and Dr. Beale and Percy Lawrence and the whole lot, in fact. Chris Owen is in the country at the moment, valuing some big nob's collection. Mrs. Ronnie Owen doesn't seem to go out much except to friends or a bridge club she belongs to. Percy Lawrence is still doing his fifteen miles every evening heel and toe, in and out and in again. Dr. Beale hasn't budged from where he lives. Your pal Alice never goes anywhere except to and from her office, and her stunt every night of watching Percy pass without any sign to show they even see each other."

"Well, then," said Bobby, relieved.

"Haven't noticed," asked Ferris, "that I didn't mention Mr. Richard Norris? Well, it looks like he's the goods all right enough."

"Norris?" repeated Bobby incredulously. "You mean that?"

"Looks like it," Ferris said. "Mr. Richard Norris, living in style in a swell flat off Park Lane out of his earnings as a writer about golf."

"He does a lot on the Stock Exchange, too," Bobby said quickly. "I believe he gets inside information, and has done well with it."

"Met that yarn before," remarked Ferris unbelievingly; "the way they all account for money there's no accounting for. Besides, there's information that the firm of stock-brokers he used to deal with have done nothing much for him for months. He may have taken his business to another firm, but they think they would have known it if he had. They gave him special terms, too, apparently. And he's been seen visiting the L.B. & S.C.S. office near Green Dragon Square."

"Yes, I know. That seemed queer," Bobby admitted.

"What's a lot queerer," Ferris said, "is that he has been trailed two successive nights down along the Embankment. He was wearing a coat with the collar turned up and his hat pulled down over his eyes, and once or twice he was seen talking to down-and-outs. Prowling about half the night he was, and what for? And if it's not to find the next to take a bath, what is his game?"

"If it's like that," Bobby said slowly, "it can't be Dr. Beale they intend to be their next?"

"Two strings to their bow, if you ask me," suggested Ferris. "Dr. Beale first, and then after him the next to be any likely bloke picked up off the Embankment. This is a long-range affair if it's anything at all."

"Yes, I suppose so," agreed Bobby.

"Everything worked out and made ready months beforehand; months, too, spent training on the next for the bath so it'll go off all right and no nasty questions at the inquest," Ferris continued. "There was another conference yesterday afternoon, you know. It seems to be pretty well agreed now that the idea was to take a bucket-shop fake—quite smart. There is no attempt to do bucket-shop business—profits in that line too small for our birds, risk too great, run too short before the people you've diddled start complaining. So what business they did was perfectly genuine and honest, only precious little of it. But it's easy enough to enter all kinds of transactions with all kinds of people out of dreamland. It'll all look genuine enough, even if most likely it wouldn't stand up to close investigation by experts, but then there's no risk of that with no one to make complaints and no one with any reason to demand an inquiry. Every bit good enough to show at an inquest on a poor chap drowned accidentally in his bath to prove no financial cause for suicide; good enough, too, to let an insurance assessor have a squint at, because, though he may smell a rat, he won't see any chance of coaxing it into a trap—and not too awfully keen either on making a stink that'll scare off clients and no certainty of proving anything. No insurance company wants a stink if they can help it, and, unless the case is dead clear, no use to scare possible clients into thinking they may get murdered if they insure, or to get a name for being difficult about payments. Given a year or two between each case for making preparation and faking the books and documents required, and a suitable stray picked up off the Embankment no one was likely to miss or make any inquiries about—it must have looked a cinch, cast iron. And, at £20,000 or so each time, a pretty paying game. And that," concluded Ferris, "if you ask me, is what your shadow man now identified as Mr. Richard Norris is doing on the prowl every night on the Embankment—picking out the next."

"If it's Norris," Bobby said, "then the others are cleared?"

"Not half they aren't," retorted Ferris with vigor. "This is a big affair—conspiracy. If you ask me, as likely as not they're all in it, the whole caboodle. Norris as chief, perhaps, the other two helping, and Percy Lawrence and Alice Yates employed as covers. And where the evidence is going to come from I don't know. Norris does the brainwork, most likely, and he'll have a perfectly good alibi for the job itself. Death in your own bath—how is that brought home to anyone? Happens often enough innocent enough."

Bobby thought so, too, and as he sat there deep in thought he wondered where in this strange and dark story there fitted in the tale he had heard of a woman sewing silently day after day, week after week, in a solitary and dreadful toil she knew must in the end cost her her sight.

CHAPTER XXI

MAGOTTY MEG

THE AUTHORITIES at Scotland Yard were beginning to grow distinctly uneasy.

The exhumation of the bodies of the other two victims of what was coming to be known at the Yard as "The Bath Mysteries" had been carried out with great secrecy, but the post-mortem examinations had revealed no other cause of death than the accidental drowning recorded in the verdicts at the respective inquests. In the William Priestman body signs were found to indicate alcoholic excess and the probable use of drugs, but, then, it had been mentioned at the inquest that Priestman had been leading a very dissipated life for the few months before his death. At the time, too, a supply of veronal had been found in his possession. More significant—of curious interest, indeed—was the fact that a trifling deformity was noticed in the left foot, and that a similar deformity had been recorded as present in the person who had presented himself for medical examination in the name of Ronald Oliver when the insurance on that personage's life was being taken out. It was probable, therefore, that Priestman, of much the same physical type as Ronnie Owen, had acted as substitute for him.

But, however suspicious this and other circumstances might seem, there did not at present appear much possibility of carrying the cases further. Only as regarded Ronnie Owen was there any proof that murder had in fact been committed, and there, too, but little chance existed of discovering satisfactory evidence to fix the guilt. Suspicion seemed to point now here, now there, and as several of those engaged in the investigation were inclined to think, both here and there with equal reason. But how to find the conclusive proof an English jury requires was for the present a problem to all seeming beyond solution.

"Of course, there's this Norris bird's prowling about the Embankment that may lead to something some day," one man remarked at one of the numerous conferences that were held to discuss the case, "and we know he's living in style with no visible income—that's always a pointer. Then we know Mrs. Ronnie Owen had had access to poison, there's evidence she knew more about her husband than she let on, and jealousy is always a possible motive; but all that's miles from proof, and how after all this time can we get her identified with the woman who appeared at the inquest, or check up on her movements the day of the murder? And we know Mr. Chris Owen was hanging round the Islington flat at the time, but that doesn't prove much except opportunity, and there seems no way of tracing the insurance money to him. It may quite well be that Lawrence is working the whole stunt with this Alice Yates girl to help—or they may be just stalking horses themselves. There's the fact, too, that Norris seems to be connected with the L.B. & S.C. Syndicate affair, and that Lawrence is as well, except that nothing is known of any of the concerns and none of them has done much business. But there's no crime in that, or else half the City today would be in jail. It looks like a complete dead end, and no wonder, when it all happened months ago. Dead cold trails lead to dead ends."

"Resignations," said the Assistant Commissioner, who was presiding, "resignations will be three a penny."

They all agreed, gloomily. They envisaged a burst of public wrath at official slackness and apathy; they saw screaming headlines in the press, a burst of furious correspondence descending upon members of Parliament, newspapers, and themselves; they all knew well that a starving tiger that has tasted blood is easier to control than the public in one of its fits of righteous—and hysterical—indignation.

But none of them knew what to do about it.

The junior in rank present said timidly:

"There's the Dr. Beale angle. That may lead somewhere if we watch it. We know there've been attempts already to get him to insure his life in favor of Lawrence."

"A philosopher johnny," observed the A.C. thoughtfully, "is just about the easiest mark there is."

And on that point, too, they were all agreed.

The A.C. looked round sternly.

"The business of the police force of this country," he declared, "is to protect law-abiding citizens even more than to bring criminals to justice."

Once more they were all in complete and even enthusiastic agreement. Having expressed that agreement with nods of the head and low, acquiescent murmurs, they all set to work to discuss how far it would be possible to use Dr. Beale's known connection with Percy Lawrence and the Berry, Quick Syndicate as a means of taking any prospective murderers in the act and before they had accomplished their purpose. It was pointed out that so long as Dr. Beale remained in his own home he was safe enough, and that therefore no action need be taken to convey to him that warning which would naturally and inevitably lead to the complete breaking off of almost the only known means of keeping in any way in touch with the suspected persons, or of discovering anything about their contemplated activities.

"No risk in his taking a bath in his own home," they decided, and one man added: "There will have to be a careful watch kept to make sure we get warning if he comes up to town any time. I suppose the locals can be trusted to do that?"

"Oh, very efficient force," commented the A.C.; and then, after a little further talk, Bobby was called in and questioned with some asperity, for apprehension had lent an edge to all their nerves. No one knew what to make of his report that Alice Yates was binding herself to such terrific toil as to endanger even her sight, but it was also agreed that the fact, if it were a fact, could have no bearing on the investigation in hand. As for Percy Lawrence's nightly pedestrian exercises, those, it seemed likely, had some significance which the careful watch being kept upon him would certainly reveal in time.

"Though what can be the object in walking fifteen miles or so at top speed every night," observed the A.C., "goodness knows—unless it is to annoy motorists. Every report, almost, talks about his walking lap bang across the road, and making cars draw up on their tails to avoid him, almost as though he didn't even see them. As for the Yates girl, she doesn't stick to her sewing quite so closely as all that. Here's a report of her having been seen again with her old associates, and another of her having spent all one evening with—er—" said the A.C. with some distaste—"Magotty

Meg. Who is Magotty Meg? Has she no—er—normal name to be used in—er—official reports?"

It was explained that, if she had any other name, no one knew it, not even, apparently, Meg herself. It was further explained that Meg, having retired through age from the exercise of her profession, still took a kindly interest in its practitioners, acted frequently as a go-between, and had developed into one of the most expert, cunning, and audacious sneak-thieves in London.

"She plays the feeble, flustered, bewildered old woman," explained the junior who had spoken before, "though really she's as spry and active as anyone a quarter her age, and when Good Samaritans have put the poor flustered old thing in the right bus, or helped her across the street, or picked up her parcels she's managed to let fall, and presently they miss their purse or wallet, the dear old lady they've helped is the very last person they suspect. We'll get her some day," declared the speaker, with more hope than confidence in his voice, "but if this Alice Yates is in with her—well, there's something up. There's more ways than one of being blind," he added, with a sideway look at Bobby.

Apprehension grew acute again with this hint that fresh developments might be expected, and Bobby, by a respectful question he managed to slip in, learned that Dr. Beale was in complete ignorance of the careful watch and guard being kept upon his movements that it was hoped would help some day or another, in some way or another, towards discovering the truth by throwing light upon the activities of those suspected. It was convenient from the point of view of the watchers that Dr. Beale's car had recently been sent for repairs and had not yet been returned, so that if he did journey up to London he would probably use the railway, though as an additional precaution the garages in the neighborhood had been asked to give warning of any order for the hire of a car received from him. He was understood, however, to be exceptionally busy both with the book he was writing—*Analysis of the Unconditioned* was known to be the title—and with some articles for a learned periodical in New York. Till midnight his light could be seen burning, his shadow on the blind was often visible as he paced up and down between lamp and window, now and again he himself in person at the window as, opening it, he would lean out, deep in thought, his glasses removed to rest his eyes, smoking the huge pipe he affected at these times, apparently enjoying the cool night air, till suddenly, with that odd, abrupt speed of movement characteristic of him, he would draw back, slam the window, and be again at his desk, writing rapidly the thoughts that presumably had come to him during that interval of repose.

"His life is in our hands," said the A.C. uncomfortably. "If we let anything happen to a man like that when we could have prevented it, we shall deserve all we get."

"He's just the sort birds like Percy Lawrence and Alice Yates are out to get hold of," observed one of those present. "Learned professors and philosophers and so on—don't know the first thing about real life, and you can't make them understand, either. No experience; innocent as lambs."

This verdict was unanimous, and, it having been delivered, the conference broke up, so Bobby, who found he had for once a little free time on his hands, went off to a secondhand bookshop he had noticed in the street in which his cousin, Chris, had his establishment. It had occurred to him that it might be a good idea if he refreshed what fragmentary knowledge of philosophy he had picked up at school and college. It was not much more extensive, in fact, than that of the gentleman who, during the world war, and under the impression that Hegel was a contemporary German general, had furiously denounced the late Lord Haldane for an expression of devotion to that philosopher. But the books upon the shelves of the shop he visited all looked so formidable that in the end he contented himself with a volume of the Home University Library, and with it in his pocket went across to Chris's shop to ask the young man in charge when his employer was likely to return.

The young man had no idea. Mr. Owen hadn't said anything about it, nor had he written. It was Lord Westland's collection Mr. Owen was cataloguing. But would Sergeant Owen please remember that that information was strictly confidential? There were reasons, apparently, why neither Lord Westland nor Mr. Chris Owen wanted it known; something to do, probably, with a contemplated winnowing at the collection.

Bobby promised absolute and complete silence, adding with a laugh that that promise must of course be taken as subject to his duty as a police officer, and the young man laughed, too, and said he didn't much suppose that cataloguing Lord Westland's collection was likely to be a matter for the police, even though there were plenty of catalogues it would be sheer flattery to describe as criminal—a word far too weak for many.

So Bobby said he would be glad to know when his cousin returned, and the young man promised to inform him, and Bobby went on to a restaurant near, where he was known, and, getting permission to use their phone, put through a long-distance call to Westland Castle, for a paragraph he had chanced to notice in the paper that morning was running in his mind.

In due course connection was made, and, in reply to his inquiry, he was informed rather testily that since, as had been stated in the papers only that morning, the castle was in the hands of the builders and decorators for extensive alterations intended to bring it more into line with modern requirements, Lord Westland was not in residence—he was, in fact, travelling on the Continent—and nothing was known of Mr. Christopher Owen. As for the famous Westland collection, that had been packed and removed to safe-deposit vaults for safety, so there was certainly no question of any fresh valuation or cataloguing for the present.

Bobby was profuse in expressing thanks for this information, thanks that were not too graciously received, and, in no happy mood, left the restaurant to return homewards.

Outside, he ran across a constable, a man named Markham, with whom he had been friendly during his own uniform days. He stopped to exchange a word with him and to ask if it were true he was now due for retirement. Markham, an elderly man, said it was, and spoke with relish of the cottage in the country, with a garden attached, where he and his wife meant to spend their remaining days, far from cars and phones and road accidents and all the rest of London's bustle; and as they chatted they were nearly the witnesses of a new tragedy. A flustered old lady, who must have been nearly eighty, though she seemed active enough, lost her head crossing the road near them and as nearly as possible got herself run over. As it was she dropped umbrella, handbag, glasses, and emitted a frightened little squawk. A well-dressed young man near by burst out laughing at her predicament; the constable and Bobby dived to her rescue. Between them they retrieved her and her possessions with no harm done, and set her on her way. She went off quite briskly, and a sudden, uncomfortable idea occurred to Bobby. Hurriedly he made sure his pocketbook was safe, and was a little relieved to find it still in his pocket. He said to his companion:

"Bit of a narrow squeak. Don't know her at all, do you?"

"Why, yes, didn't you?" answered Markham. "It was Lady—" And he named the mother of a well-known Cabinet Minister at the moment much in the news. "Lives in the square just round the corner," he added.

"Oh, is that she? No, I didn't know her," Bobby answered, thankful he had not betrayed his passing suspicion that so influential and important a lady was Magotty Meg.

"Did you see that fellow laughing?" Markham added indignantly. "I nearly said something. A fellow who thinks it funny when a woman old enough to be his mother is nearly run over—well, he's got the mind of a murderer."

"So he has," agreed Bobby, and went on his way.

CHAPTER XXII

MISS HEWITT'S STORY

IT WAS ODD how tenaciously every detail of this narrow escape an old lady had had from being run over clung in Bobby's mind, thankful as he was that he had not betrayed his momentary impulse to identify the respected mother of a Cabinet Minister with Magotty Meg.

He was worried, too, by the report that Alice Yates had spent an evening with that disreputable and almost legendary character. He himself had never come in contact with her, but he knew that the oddest tales were told about the old woman, most of them highly discreditable and improper, and often showing an odd twist of mischief or of malice. One of her favorite hunting grounds, for instance, was charity bazaars, or those meetings at fashionable houses where fashionable women assemble, sometimes for moral and intellectual uplift, sometimes to consult how, with dance and song, to do good to the poor at the rate of two guineas a ticket, including a champagne supper. Who could suspect the earnest, attentive old lady in quaint, old-fashioned clothes of the best quality, grown a little feeble evidently and continually fumbling with her glasses so that her hands were never still, of being in any way responsible for purses missing from handbags their owners were certain they had never left hold of for a moment? Or if—for Magotty Meg was no despiser of small things—a shortsighted old lady mistook a thirty-shilling silk umbrella with a gold-mounted handle for her own, and was stopped just as she was toddling away with it, no one could be so churlish and suspicious as to refuse to accept her flustered apologies and protestations that it was exactly like her own someone else must have gone off with by mistake, since it was nowhere to be found. But the necessity for offering such excuses were rare indeed, for Magotty Meg could nip into a taxi or round a corner with astonishing speed. There was this to be said for her, too: that, though her avowed object was to accumulate savings large enough to permit her, as she put it, "to retire to a little country cottage," every girl in her former line of business knew that, when times were hard and luck was out, Magotty Meg could always be relied on for a friendly loan.

And it is a fact that only under the stress of such hard necessity as prison, sickness, or death—the last contingency not infrequent in the profession with the highest death rate—was default in repayment any but the rarest of occurrences.

None the less, it was sufficiently disturbing to the picture beginning to frame itself in his mind, though with outlines as yet both blurred and dim. No very good interpretation could be put upon a visit to Magotty Meg, old and experienced in evil, a notorious go-between, though one who always made sure that both parties knew and understood what they were doing and all probable consequences—it was another odd trait in her character that, being possessed of a certain amount of medical knowledge, said to be due to her having been a nurse in her young days, she was—her one vanity—extremely fond of showing it off in frankest detail. This story, therefore, of a visit paid the old woman by Alice troubled Bobby curiously. It was difficult to understand;

it was only too likely to mean that the girl's resolution had broken under the strain of the enormous toil she had been inflicting on herself, and that she was now drifting back into her old ways.

A pity, he thought; and he wondered uneasily if his reminder to her that she was losing her sight had anything to do with her relapse. What he had said might, he supposed, have made her realize with sudden force the inevitable consequences she was facing, and so might have made her decide, in abrupt panic, that she could not go on.

Bobby told himself wryly that those hasty words that had, as it were, got themselves uttered by his tongue before his mind had had time to weigh them, had involved, apparently, a heavy responsibility, one little to his taste. And he was aware, too, that this suggested interpretation, if it proved fact, proved entirely false the picture of events that had been vaguely and dimly forming itself in his mind.

By an effort he put such thoughts aside and went back to the Yard, chiefly with the idea of seeing if anything fresh had come in, and there presently a colleague found him sitting with his Home University Library book open before him, but obviously not reading it.

"Don't wonder," said the colleague, looking askance at the title. "What on earth are you going in for now?"

"I thought I would like to know something about the theory of monads and about Hegel's—realism," Bobby answered slowly. "It's all very instructive—and jolly puzzling. If I can get time, I want to run down to Oxford and find some professor of philosophy to put a few questions to."

"Better put in for a day's leave and tell 'em why," observed the colleague with deep irony. He added accusingly: "All the same, you weren't reading, unless you read upside down."

"Upside down? So it is," agreed Bobby, surprised. "No, I wasn't reading—I was thinking about an old lady I saw nearly run over."

"What about it?" demanded the other. "See that every day in every street, nearly, don't you?"

"It's no laughing matter, anyhow," Bobby observed.

"Who said it was?" came the sharp and somewhat indignant response; and then, as Bobby did not answer, the continuation: "I came along to tell you there's a girl turned up wants to spill something she thinks she knows about those City bucketshops we've been chasing round after. It's your case, so you're to see if there's anything in her yarn. Is it true they're going to pinch the Norris bird?"

"Not that I know of," said Bobby, startled. "Is there anything fresh against him?"

"The fellow he was talking to on the Embankment was brought in this morning. Didn't you know? Always the way, us chaps don't get told a thing, but we're supposed to know it all, all the same."

For a moment or two the speaker expanded on this perennial grievance of the junior ranks; and Bobby expressed heartfelt acquiescence, and wondered what information the man from the Embankment had been able to give, and his colleague said he had no idea but he understood the papers in the case had now been put before Treasury counsel. It was believed the A.C. thought there was enough to risk an arrest on; and a good chance that the search of Norris's flat an arrest would make possible would reveal further information to justify it.

"The fact is," said the colleague confidentially, "the old man's got the wind up for fear someone else gets bumped off, and he'll get it in the neck for not having had the gumption to save him when there was previous warning."

"It's worrying me, too," observed Bobby; and his colleague said it wasn't worrying him. He added thoughtfully that a few resignations high up always made things livelier down below, and Bobby said he must get along and interview the young lady who thought she had something to tell them.

"Don't let her keep you too long," said his colleague cheerfully. "I'm signing off—done my eight hours, thank the Lord, and it's me for my little home in the west."

With that he departed to catch a train for Acton, and Bobby made his way to a room where a very nervous young woman who gave her name as Harriet Hewitt was waiting for him, and protested eagerly that she had never had anything to do with the police before and wouldn't have come now, only her boss said she must, and was sure to ask about it in the morning, and quite likely to give her the sack if she said she hadn't been.

"He's so down on outside brokers," she explained, "we all think he must have been bitten by one some time. So you see I had to come, hadn't I?"

Bobby agreed upon the necessity and hinted gently that he would be glad to know what it was Miss Hewitt knew. So Miss Hewitt opened her eyes to the widest and said:

"Oh, but I don't know anything, not really."

Bobby waited, knowing that this was a quite hopeful beginning, since often those know the most who are the least aware of it.

"It was so funny, and such impudence as well," Miss Hewitt continued, "not but that I was glad to go in a way, especially with a month's salary when I couldn't have asked for more than a week's, being all you're entitled to when paid by the week. Of course," she added, looking thoughtfully at Bobby, "I saw at once what it meant."

"Yes," said Bobby, "it meant—?"

"Meant she was in love with him," explained Miss Hewitt, searching in her handbag for a handkerchief so that she might wipe her eyes, into which tears had come at the very thought of that tender passion. "She wanted him," said Miss Hewitt, applying the handkerchief to each eye in turn, "and she jolly well meant to have him, and that's partly why I gave in so soft-like, only you don't want to be a spoil-sport, do you?"

Bobby agreed that you didn't, and dropped another gentle hint that he would like to know who the "he" and the "her" were.

"Why, it's them I'm telling you about," Miss Hewitt pointed out patiently. "You could see it all over her, just like the films when the big business man comes in and sees the new secretary and it's ever so exciting because you know just exactly what's going to happen. Only what I say is, every one has their own choice, and if there's some who go soft for what's more like a walking corpse straight out of the coffin than anything else—well, it's nothing to do with anyone else."

"Certainly not," agreed Bobby. "You mean Mr. Percy Lawrence?"

"Well, it's him I'm talking about, isn't it?" demanded Miss Hewitt, less patiently this time. "Gave me the shivers, he did, first time I saw him, but always the perfect gentleman, that I will say. Me being hard up and out of a job through Brown, Jones & Son's crashing. I was five years with them before—well, I was glad enough to take it on, though all the time meaning to get something better as soon as I could. There's some in the City," she added, growing thoughtful again, "such smart Alecks it would be all the better if they were living corpses, too, or dead ones either, wouldn't it?"

Once more Bobby expressed agreement, and, by dint of discreet questioning, discovered that Miss Hewitt, out of work for some time and finding it difficult to secure fresh employment, had been glad to take the post offered her by Mr. Percy Lawrence on behalf of the Berry, Quick Syndicate.

From the first she had been uncomfortable and uneasy. For one thing, there appeared hardly any work to do—a disconcerting experience to one used to a busy office. Then it had been lonely, for there was no one else employed by the syndicate—not even an office boy—except Mr. Lawrence himself; and his silence, abstraction from all apparent interests, utter indifference to his surroundings, had soon begun, as she put it, "to get on her nerves."

"You couldn't hardly believe sometimes he wasn't just a dead corpse walking about because no one had remembered to bury him," Miss Hewitt declared; and Bobby nodded understandingly, remembering that he, too, the first time he saw Lawrence, had had something of the same impression. "It was like he was always remembering the past," she went on, "always going through it again in his own mind, and what was actually happening round him wasn't half so real. That was bad enough, and then no one to say a word to all day and hardly any work—not that I'm a whale for work in the ordinary way," added Miss Hewitt frankly, "but almost anything's better than sitting with your hands folded all the blessed day. Properly fed up I got, I can tell you."

"There was very little business done?" Bobby asked.

"Not enough to pay the rent, or even the electric light bills, if you ask me," declared Miss Hewitt. "Now and then we sent out circulars. Hardly ever got any reply; no reason to; nothing in them."

"What sort of circulars?"

"Oh, advice what shares to buy and what was likely to go up and what to go down—ordinary stuff copied out of the papers, most of it, I thought. And I never saw the books. They were kept locked up. Sometimes I saw Mr. Lawrence busy with them, making entries. Beats me what he had to enter. It all seemed funny to me, only nothing wrong you could put a finger on, only you felt there was more behind. Funny it seemed, didn't it?"

"Very funny," agreed Bobby gravely.

"Not short of money, you understand," she continued. "Every bill that came in paid at once, only nothing to show where the cash came from, and I got so I made up my mind to leave just as soon as I could get another job, even if it meant less money and more work. Jobs aren't so easy to find, but a friend of mine told me there was likely to be a vacancy soon where she worked, and I should stand a good chance if I put in. So I did, and then, before I got a reply, one day I came back from lunch to find another girl sitting at my desk, large as life, hat and coat hung up and pounding away at the typewriter as if she had been there for years. 'Hullo,' I said, taken aback like; and there were two five-pound notes on the table, and she looked up and pushed them over with a letter Mr. Lawrence had signed—if he had signed it; his name was there, anyhow, just as he wrote it, only afterwards I thought it hadn't looked quite the same. The letter was sacking me, and there was an A1 reference, and while I was sort of gasping the girl said: 'Mr. Lawrence very much regrets he can't continue your engagement. The work in the office does not justify it. There is ten pounds in lieu of notice, and he hopes the reference is satisfactory.' Well, ten pounds is ten pounds, and I was pretty sure of the other job, and I couldn't have asked for a better reference, and deep down in me I was glad and thankful to be off. I said: 'You taking the job?' She didn't answer that, only something about how sorry Mr. Lawrence was for any inconvenience caused, and then in walked Mr. Lawrence himself. Believe it or not, I'm as sure as anything you like he didn't know a thing about it."

"About what?" Bobby asked.

"About her being there, or the two fivers, or the letter he was supposed to have signed, or the reference either. He had been sitting in his room, just remembering same as always, and if he had heard anyone come in he must have thought it was me coming back from lunch. But he knew her all right. You could see that. You could see he was puzzled. Didn't understand it, or why she was there, or how she got there. That was plain, but what was a lot plainer was the way she looked at him—like he was It, and all she wanted was to go down flat and lick his boots for him. All sorts to make a world, of course, and all have their own tastes, but living corpses aren't mine—not by a long way. She said: 'Miss Hewitt is leaving and I am taking her place.' He looked at her and he looked at me, and you could see what he was trying to do was to come back out of the past where he lived, so he could understand. Only he couldn't, because it needed too much effort, so he didn't say a word but went back into his own room, sort of leaving us to it."

"What happened?" Bobby asked.

"We just stopped there like that, me with the two fivers in my hand and her looking half 'I'll tear your eyes out if you don't go quiet' and half 'You don't want him, and I do, so won't you go, please?' and another half saying it was all her life to get him, the way they try to look in the pictures only they never do, not like her. I was glad in a way to be out of the place, and ten pounds is ten pounds, and more than often comes your way as a gift like, and I knew this other job was waiting in a manner of speaking, and her watching me as much as to say she would be grateful forever if I gave her her chance, and if I didn't she would fight down to the last drop of blood. I was sort of scared of her and sort of sorry, too, never having known that wanting a boy was like that, which I suppose you never do till it gets you real bad like it had her. Before I knew I meant it, I had the two fivers and the reference in my handbag and I said: 'Cheerio—best of luck,' and I went off just like that, and, believe me or not, all the way down in the lift there seemed to be a sort of whisper in my ear, same as if she was saying, 'Thank you.' Funny, wasn't it?"

CHAPTER XXIII

DEATH OF ANOTHER

THAT IT might be added to the enormous collection of documents forming the dossier of the case, Bobby wrote out a full report of this interview before he left the Yard for home.

But for himself he did not see that it advanced their knowledge greatly, or helped them to ward off the menace and threat of murder to come that hung so heavily upon their apprehensions. They had known well enough that some connection existed between Lawrence and Alice, and the coffee-stall keeper's story had already told of what seemed to be its beginning. How that connection had developed, what its significance now was, what bearing it had upon the sequence of events, were the important questions, and upon them Miss Hewitt's tale seemed to throw small light. What was troubling Bobby much more was the report that Alice was renewing intercourse with her old associates. Stirring him to a bewildered yet profound sympathy had been the picture in his mind of the unceasing toil, the fierce enduring discipline to which the girl had subjected herself of her own free will. There had seemed to him to be shown in it more than a touch of heroism—of heroism, too, of that unknown and solitary sort which is most rare. But to these new reports, especially to those that told of visits to the woman known as Magotty Meg, it was difficult to attach any good meaning. Nor did he see what aim or purpose the girl could have that demanded both the willing and deliberate sacrifice of her sight and the assistance of that old woman of evil life and worse repute.

Only too likely did it appear that her first determination had broken down and that by the aid of Magotty Meg she was seeking to return to easier ways.

When Bobby had finished writing his report, he took it to Inspector Ferris, and was surprised to find much bustle and preparation proceeding. Evidently some special action was being prepared, and Ferris said to him:

"Oh, you hadn't heard, had you? It's that bird they pulled in off the Embankment. He's come clean."

"The one Dick Norris was seen talking to?" Bobby asked, a good deal disturbed.

"That's right," Ferris answered. "Not much in this," he added, running his eye over Bobby's report. "Plain enough there was something between Lawrence and Alice Yates when they were both working together—they wanted to get the Hewitt girl out of it for fear she'd blab, and they fixed up to do it like that."

"Well, sir, the only thing I thought might be worth remembering," Bobby remarked, "is her idea that Miss Yates is in love with Lawrence."

"Oh, lots of women can't see a girl and a man together without thinking they're in love with each other," answered Ferris. "Sort of fixed idea with 'em. Doesn't matter, anyhow. We're pinching Norris tonight and Lawrence as well, and that ought to get us material enough to put them away on."

Bobby felt a good deal surprised and a little worried at

this information. He had had no idea things were considered in higher quarters to be so far advanced, and for himself he was inclined to think that the action about to be taken was probably a little precipitate.

"It's all straightened out now, then?" he ventured to ask. "I suppose on what this Embankment bird says?"

"That's right," agreed Ferris, who was in a genial mood at the prospect he thought he saw of a cessation in the torrent of reports by which he had been overwhelmed recently. "Norris made a bad bloomer. Picked on a fellow with some brains. Talked too freely, too. The chap didn't half like it. Norris practically gave the show away—that is, to anyone who knew something already. Talked about it all—insurance, everything; even the bath business as well. The chap he talked to got the wind up, it all seemed so queer, and, when we tackled him, he wasn't half ready to tell us all about it. What it means is absolute, cast-iron proof Norris knew—and how did he know if he wasn't in it from the start? No answer to that, eh?"

Bobby, trying his hardest to think out clearly all the possible implications resulting from Ferris's story, did not reply. Ferris went on:

"His story stood up right enough, and the A.C. said to pinch both Norris and Lawrence and make a thorough search of Norris's flat, and of both the Berry, Quick office and the L.B. & S.C. place as well. Dead sure thing they'll find enough one way or another to clinch the case and clear up the whole thing. I shan't be sorry, either. And it's long odds they'll find enough to bring in Mrs. Ronnie and Mr. Chris Owen as well. It's been a big show, and there must have been a lot of them working it together."

He turned again to his work, and Bobby drifted away. He would very much have liked to accompany one or other of the raiding parties, but that, it seemed, was not going to be allowed. Others had been assigned to the duty, and for him there was nothing left but to sign off and go home.

He had to admit to himself that it did in fact look as though the case were drawing to an end, for indeed the knowledge that Norris had displayed of the methods used appeared quite incompatible with innocence. That admitted of no doubt, it seemed, and yet Bobby could not help a feeling that the picture was not complete; he thought there were still odd bits lying about not yet satisfactorily fitted into the general pattern. But he knew how generally successful it was, when guilt was believed to be clearly established but formal proof was still wanting, to trust to an arrest providing material to fill up any gaps remaining. Almost invariably the guilty man who has been arrested feels that, since the police have gone so far, they must know all, and, with that belief working like yeast in his mind, hardly ever has he sufficient strength of mind to prevent himself from offering explanations, excuses, comments, that serve only for additional proofs of guilt.

Yet Bobby was still inclined to think that this time his superior officers had acted too hurriedly, most likely under the spur of their apprehension that fresh murder was on the way and that prompt action must be taken to prevent it. The fact, however, still remained that proof was found of knowledge possessed by Norris of all that had happened in the past.

The bus he had travelled on put Bobby down some distance from his lodgings. Completing the distance on foot he turned into the quiet, old-fashioned crescent, little used save by the residents, in which his landlady's house was situated. As he did so he saw, a few yards in front, Alice, approaching from the other direction, returning, he told himself grimly, for this was an hour at which it had been her custom to be bent over her sewing, from some fresh interview with Magotty Meg.

To his surprise she did not seem to recognize him; and then he perceived that there was something not quite ordinary about her walk and bearing. Looking again, he saw that she was guiding herself with one hand against the area railings of the houses and that her eyes were tightly closed.

Wondering what this meant, he pushed on ahead, but on the opposite side, by the patch of enclosed, ill-tended garden that divided the crescent from the street from which it opened, and, looking back, was able to see that her eyes were still closed as she groped her way along. Her lips were moving, too, and he had the impression that she was counting her steps. When she had nearly reached the door of the house where they both lodged, she stopped, and felt along the area railings. The head of one was broken. On this her hand rested for a moment, as though it were the landmark showing her where she was, and then she went on briskly and up the steps to the front door. Bobby ran across after her. She was still keeping her eyes shut as she felt for the keyhole and let herself in. Bobby followed, asking himself if what she had risked, had happened, and her sight had indeed abruptly left her.

She must have known that someone was behind her, but, though he could see she was listening, she did not speak or hesitate. Groping her way to the foot of the stairs she began to ascend them, guiding herself by the banister rail. Still Bobby followed, and, on the landing, outside his room, she paused.

"I think it's you," she said, still with closed eyes. "Isn't it?"

"Yes," he answered. "Has anything . . . ?" He paused and hesitated. She waited. He went on awkwardly: "I mean . . . I wondered . . . "

"I was only seeing what it is like to be blind," she answered, whispering the last word with an infinite dreariness as though into it were compressed all those long years of darkness she foresaw.

He did not know what to say. He stood there, looking at her, wondering. Her eyes were open now, and she was looking not at him, but far past him. She might have been straining her vision to store up every physical detail it could reach. She said with the same accent of infinite dreariness:

"I suppose for a long time I shall go on saying 'seeing.' "

"Why?" he asked. "What for—I mean, what are you doing it for?"

Her eyes that had been steady before began to blink again, and she made that characteristic gesture she had of wiping away something from before them.

"It'll be worse than spiders' webs being there all the time," she said.

She went on up the stairs to the top where her own little room was situated. He followed her. She left the door open, and, while he watched her from the landing, she began with a kind of feverish and hurried impatience to get out her sewing. Bobby found himself saying abruptly:

"Don't do that."

"I must," she answered. "There's so little time."

"What for?" he asked. "Why are you . . . I mean, what are you doing all that for? It's crazy."

"If you have no money," she said, but a little to herself, "you are so helpless—helpless."

She came towards the door then to shut it, and he said:

"I wanted to tell you I have had a talk today with Miss Hewitt."

"Miss Hewitt?" she repeated, as if the name were not at first recognized, and then, remembering: "Oh. Yes. How did you find her?"

"We've found out a good deal," he told her, "but not why you came here to lodge, or why you are trying to work yourself—blind."

She shivered a little at the word, and again he was aware of that feeling of brutality. He said:

"Is it to help Percy Lawrence?"

"I suppose you know all about him," she said slowly. "All about me, too. Don't you? You're so clever at finding things out."

"Why not tell us yourself?" he asked. "We might be able to help you. I think we could, perhaps. I think there may be need. But how can we, if you won't tell us anything."

"What would be the good?" she asked. "A street woman, a convict, you wouldn't believe us; you would twist and turn everything we said. Can you see such as we are asking policemen for help?"

"Yes," he answered. "I think that is why you came here, because you thought you might want me."

She made no answer to that, but went back to her sewing, and, sitting down, began to work. She pushed the door to, and he went away down the stairs, remembering her sitting bending over her work, her busy needle moving to and fro, the shadows heavy all around in that small, dark, and awkward room.

"If she wanted to make sure of finishing off her sight, she's chosen the right place for it," he thought.

Almost immediately the phone rang. He had had an extension put into his room so that he could answer without going into the hall. The message was from the Yard, and directed him to hurry immediately to the Park Lane flat rented by Dick Norris.

"Get a move on," the voice over the wire enjoined. "They had a bit of a shock when they got there—Norris dead in his bath."

"What? What's that?" Bobby shouted; and the thin distant voice repeated:

"They had to break in, and that's what they found. Bit of a facer—oh, and Percy Lawrence was recognized leaving the building just about half an hour before. There's a general call out for him, and they want you along at once, as you have seen him."

"I'll be there right away," Bobby said, but he took time to run upstairs and knock at Alice's door. When she answered, he pushed it open, and said:

"I've just had word a man named Norris has been found dead in his bath. Lawrence was seen leaving a little before."

She listened, but gave no sign of emotion. Below her breath, so that the words were scarcely audible, she said:

"I thought so."

CHAPTER XXIV

ROUTINE WORK

When Bobby reached the Park Lane flats he found the general routine of such affairs in full progress, and he also soon found that he himself had been sent for in such haste through a misunderstanding. As soon as it was known that Lawrence had been seen leaving the flat shortly before the discovery of Norris's death, someone had mentioned that Lawrence was well known to Sergeant Owen, and someone else had at once suggested that Sergeant Owen should be sent for to provide a further description of the wanted man. Only after the message had been sent off had it been realized that of Lawrence, an ex-convict, a perfectly good description, photograph and fingerprint record included, was already in existence.

However, as he was there, he was told on his arrival to stand by in case he was wanted, and from one of the others present he learned that radio instructions had already been sent out for Lawrence to be found and brought to the Yard for questioning. Bobby's informant added:

"I was out chasing round after Magotty Meg when I got word to turn up here. The old girl's been at it again."

"Has she?" Bobby asked, interested. "What is it this time?"

"Pinching a suitcase in a bus," the other answered. "Lady getting out at Cannon Street found her suitcase missing, and then the conductor remembered Magotty Meg had been a passenger. Lively old girl, isn't she? The conductor knew her because he had been in court once as a witness against her, though he hadn't been able to place her at first, not till the lady complained. By the time we pick her up Meg will have got rid of the suitcase and everything identifiable, and butter won't melt in her mouth."

"Was there anything valuable in the suitcase?" Bobby asked.

"No; she's not got much this time. A library book, some knitting, and a few odds and ends."

"Curious," Bobby muttered, and the other nodded agreement.

"The old girl generally does better," he said. "Got a keener nose for a good thing as a rule—most likely she just saw a chance and took it. Not one of her thought-out do's. I might just as well have gone on having a try to land the old lady before she got rid of the stuff. There's nothing to this case; not much to it when a bird with Lawrence's record is seen leaving a flat and a dead man is found in it half an hour later."

"How do they know it was Lawrence?" Bobby asked. "Did someone recognize him?"

"Gave his name to one of the porters when he was asking for the flat," was the reply. "Said he had an appointment with Mr. Norris and would they phone up and see if Mr. Norris was in, and Norris phoned back to send Mr. Lawrence up."

"Then he gave his name himself quite openly?" Bobby remarked.

"Well, most likely he didn't come meaning to do Norris in," the other answered. "You know Lawrence's record?

Got the cat in jail for an assault on a warder."

"Yes, I know," Bobby answered. "I thought it would be interesting to get particulars. I got a man I know to write a chap he knows who was a warder at the time. There ought to be a reply soon."

"What particulars?" his colleague inquired. "It was just that he went for a warder and tried to kill him, that's all. Some of them try it till they find it only means the cat. Pretty tough record Lawrence has all round, from what I can make out. And now this."

"They found Norris dead in his bath, didn't they?" Bobby inquired.

"Yes. No answer when they knocked, and they made sure he had got word he was wanted and made a getaway. But they hammered a bit more, and some of the staff came along. Didn't like it one little bit; scared of their lives of a scandal and the other tenants not appreciating it and leaving, and then their going themselves, too, because the management blames it all on them and sacks the lot. But our people told them they had to get in, so the manager was sent for, and he opened the door with his key. Everything looked a bit upset, and when they went into the bathroom, there was Norris, in the bath, dead. And the first man who tried to get him out was nearly a deader, too."

"Why? How?" Bobby asked.

"The sunray lamp at one end of the bath had fallen into the water and it was charged with electricity; current running through it. Rummy stuff, electricity. First man took a bad knock—nearly a knockout. Second man didn't even know what was the matter. He had rubber soles to his shoes."

"Nothing to show how the lamp got into the water?" Bobby asked.

"No. Norris had one hand on it as if he had taken hold of it for some reason—to lift it somewhere out of the way perhaps. But the flat people swear the thing was securely bolted down, and could only have been loosened on purpose and with the aid of tools."

"Was that what caused death, do you know?" Bobby asked. "Electric shock, I mean?"

"They don't seem sure. I suppose they'll find out at the post mortem. His head was under water all right, but it seems a question whether the shock killed him or the drowning. The doctor said perhaps they would never know for certain."

The speaker's name was called just then, and he vanished on some errand. Bobby, standing by as he had been instructed, but keeping out of sight as much as possible for fear of being told he was not needed, continued to watch unobtrusively the progress of the investigation, and to pick up as many details as he could from what he could overhear.

He learned that Norris's evening clothes had been found laid out in the bedroom, so that apparently he had been having a bath before dressing for dinner. The first idea entertained, therefore, that he had perhaps committed suicide, on hearing in some way that his arrest was contemplated, seemed to be disposed of. A man intending to commit suicide would hardly take the trouble to get out dinner jacket and dress shirt first. There remained the possibility of accident, but against that was the fact of the presence in the water of the electrical apparatus that according to the testimony of the flat management could not be there as the result of any mischance, and the further fact that the flat showed signs of having been hastily ransacked, apparently for documents, since such signs were plainest in the disturbed contents of the drawers of the writing table and of a deed-box of which the lock had been broken. A cupboard and other drawers looked as if they had been searched, too, but whether anything had been taken it was, of course, impossible to say as yet. A careful examination of the rooms was still in progress, and fingerprint experts were busy.

"We know Lawrence was here," one of them remarked to Bobby; "there's the evidence of the staff of the flats for that. But he may have had pals. There's a girl works in his office with him; she may have been here, too. Though if she were she'll have worn gloves. They all do that all right."

Another of the searchers had made a discovery—an insurance policy for a large amount; £20,000 in fact.

"Here's what it was done for," he exclaimed excitedly. "Twenty thousand pounds again; always the same amount." Then he gave a low whistle. "Oh, lumme," he said, "it's only for an accident caused to a train or other public vehicle in which policyholder was a fare-paying passenger. That knocks it clean out for this business."

Looking very dissatisfied, he continued his inspection of the different letters and papers he found; and then the senior officer in charge noticed Bobby, asked him what he was doing there, and told him to get off and take part in the general hunt for Lawrence that was now on foot.

"Nothing you are wanted for here," he said. "Oh, wait a moment. It is you who reported on a man named Beale—Dr. Beale, isn't it? A professor or something. You know his address?"

"Yes, sir," answered Bobby. "Dr. Ambrose Beale. I don't think he is a professor, as I understand it; he is a writer on philosophy. I think he is busy with a new book now. He was talking about investing money through the Berry, Quick Syndicate—£20,000—and apparently they wanted him to insure his life for that amount as a protection against loss. The local police have been asked to watch and report if he comes to town, in case of any danger."

"In case he was meant to be the next," observed the senior officer. "Yes, I remember. Ring up the local people and ask if they have anything to report, and if he has been at home today. He may be able to give us some information."

Bobby went to carry out these instructions, but it took him some time to get through. When he did succeed, he received an emphatic reply to the general effect that Dr. Beale had been working in his study as usual. He had not been seen to leave the house at any time all the day. He had been seen once or twice leaning out of the window and smoking his pipe, or sometimes a cigarette, as was his custom, and his typewriter had been heard going continuously. At the moment of phoning—for by now it was late—his lamp was burning, and his shadow could at times be distinguished on the blind as, in his usual way, when presumably thinking how to frame his next sentence, he paced up and down the floor of his room between lamp and window. Bobby suggested they might take steps to assure themselves it was in fact Dr. Beale who was there, and they grumbled back that it was quite unnecessary but they would do so all the same. And in fact, an hour after Bobby had gone, a message came through from them to the effect that one of their men had made an excuse to look up Dr. Beale on some pretence of an automobile accident of which it was thought he might have been a witness. Dr. Beale had been very annoyed at being bothered at such a late hour, knew, of course, nothing of the imaginary accident, and had not accepted too graciously the apologies profusely offered for his having been troubled. But at any rate it was quite certain that it was Dr. Beale in person who had been seen and spoken to.

Before this piece of information came through, however, Bobby had departed homewards, though not before he had learned that the search for Lawrence had so far been unsuccessful. It was known that he had gone to his lodgings after leaving the Norris flat, for his landlady had been questioned and had said that he had been in for supper as usual, and as usual had gone out afterwards. Also one of the patrolling police-cars had seen him on the accustomed route of his evening walks, well on the way to Acton, but had lost sight of him in the traffic through a change of the control lights that had released a flow of cars between it and him. After that he had vanished, presumably having realized that he was being looked out for, and so having changed the ordinary routine of his walk.

"We'll pick him up all right, though, sooner or later, and more likely sooner than later," declared Bobby's informant, and Bobby agreed, and, returning home, found the letter waiting for him which he had been expecting, giving full details of the assault upon a warder for which Lawrence had been punished while serving his sentence.

Bobby read it with interest, and sat down for a time to think. Then he got up, and, late as the hour was, went out and, finding a late taxi prowling homewards in the direction of the Edgware Road, bargained for a cheap ride thither.

"Bit late out, aren't you?" remarked the taximan, who knew Bobby by sight, taximen having a wide acquaintance with the police. "Looking out for someone?"

"That's it," said Bobby, gave the man his promised shilling, and from the Edgware Road turned into the street where Lawrence lived.

There was no one watching, for it was not thought likely that if Lawrence knew of the search being made for him he would return home, while if he did not know he would be safely there in the morning. But when Bobby got to the house he saw there was still a light in one of the rooms, and, when he knocked softly, it was Lawrence himself who came at once to the door.

"It's you, is it?" he said, recognizing Bobby. "You've come about Mr. Norris's murder, I suppose?" The light from the hall lamp shone on his face, showing it clearly. He was smiling to himself, his worn and tortured features, as it were, entirely changed, so that they seemed to show an infinite content. "Come in a moment while I get my hat and I won't keep you," he said.

Bobby said to him:

"How did you know Norris had been murdered?"

CHAPTER XXV

RESURRECTION

Bobby followed Lawrence into the sitting room where he had gone to get his hat. Did he live entirely in his memories, Bobby asked himself; and Lawrence, who had picked up his hat from the old horsehair sofa that stood limpingly on but three sound legs, said to him:

"I'm ready."

Bobby turned his attention from the room to its tenant. He looked thinner even than when Bobby had seen him before, his eyes more deeply sunk, the black rings round them more clearly marked, his cheeks more hollow. The expression Miss Hewitt had used—"living corpse"—returned to Bobby's mind with a fresh impact of appropriateness, so remote from life Lawrence seemed, so far removed from all contact with the things around.

"I want to ask you some questions," Bobby said.

"Questions?" repeated Lawrence vaguely, as if wondering what they were. "Why? I shan't answer," he added, not with any air of defiance, but simply as stating a fact for which he himself had no responsibility.

"Not even if I ask you how you knew Dick Norris had been murdered?"

Lawrence's small, indifferent shake of the head was so slight as to be hardly visible.

"You seem to want to get yourself hanged," Bobby snapped out angrily.

Lawrence let this drift by him as though he had not

even heard it, as though it concerned him not at all.

"You see," Bobby went on, "my trouble is this. I happen to be fairly sure you had nothing to do with Norris's murder."

But to this statement, too, Lawrence paid no attention; it affected not in the very least that terrible aloofness from every human concern that seemed to be ingrained in all his being. He merely said:

"I'm ready if you want me to come with you."

"You've no right to play the silly fool like this," Bobby almost shouted, his temper quite gone, and this time Lawrence was moved to show a faint surprise, as if a little astonished at the other's vehemence.

"Well, why not?" he asked.

"I've been making a few inquiries about you," Bobby said. "I've got to know quite a lot."

"Your duty, I suppose," Lawrence said.

Bobby, who had sat down on one of the slippery horsehair chairs, jumped to his feet. His face red with anger, he said furiously:

"For two pins I'd punch you one in the eye, and what would you do then?"

Lawrence appeared to be considering the question, which apparently had interested him enough to get below the armor of his indifference.

"I shouldn't do anything," he decided at last. "Why should you mind a punch in the eye when you've had a dozen strokes with the cat-o'-nine-tails?"

Very greatly relieved, Bobby sat down again on his slippery chair.

"Now we're getting on," he said with satisfaction. "I

had a letter about you tonight. You were sentenced to five years' penal servitude for embezzling money. You were a bank clerk at the time, so you had every opportunity, and the judge said you had betrayed the confidence of your employers."

"He was quite right," Lawrence said. "So I had."

"You pleaded guilty at the trial and you didn't say anything in explanation or excuse. It's no excuse, of course, but you had taken the money because the girl you were engaged to had been flashing around and had got herself into the hands of moneylenders. She had been doing a bit of forging on her own account, hadn't she? And if you hadn't found that five hundred for her, she would have gone to prison and not you."

Lawrence said harshly and angrily:

"What business is that of yours?"

"Other people's business is a detective's business pretty often," retorted Bobby. "While you were doing time, the young lady concerned married someone else. A good match, too. It was the manager of the bank where you had worked. She got him by playing a broken heart at her discovery of your wicked dishonesty. He felt it was up to him to mend what one of his staff had broken, and she felt his salary of a thousand a year or so would do the trick all right, and anyhow was a jolly sight better than waiting five years for an ex-convict."

Bobby paused then, and Lawrence said very slowly:

"I never expected her to wait. I knew it was finished—an ex-convict. She acted—sensibly."

"While you were in prison," Bobby went on, "your mother—died. She was found drowned. The coroner made some remarks about recent distressing experiences she had passed through. The verdict was a kindly one—'temporary insanity.'"

Lawrence's face was livid now. All his indifference had gone. It had become human again, by a paradox, human through the awful animal ferocity it showed. He said, muttering the words through firmly clenched teeth:

"Take care—take care."

"I'm a bigger man than you," Bobby answered dispassionately, "and I'm in training, and your condition—well, rotten, isn't it? If I have to, I'll knock you down and sit on you while I finish what I have to say. I could get away with it, too. 'Resisting the police in the execution of their duty,' I should put in my report. That's like charity. It covers a multitude of—incidents."

Lawrence, standing opposite, stared bewilderedly at Bobby.

"You are police, I suppose, aren't you?" he asked. "I don't know what you're getting at."

"What I'm getting at," retorted Bobby, "is that you can't put the Embankment trick over on me."

"What do you mean?"

"I mean the fellow you scared on the Embankment by looking at him," Bobby answered. "I've heard about that, too. But it won't go with me. Never mind that, though. Let's get on. I ought to be hauling you off to the Yard, but there's a lot I want to say first. While you were in prison, you assaulted a warder; nearly killed him. You got the cat for it."

"Would you like to see the marks on my back?" Lawrence asked.

"No," Bobby answered slowly, "for I do not think those are the marks that matter."

Lawrence seemed about to make some angry remark and then changed his mind. He was sitting at the table now, and they were both silent. Bobby, watching closely, saw by the flickering and uncertain light that came through the broken mantle on the gas pendant how Lawrence's expression had altered. His utter, frozen indifference had been broken now; it was as if he had become aware of his environment; his eyes were no longer aloof but living, as if these stories of the past had drawn him from his perpetual contemplation of it and made him more conscious of the present. Bobby continued:

"The letter I got tonight said the reason you went for the warder, and got flogged for it, was because you had seen him put his foot on a mouse."

"It wasn't that so much," Lawrence explained in hesitating, doubtful tones, "it was the way he did it—deliberately, as if he thought it fun. I suppose, in a prison, a mouse means a lot; it comes and goes, and you can watch it; you can't come and go, but the mouse can, and so you watch. When he did it, I hit out at him without thinking—I mean without thinking who he was and what I was. I was in good condition then, whatever I am now, and I had him down in a moment. Some other warders came up and went for me, and I lost my head a bit, I suppose, and went for them, too. So after that they tied me up and flogged me. You don't know what it is, to be tied up and whipped. I think they whipped the soul and heart out of me."

They were both silent again, both thinking deeply.

Lawrence muttered:

"It was being tied up and whipped. It was deliberate ... like the mouse. Deliberate. It was afterwards I heard about mother. She had stood it about the five years, but when she knew I had been flogged with the cat—she couldn't."

"No," said Bobby, "no."

"It wasn't that it hurt so awfully, it wasn't the pain—it hurt all right, but anyone can stand pain if they've got to. It was its being done so deliberately," Lawrence said, and added: "Like the mouse under that warder's boot."

"I expect," Bobby mused, "only the very best and the very worst can go through a flogging and remain unchanged."

"I was changed, I think," Lawrence said. "Afterwards I felt somehow I wasn't like a man any more."

"Afterwards," Bobby said, "they found out things about that warder and he got the sack, didn't he? But they couldn't unflog you."

"No," agreed Lawrence, "and they couldn't make me feel a man again—nothing can. I'm just a thing that's been tied up and whipped. Not even God can alter that."

"I suppose God can do what He can do," Bobby said.

Lawrence seemed to be sinking back into his former abstraction.

"It's all past now," he said.

"You're making it the present," Bobby told him, and went on in a tone he tried to make hard and sneering: "Oh, yes, you talk about cruelty—cruelty to a mouse, cruelty to a girl when you saw a man putting a lighted cigarette-end on her wrist. All that upsets you a whole lot, doesn't it?"

"Cruelty always did, somehow, I don't know why; seeing helpless things ill-used always upset me. I dare say it wouldn't now. Who told you about the Embankment?"

"Well, we'll be getting on," Bobby said, "but I wouldn't talk about cruelty to helpless things upsetting you if I were you—not while you're trying your best to poke a helpless girl's eyes out. Worse, if you ask me, than squashing a mouse; worse than putting a lighted cigarette to her wrist. Not that you care, you and your talk about cruelty."

"I don't know what you're talking about," Lawrence said, staring at Bobby in bewilderment, his tones more human than any he had used before.

"I'm talking about a girl who is going blind," Bobby answered, "going blind because she's working her eyes out to get money to help you and all you do is keep your hands in your pockets and look on."

"I don't know—"

"Of course you don't," Bobby interrupted sharply. "Why should you? The fellow who flogged you didn't know either. Why should he? That made no difference. You were flogged and her sight's going."

"You mean Alice—Miss Yates?"

"It doesn't matter," Bobby answered, shrugging his shoulders. "It isn't you, anyhow, so that's all right. We'll be getting along—gross breach of duty wasting all this time talking. After all, there's been murder done, and they're wanting to see you at the Yard. I don't happen to think you had anything to do with it, but that doesn't matter."

"No," agreed Lawrence; "besides, you see, I had."

CHAPTER XXVI

LAWRENCE'S STORY

WHEN HE had said this, Lawrence relapsed again into silence, but a silence different entirely from that which had before possessed him. For that had been a denial and a withdrawal, a refusal of that common manhood by which we are all members one of another, a silence, in fact, of an inhuman indifference. But now this new silence of his was an outcome of doubt and of bewilderment, of terror, of a whole tumult of long-repressed emotions stung all suddenly into violent being once again. Whereas before his immobility had been that of unknowing stock or stone, now he seemed a man again, for he was suffering.

Not that Bobby at the time understood all this in such plain terms. But he did realize well enough that he had achieved his main purpose of awakening Lawrence from the lost dream of the past in which he had been living, and bringing his mind back to that strange aspect of reality we call the present; and he realized, too, that this ferment of the other's re-awakened mind had best be left for the time to work out its own conclusions.

The thought came oddly into his mind, as he and Lawrence left the house together and went down the street towards the main road, that it was almost as if it was by the side of one risen from the dead that he walked. He found himself wondering if those who had walked with Lazarus, or with the son of that widow who had but the one child, had felt a little as he felt now toward Lawrence.

By good luck, before they had gone far, they met a cruising police car. In it they were conveyed to Scotland Yard, and there Bobby was much puzzled by the reception given to Lawrence. It is true that between the professional criminal and the professional detective there often exists an odd kind of fellowship, as of those who know and understand each other and take each other as part of the necessary framework of the world. There is no malice on either side, provided that the decencies are observed, and the arrested criminal may always be sure that any reasonable request he makes will be granted. While if he does manage to wangle a "not guilty" verdict out of the jury, he will probably get from his defeated opponent of the police a hearty slap on the back, a word of congratulation on such undeserved good luck, and a warning to change his ways while there was time, since good luck does not last forever.

But tonight there was a warmer, almost an apologetic, tone about the formalities ensuing on Lawrence's arrival. Bobby even had the impression that had Lawrence insisted he might have been allowed to go home again. He showed himself, however, amenable to every suggestion, content to be passive in their hands, though still not so much indifferent as too absorbed in his own thoughts to have time to spare for other matters. There was no objection whatever on his part to the suggestion that he might be willing to spend what remained of the night at the Yard, so that there would be no delay in the morning in beginning those interviews, by his consent to take part in which, the C.I.D. officials explained, they would feel themselves put under so great an obligation.

As for Bobby, convinced by all this that either the case against Lawrence was very black indeed, and probably blacker still against someone else, or else that no case existed at all, he was told he had done well in producing Lawrence, and even better in performing that feat on a footing of such amiability and friendliness.

"Always best, to bring 'em in as if you loved 'em," the officer in charge said to him approvingly; and, by way of reward, told him to be sure to be on hand in good time next day—next day being purely a figure of speech, since by now it was nearly five in the morning, all this and the formalities on Lawrence's arrival having taken up a good deal of time.

So Bobby returned home, went upstairs to look longingly at his bed, passed a contemplative and affectionate hand over the unruffled smoothness of its pillow, then treated himself to a bath and a shave, and to a breakfast consisting largely of hot, black coffee of a strength to daunt the boldest, and so returned to the Yard, where he was greeted with the news that Lawrence was asking for him.

Bobby went accordingly to the room where Lawrence was waiting, and was surprised to find him standing at the window, smoking a cigarette.

"I didn't know you smoked," he remarked, after they had exchanged brief good mornings.

Lawrence, with an air of considerable, even comical, surprise, contemplated the cigarette between the fingers.

"I don't," he said. "I mean, I haven't for years. But one of your people gave me a packet, and I forgot I didn't."

He took another whiff, and seemed to enjoy it and yet still to be surprised at what he was doing. He laid the cigarette down, and said, leaning against the window and looking sideways out of it to where the river flowed brightly in the morning sunshine:

"I wanted to ask you . . . you told me . . . you said . . . I mean, is that true what you said about Miss Yates?"

"Yes. Why not?" Bobby answered, in as careless a tone as he could assume. Exaggerating a trifle, he added: "Her sight may go any minute almost—and, when it goes, it goes for good."

"What . . . I mean . . . what for?"

"How should I know?" Bobby retorted. "I never asked, and I don't suppose she would have told me if I had." After a pause, he added: "I saw her trying it out the other night."

"Trying what out?"

"Blindness. Trying what it would feel like."

He told curtly, and rather roughly, how he had watched the girl groping her way along the pavement and up the stairs of the house to her room. Lawrence listened with an intensity of interest far removed indeed from the dreadful, frozen indifference that hitherto had seemed to remove him so far from common humanity. But he made no comment at first as he moved restlessly up and down the room, pressing his hands together, fidgeting with the buttons of his coat, trying to moisten with his tongue his dry and twitching lips. He burst out presently into a low cry:

"But why? What for? I can't make it out."

"Well, it's your affair, not mine," observed Bobby, with a yawn that began by intention but soon passed beyond control as it cavernously expressed a whole night out of bed. "By the way, what did the Berry, Quick people pay you?"

"Pay me?" repeated Lawrence. "Why? It was never settled exactly. There was always money in the bank, and I took what I wanted when I had to."

"Then you have no cash by you? I mean, if you wanted to go away somewhere—abroad, for example—in a hurry, perhaps—you couldn't do it, because you have no money by you."

Lawrence was looking puzzled now. He felt in his pockets, and produced a shilling or two and some copper.

"That's all I've got," he said, in the same puzzled way. "I get a bill for board and lodging every month, and I draw out money to pay it. Or if I want anything else—I don't often—a new hat, I mean, or something like that... and I don't want to go abroad in a hurry. Why should I?"

"Someone else might think there might be need some day," observed Bobby; and Lawrence came and sat down opposite and stared at him, though not much with any air of awareness of his presence. He gave, indeed, somewhat an impression of one attempting to recall things seen and experienced on and from a sick bed, between intervals of recurring delirium. At last Bobby broke the silence by saying twice over: "Well? Well?"

"You don't mean," Lawrence asked then, as it were a great wonder showing itself slowly on his troubled and bewildered features, "you don't mean she's losing her sight scraping coin together so that I could run for it if I had to?"

"Better ask her," Bobby said, perpetrating another atrocious yarn. "Sorry," he apologized. "Who wouldn't give a kingdom for a bed? Didn't some johnny say that once, or something like it? Well, never mind. Nothing to do with me. I suppose it's a natural idea that police couldn't be trusted to give a fair show to an ex-convict when they had proof of dirty work at the crossroads and they knew he had been hanging around, and so the best thing would be for him to bolt. You aren't listening, are you?" he went on, noting with satisfaction that this chatter had passed unheeded by a Lawrence profoundly lost in his own thoughts. "But tell me this." He called Lawrence back to his surroundings by the crude method of poking him violently in the ribs. "Did you never wonder how it was the Yates girl turned up at the Berry, Quick Syndicate?"

"I don't think so," Lawrence answered slowly. "No, I didn't—I suppose, if I thought about it at all, I thought he had sent her."

"Didn't you recognize her?"

"Not at first; not for a long time, I think. Then I did."

"And it didn't occur to you to wonder . . . ?"

Lawrence shook his head.

"I never wondered about anything," he said. "I never cared enough. It didn't matter. I was only waiting—I think," he said slowly and carefully. "I think I felt I was as good as dead. I felt I had died long before, and I was just waiting for—for a grave."

"Who do you mean by 'he'? You said, you thought probably 'he' had sent her."

"He brought a fur coat for her once," Lawrence said. "He said I was to give it her; it was an old one his wife had done with, but Miss Yates might be glad of it as we didn't pay her much. So I thought he knew about her, but—now I'm not sure he even knew there had been a change and she had come and the other one gone."

"Who do you mean—'he'?" Bobby asked again.

"I don't know," Lawrence answered. "Though I think perhaps you do."

Bobby looked at him doubtfully.

"Never mind what I know," he said. "How do you mean, you don't know? You must. How can you help?"

"I never saw him in the light," Lawrence answered. "It was dark when we talked on the Embankment. At the office, it was always dark, too, always late at night when he came. Generally I got a typewritten letter to say what I was to do. Or he rang up. But sometimes he came himself. Then, if I was already there, he switched off the light before he came in. If he was there before me, he would have taken the bulb off. So I never saw him. He said he had to be careful because of certain reasons."

"You never asked him what they were?"

"No. Why should I? They were his reasons, not mine. He said something once about an official position he held, and so he didn't want it known who he was."

"Did you believe him?"

"I didn't care. What did it matter? Sometimes I think I was glad I didn't know. But generally I never thought about it. Why should I?"

"Most people would," Bobby grumbled.

Lawrence seemed to be thinking.

"I wasn't a person," he muttered, more to himself than to Bobby. "They had made me just a thing."

"Oh, rot," Bobby snapped impatiently. "You mean, you liked to sit and feel sorry for yourself."

"Well, well," Lawrence said, a trifle uneasily. "I don't think it was that," he protested, but with some doubt in his voice.

"Yes, it was," Bobby declared positively. "Anyhow, you heard the chap's voice—you would know that again?"

"Yes, I think so; yes, I would. He had a slight stutter. Very slight, but you noticed it. When he began speaking, generally."

"Oh, a stutter," Bobby muttered. "A stutter," he repeated.

"I know his name, too," Lawrence continued. "It's the same as yours: Owen—Chris Owen. After he had gone once, when I put the bulb back, I saw he had dropped some envelopes on the floor. I suppose he hadn't noticed in the dark, pulled them out by mistake somehow, and let them fall and never knew. I saw the name. It was Chris Owen."

"The—the address?" Bobby asked, his voice gone small and dry.

"I didn't notice. I tried not to," Lawrence said. "I knew he didn't want me to know, so I didn't look. Besides, I didn't care; it didn't matter. But I had seen the name. I remembered it."

"Chris Owen?" Bobby repeated dully. He said, with extreme irritation: "Did you never get to know anything more? You hadn't much curiosity?"

"None," Lawrence answered. "Dead things have none."

"Not even at first—the first time you met him."

"No. I told you. It was dark. He talked to me. He didn't even ask me my name, so why should I ask his? He told me to think it over, and, if I agreed, then to leave a message at a coffee stall that 'William Priestman agreed.' He said William Priestman was as good a name as any for the time."

"So it was," agreed Bobby, grimly remembering.

"Afterwards, he said, I could use my own if I wanted to. I was hungry. He gave me food. That was all I knew or cared to know."

"It seems—funny," Bobby said, with doubt in his voice.

"Yes. I dare say. You don't understand. How could you? You have never come out of prison after five years there. You don't know what it's like. I went in a man. I came out a thing. There had been the cat—and mother; what happened to her, I mean. She couldn't stand it—the cat, I mean—knowing I had been tied up, flogged. Got on her nerves, I suppose. Perhaps it did on mine, too. I had heard of it, of course, but I didn't know it was like that—not so much inhuman, if you know what I mean, unhuman rather. You felt you weren't a man any more, just a thing to be tied up and whipped or anything. It's silly talking like this—no one can understand. After I came out I felt like a dead man come from his grave, and I wanted to die again and go back and be done with the filthy thing that's life, but somehow I couldn't kill myself—I don't think I was afraid; I hadn't the will, perhaps, or else it was because of what mother did. I used to wander about the Embankment and the parks—like the others. One night, on the Embankment, I had a turn up with the fellow who was bullying a girl. It was when I saw him pushing a cigarette-end against her wrist . . . something took hold of me. He went away or I expect I should have killed him—something had come upon me. I felt as if I could have torn him in half as easily as I could a scrap of paper. I never thought of him or the girl again. He had gone, and I told her to get on with her job—easy to see what it was. I don't think I should ever have known it was her again at the office, only for the way she had of looking at me as if . . . as if . . ."

He paused, letting his voice sink away in wondering bewilderment, and Bobby said:

"As if—what?"

"What I wouldn't believe. I knew too much to be taken in any more. I was beginning to understand then why I had been picked up from the Embankment; what I was for—a useful thing again. Well, I didn't care. Things don't care; men and women may, but not things. Besides, he had given me food when I had had nothing to eat for a day or two and not much before that for long enough. A lot of it is all a blur, but I remember the coffee well enough, and how the strength of it went into me, and I remember the sandwiches he bought me, and how hard it was to get them down fast enough. Funny, I mean, funny what coffee and a sandwich mean. Even when your mind's like mine was then—even then, coffee and a sandwich mean a lot. Body and mind, you may be both, and God knows which counts most. Well, he got me a bed as well, and a job, too, and I thought at first—but that doesn't matter, only I was growing human again with a kind of warmth of gratitude, and then I began to understand what was behind it all."

"What?"

"Money and death," Lawrence answered dreamily. "His money and your death. I didn't care, only I felt myself grow like a stone again, just as I had been before. I was glad really, I suppose—after all, it was only paying a debt. He had given me food, given me a bed. You don't know what a bed means."

Bobby, thinking of his own unoccupied so long, was not so sure, but he made no comment.

"When I understood, at last, what it all meant," Lawrence went on, in the same dreary, reminiscent tone, "I had to laugh."

He fell silent once again, and Bobby could almost fancy that he heard that laughter, so lost and desolate, so full of —acceptance.

"I had to laugh," Lawrence continued. "Just for a moment I had let myself think the world wasn't quite what it seemed—not altogether a place where old women drowned, and young girls lied, and men were tied up like packages and parcels. But when I understood just why I had been given that coffee and those sandwiches, just why I had been picked up off the Embankment, why, then I had to laugh because I saw it was all of a piece."

"So it is," agreed Bobby. "Including girls who are fools enough to sew themselves blind for money to help someone else. It takes all sorts to make a world, they say, and I suppose she's that sort."

"I suppose she is," agreed Lawrence, drawing his brows together in a heavy frown. "I suppose she was the person who warned Norris."

"Warned Norris?"

"Yes. He had had a letter. That's why I went there. He sent for me."

"You knew who he was, then?"

"He used to come to the office—to the Berry, Quick office; and to another near Green Dragon Square—the London, Brighton & South Coast, they called it. At first I thought he was doing it all, and that the man with the stutter was a tool, like I was. But afterwards I got to understand Norris was meant to be the next after me, and so he was safe till then."

"What . . . what are you getting at?" Bobby muttered. "You mean . . . ?"

"Didn't you know?" Lawrence asked, with a kind of dreadful calm. "Didn't you know I had been insured for £20,000?"

Bobby felt his mouth and lips had gone dry. Incredulously he stared at this man who incredulously related how he had acquiesced and helped in the steps that he had known were the preliminaries to his death.

"I . . . I . . . " he muttered again. "You knew all the time . . . ?"

"Not all the time," Lawrence corrected him. "I got to understand after a while, that's all. It wasn't difficult. Easy enough to see what it meant. I found out it had happened before. That was why someone was wanted who had no friends, no relatives, to make troublesome inquiries. That was why the man who was planning it all kept away from the office; why I got all my instructions by phone, or letter; why I got long lists of what I was sure were imaginary deals on the Stock Exchange to enter up in our books—that was so it would look like a genuine business. There was a Dr. Beale as well. I was told to try to get him to insure himself, too, for the same amount. He wouldn't. I think he is marked down to be the third, after me and after Norris. You ought to take care of him."

"Oh, we will," said Bobby.

"Don't be too late," Lawrence warned him gravely. "Too late as I was with Norris. I used to be afraid, sometimes, they were operating, in a way I knew nothing about, through that other office they rented. Dr. Beale ought to be told."

"He'll be told all right," Bobby repeated; and Lawrence looked at him a little doubtfully, as if not quite understanding his tone.

"It was too late with Norris," he said. "I was so sure I was the next, and that when everything was ready, and enough time had gone by since the last one, I was to be found dead in a bath. That was all right. I didn't mind. I was glad to think I should be out of it all without any trouble, without having anything to do myself. Somehow I felt I had lost all power to do things myself, and, if he would manage it for me, all the better. And if it brought him in £20,000, I didn't mind—why should I? I felt I had been thrown out—the world had thrown me out, and why should I care what happened in it? I didn't—belong."

"Rough luck on the next man—on Norris, if you thought he was to be the next," Bobby said, a little sternly.

"I didn't mean there to be a next after me," Lawrence answered. "I was willing to be the next myself, and glad enough, for that matter, but I meant it to end then. I wrote a letter and put it in the office safe, where I knew he could find it—only he and I knew the combination. I told him in it I knew exactly what was going to happen, and how he meant to do it. But I told him, also, he had to stop, because I had left all proofs and particulars with a friend, a lawyer, who would send them at once to the police if anything else of the same sort ever happened again."

"A friend? Who is he?" Bobby asked quickly.

"He doesn't exist," Lawrence answered. "I had no

friend; no proofs either. I knew. I knew all right, but only because I had guessed and understood, not because of proofs on paper. But I was certain what I said in the letter would make him give it up. It couldn't help. I told him he needn't worry about me—I was a consenting party. I couldn't bring myself to do it myself; somehow it seemed too—deliberate. But I wasn't sorry someone else meant to do it for me—that would end it all."

"What about the insurance company that was going to be done down for £20,000?" Bobby asked.

Lawrence stared at him with quite absurd surprise.

"I don't believe," he said slowly, "I ever once thought of them. But, if I had, I don't think I should have cared."

"What about those walks of yours?" Bobby asked. "Every evening, I mean, round by Kew and Acton and that way?"

"I had to sleep," Lawrence answered. "I used to lie awake and think, and then I felt that I was going mad. But if I walked for two or three hours—then, sometimes, I slept."

"Did you ever notice Miss Yates? During those walks of yours, I mean?"

"No. Why? Why should I?"

"Oh, nothing," Bobby answered, convinced the girl had merely watched Lawrence pass; possibly, on his return, to make sure he had come back safely. He added: "Do you think Mr. Norris had any suspicions?"

"Yes. Not at first, but afterwards. Only he didn't know who to suspect. He thought it was me at first. He began asking me questions. I never told him much—I didn't know much, for that matter. Then he tried to find out, hanging about the Embankment and asking questions there—he hadn't got it right. Only, he was beginning to feel he had to be careful, and then he got an anonymous warning. I couldn't think who that could be at first, but now I suppose it was Alice. I expect she was getting nervous. But I don't think he quite believed what it told him. I ought to have said more. Only he didn't give me much chance; he still thought perhaps I was at the bottom of the whole thing. And I still felt so sure he was safe, because I was so certain I was marked down to be the next. I suppose it comes to my being responsible for his death. I told you I was. But I was so sure it was to be me, not him. So I told him he was safe enough, and perhaps that put him off his guard—I mean, that's what I told him when I was at his flat. He tried to make me tell him what I didn't know—who it was working it all. He said he had proofs of everything except that. But I didn't know either; all I knew was a name I was sure wasn't his own—that and a stuttering voice in the dark. But after I had gone away I thought that, if Mr. Norris really had the proofs he said he had, he might be in more danger than I realized—perhaps it might be him next, not me. And, while I was thinking that, I saw some of your men in a police car looking at me. I knew at once they were after me—you can always tell, the way they look. There was a lot of traffic between us just then, and a bus came along. I made up my mind I would go back and tell Mr. Norris he was in more danger than I thought. But when I got back where he lived, there was a crowd hanging about, and one of them told me what had happened."

CHAPTER XXVII

TRIP TO OXFORD

RETURNING thoughtfully towards his desk from his interview with Lawrence, Bobby met a colleague, who said to him with a cheerful grin:

"They've pulled in Magotty Meg and now they jolly well wish they hadn't."

"Why?" Bobby asked.

"Nothing on her," the other answered. "She's got two girls to swear she was with them at the time the bus conductor says he saw her. Lies, of course, but there it is. And no sign of the suitcase or its contents. Not that there ever was much chance of getting her unless we traced the thing to her."

"Nothing of much value in it, was there?" Bob asked.

"No, and there's a report a man was seen to throw a small attaché case over Southwark Bridge into the river and then run for it when he was asked what he was up to. Said it was an accident and scuttled off. Looks as if Meg had given it to a pal to get rid of when she found there was nothing in it worth much."

Bobby agreed that might be what had happened, though, from what he had heard of Magotty Meg and her thrifty ways, it did not seem likely that anything pawnable, even for a few coppers, would go into the river if she had anything to do with it. The story stuck in his mind as he went on to report to Ferris and tell him Lawrence was now apparently ready to tell all he knew, but that in spite of all their expectations that all amounted in fact to very little—not to much more than how vague suspicions had ripened slowly into certainties, and how at one time he had been inclined to believe Norris was the head of the conspiracy the Berry, Quick Syndicate masked, but that all he really knew was that that unknown's name might be Chris Owen and that he spoke with a slight but noticeable stutter.

"Chris Owen?" repeated Ferris. "Isn't that the name of that cousin of yours? The bird with an eye for the ladies, said to be in with the widow of one of the deaders, known to have visited his flat and never said a word about it? I say, that looks—"

He left the sentence unfinished, except for a low whistle, and Bobby agreed that it did, and said he thought he would like to spend the day taking a trip to Oxford to see an old tutor of his. Ferris agreed that things became awkward when a member of a man's own family, even if only a cousin, came under suspicion.

"You think," he added doubtfully, "Lawrence is really ready to make a statement? He won't shut up again?"

"Oh, I don't think so," Bobby said. "I should put it he has had concussion of the soul, but that's passing now and he's getting normal."

"What do you mean—concussion of the soul?" demanded Ferris.

"A result of what's happened to him," Bobby explained. "He's been living in a kind of dazed condition, only half conscious, about one percent awake, or less, to what was going on round him."

Ferris grunted and did not seem to think this very enlightening. He said:

"Anyhow, if he talks, he ought to be able to tell all about it."

"I don't think you'll find he has more to tell than he's told me," Bobby said. "Whoever it is has been engineering all this business has been careful never to let Lawrence see him. Lawrence only met him at night or in rooms in the dark—all the lights turned out. All instructions came to him typed: all the figures he was given to copy into the firm's books were typed and so on. And, in the dazed sort of condition he seems to have been living in, I don't think he ever made any attempt to find out anything. All he did was to try to make sure he should be the last in the list." Bobby explained briefly the precautions taken by Lawrence to come into effect after his death which he anticipated so passively. He added: "There's evidence now, isn't there, to show Lawrence had nothing to do with Norris's death?"

"One of the occupants of one of the other flats," Ferris explained, "has come forward to say he saw Norris come out into the corridor with Lawrence, and wait, talking to him, till the elevator came up. He saw Lawrence go down in the elevator and Norris go back to his flat. And there's no evidence Lawrence returned afterwards and a good deal to show he didn't. Seems to rule him out so far as that's concerned."

Bobby thought so, too, and departed to acquaint Higher Authority with his Oxford project. Higher Authority was too worried and busy to be really interested. Bobby, told off for special duty in connection with the Ronnie Owen investigation, was not yet returned to ordinary routine, and so his name was not in any list of those detailed or available for duty. Higher Authority supposed Bobby might as well spend the day at Oxford as anywhere else, and if Bobby could dig up any fresh evidence in that unlikely spot, so much the better. It was badly wanted. At present there was hardly evidence even to prove murder, let alone to prove the identity of the murderer. A coroner's jury could easily and reasonably return a verdict of "Accidental Death."

"Not enough proof to convict a small boy in an orchard of being there to steal apples," grumbled Higher Authority; and expressed a strong opinion that, unless Lawrence had more to tell them, it would be another washout.

There was, for instance, nothing to show that the apparent search of the room, of which it was thought traces were discernible, was not merely due to Norris himself having mislaid something and looked for it. He was not known to have had any other visitors than Lawrence, who seemed to be fully cleared by the proof that Norris had been seen to accompany him to the elevator in which he had descended. Nor were any valuables missing so far as could be told; money, gold watch, studs, and so on, were all in place. The only real bit of evidence was the fact that the electrical apparatus found in the bath had been deliberately loosened with the aid of a screwdriver. But the only fingerprints—and they were plain—on the handle of the screwdriver were those of the dead man, and it was quite conceivable that he himself had loosened the thing for some reason of his own.

"What's this about Lawrence and soul concussion you've been talking about?" Higher Authority added.

Bobby tried to explain, not very successfully, and Higher

Authority didn't seem very interested, but thought and hoped that Lawrence, having said so much, would be willing and able to say more.

"Once they begin, they go on," said Higher Authority from long experience; "it's the birds that keep dumb all the time are the trouble. And he's given us two good pointers. By the way, this Mr. Chris Owen—name only a coincidence perhaps, but the Chris Owen—that's a cousin or something of yours speaks with a slight stutter, doesn't he?"

"Yes, sir; not much, but it's quite noticeable."

"Let me see," mused Higher Authority, "wasn't there some report? Wasn't he thought to be cataloguing some collection and then it was found he couldn't be, because it was in cold storage somewhere, and no one seemed quite to know where he actually was?"

"Yes, sir," agreed Bobby impassively.

"Great ladies' man, too, I remember," mused Higher Authority; and then dropped the subject, but thought that if Bobby wanted to spend a day at Oxford, looking up old friends of his undergraduate days, there was no objection at all. Sergeant Owen had done a good deal of work—quite useful work—and deserved a day's rest and change. Higher Authority was, in fact, quite benevolent about it, and Bobby expressed his gratitude and retired, fully convinced it was thought just as well he should be out of the way for the time.

"Mean to haul in poor old Chris," he thought, "and don't want me around. Nothing I can do."

He returned to his rooms, and was glad to find waiting for him the report he had been promised of the address given by Dr. Ambrose Beale to the local literary and debating society. Bobby put it in his pocket to read in the train, and during the journey from Paddington to Oxford did his best to carry out that intention, but soon found himself in acute sympathy with the members of the literary society. He supposed the words made sense; they seemed to be put together in grammatical sequence, a good many of them he even recognized as being in ordinary everyday use, the meaning they conveyed to him was just none at all.

Sighing, he put the document in his pocket, and on arrival at Oxford, and after evading the various guides who assured him that unless he accepted their services he would see very little of the place, he found his way to the rooms of a Reader in Philosophy with whom his own acquaintance in his college days had been chiefly confined to the receipt of violent exhortations from the towing path, when he was being tried out for the college boat and the philosopher had been transformed into a coach.

The Reader, Mr. Allen by name, was out, and Bobby, awaiting his return, found a volume of Hegel in which he was somewhat doubtfully immersed when Mr. Allen appeared and noticed at once the book in Bobby's hand.

"I heard you had taken to tracking down the nightly burglar and the festive forger," he said. "You don't expect to find one in Hegel, do you?"

"No," Bobby answered, "it is a murderer I am looking for."

"Dear me," said Mr. Allen, from whom many years of experience of undergraduates had taken all capacity for surprise, "in the *Logic*. Had any luck?" he added with interest.

"I think so," Bobby answered. "One of our uniform men gave me a tip when I saw an old lady nearly run over, and it looks as if Hegel confirms. Would you call Hegel a philosophic realist?"

"Would I call Zeno an Epicurean?" retorted Mr. Allen, growing sarcastic.

"The monad theory?" Bobby asked. "Do you find that in Spinoza?"

"You do not," replied Mr. Allen, feeling sarcasm was useless here and falling back on patience. "You find it in Liebnitz." He returned to sarcasm. "If you want to ask any more questions like that, go and find some ten-year-old schoolboy—backward, of course."

"But I want to ask you," Bobby protested. "Oh, do you mind looking at this?"

He handed Mr. Allen the report of Dr. Beale's paper and retired to the window, whence he was recalled by various sounds of indignation and contempt and finally by that of the typescript being flung violently on the table. From one of the shelves Mr. Allen took down Whitehead's *Process and Reality* and opened it.

"That stuff," he said, with an indignant glance at the typescript on the table, "is a muddled-up copy of the beginning of this chapter. It hasn't even been copied right—whole paragraphs missed out. Is it a joke or what?"

"I shouldn't call it a joke," Bobby answered gravely. "Did you know a Dr. Ambrose Beale? I've been looking him up. He got his doctorate of philosophy in 1903 for a thesis on 'The Conditioning of the Unconscious.'"

"A very fine piece of work, too," declared Mr. Allen. "I remember it well. It suggested ideas that were entirely novel then, though they are common enough now. In its way, a landmark of thought. He went to Australia to study the Unconscious in the Primitive Mind."

"To Australia?" repeated Bobby, remembering that Australia had been mentioned in the Priestman case.

"Yes. There was an article in *Mind* giving some tentative conclusions, and I've always hoped he would follow them up some day. Very brilliant man, most original outlook, wonderful grasp of his subject. I should be glad to get in touch with him again. Do you know anything about him?"

"It was he who wrote that," Bobby said, nodding towards the typescript.

"He did not," said Mr. Allen, very positively.

"Why?"

"Because he was not a humbug, a charlatan, an impostor," declared Mr. Allen heatedly. "That typescript is ignorant rubbish—unless it's a practical joke?" he added, relenting a little.

"I don't think it's a joke," Bobby answered; "anything but a joke indeed."

"What is it, then?" demanded Mr. Allen.

"The gallows, I hope," Bobby answered grimly, and went away.

CHAPTER XXVIII

SUFFICIENT EVIDENCE?

But in the train, on the journey back to Paddington, Bobby felt he had after all drawn only very little nearer to his goal. True, he was assured now that Dr. Ambrose Beale was an impostor, with no right to the name he had assumed, no right to call himself a doctor of philosophy, ignorant indeed of the very elements of that study. Yet between the proof of all that he now held in his hands, and proof to satisfy a jury that Beale was actively responsible for the long series of murders under investigation, the gap was wide; nor did Bobby at the moment see any means of bridging it.

He had no doubts himself. He felt he ought to have guessed the truth at the moment when Beale, thinking himself safe talking to a policeman—probably he was more cautious with people he supposed better educated—had babbled absurdly of Hegel's realism and had attributed the Liebnitz theory of monads to Spinoza.

He wondered if ever before in the history of crime a better knowledge of philosophy would have led to a quicker detection of a murderer's guilt. But he had also to admit to himself that there had been other indications that might have roused direct suspicion in him, instead of only that vague unease which it had needed the casual remark of Markham, the uniform man on street duty, to crystallize into conviction of the truth. For, though he was not instructed in higher mathematics, he did know enough to be aware that equations are seldom represented by such neat columns of figures as Beale had on his blotting pad, and that were in reality no doubt, the imaginary stock and share transactions sent to Lawrence to be copied into the books of the firm in readiness for the possible inspection by insurance company assessors that was being prepared for. In the same way the clean, unsoiled, in a way untouched, appearance of the books on the shelves in Beale's study might have let him guess they were there only for show and deceit.

Looking back, now he was assured of the truth, every detail seemed to fall into place.

But it was a good deal less certain that all of it put together amounted to anything like that direct, simple, and unquestionable proof the law requires.

The coat of ocelot fur, for instance, that had been mentioned as having been worn by the supposed Mrs. Oliver at the inquest on the unfortunate Ronnie Owen, and that it was now fairly certain had been passed on to Alice in order to confuse the issues, as well as, most likely, to get rid of a possibly dangerous identification—what was there to show it was actually and in fact the same coat? "Fairly certain" and "most likely" are not phrases that can be used in courts.

Obvious, too, that the supposed Mrs. Oliver had been in reality Mrs. Beale, the timid, nervous woman, at home only in her kitchen, of whom he had once had a glimpse. Probably she had been provided with a dark "transformation" to cover her own fair hair, and other steps would have been taken to give her a superficial likeness to the genuine Mrs. Ronnie Owen, but there again, what proof of all that could be produced? Most likely, too, she had had no guilty knowledge of the purpose she was being used to serve, but had simply done as her husband bade her, partly coerced, partly persuaded, accepting some such explanation as that it was all part of obscure business transactions, credits, loans, debts, financial arrangements, that she herself neither could nor was expected to understand. Any evidence she could give, even if it could be obtained, would probably be useless, and at such a distance of time there would be no hope of there being obtainable proof of her identity with the self-styled Mrs. Oliver.

Everything, Bobby told himself gloomily, had been prepared and carried out with the utmost care and foresight. No doubt it was when Beale was in his study, ostensibly writing his philosophical treatise, that he composed the imaginary transactions to be entered in the books of his syndicates with such care and detail that the accountants who had examined them had noticed nothing suspicious, and had accepted the entries as genuine. The precaution had even been taken of showing a moderate profit, on which income tax had been duly paid—and there is no document on earth more satisfactory and convincing in its stark, bare realism than a demand note or a receipt of the Income Tax Commissioners. In the safe seclusion of his study, too, Beale had probably prepared the necessary forged documents, marriage certificates, and so on, that had been necessary to satisfy the insurance companies and prevent their suspicions developing into a refusal to pay.

No doubt it would be easy to establish that the business of the Berry, Quick Syndicate and other concerns had been entirely imaginary, but there is no legal offence in inventing business transactions or in paying income tax on non-existent profits, and in them is no proof of murder, however suspicious they may seem. Bobby supposed that very likely evidence on such points would not be admitted at a trial, unless and until it could be linked up with more direct proof. Confirmatory testimony was all that could be considered.

Nor was there any hope that Lawrence could give evidence of identity. Plainly he had had no suspicion of Beale; he had regarded him simply as a prospective victim, though one safe for the time, both because Lawrence believed he was himself first on the list, and also because Beale had been wise enough to refuse to insure his life.

Bobby had learned, too, in further conversation with Mr. Allen, that the genuine Ambrose Beale had been a little over thirty when he received his doctorate in 1903, so that his age, if he were still alive, would be somewhere about sixty-five. And that was why the sham Beale had professed that age, though Bobby was now perfectly certain he was at least fifteen years younger.

"I ought to have followed that pointer up," Bobby told himself with self-reproach.

Actually, though a vague unease had troubled Bobby almost from the moment of his first meeting with Beale, it was the subtle manner in which that gentleman had transferred himself from the category of possible suspects to that of probable victims which had succeeded so well in diverting suspicion. In the same way, this aspect of yet another dupe and victim he had succeeded in giving himself had prevented any risk of Lawrence growing suspicious. One does not readily suspect the fly hovering over the web, and apparently about to alight on it, of being in fact the spider that has actually spun the web.

Bobby supposed, too, that it was the gossip started by the porter, who had recognized him as a police officer on the occasion of his first visit to the Berry, Quick office, that had reached Beale and brought him so promptly on the scene in his character of yet another prospective victim. All the scene that day with Lawrence must have been carefully arranged; Lawrence in his condition of apathy and indifference being ready to agree to anything asked of him, without troubling to require any explanation.

The precautions he had taken to insure that his own death should end the series had satisfied him. These effected, he had been willing to drift on the current of events to an end clearly foreseen and willingly accepted.

So vague and doubtful, in fact, had been Bobby's own suspicions that there had been needed the casual remark of the uniformed constable he had been chatting with one day, to the effect that a man who could laugh at an old lady's narrow escape from being run over had a murderer's mind, to crystallize them into certainty, as sometimes in chemistry the addition of one element to others held in solution will make clear the nature of them all.

Clear and certain as all this was now in Bobby's mind, yet, go over and over again, as often as he liked, his arguments and inferences, he saw no line to follow leading to absolute proof.

Beale was certainly an impostor, and that much no doubt could be proved, but imposture is not murder. Indeed, in two of the tragedies that had taken place there was no proof of murder at all. Bobby himself was convinced that murder had been carried out by some simple process of making the victim drunk or drugged, or depriving him of consciousness in some way, and then getting him into his bath, there to drown; but in each case the verdict of the coroner's jury had been "Accidental Death" and would not be easy to upset. In the other case—that of Ronnie Owen—there was indeed this proof of murder, since it could be shown that poison had been administered, but nothing could be brought forward to implicate Beale.

And in the case of the death of the unlucky Dick Norris, there was nothing again to show that Beale had been in any way concerned, or even anywhere near at the time. Possibly he had been concealed in the flat somewhere, but that was a pure guess, and Lawrence apparently had seen no sign of him. There was, in fact, nothing to prove that Norris's death had been anything but a deplorable and unfortunate accident.

Bobby was certain for his own part that Norris had begun to entertain suspicions pointing towards Beale; that this was the cause of his nocturnal wanderings on the Embankment which had roused suspicions of himself; that he had accumulated certain evidence; that Beale, therefore, had found it necessary to remove him, adopting for that purpose his well-established and successful technique of the bath; and finally that it was Beale's collection and removal of such written testimony as Norris might have succeeded in getting together that accounted for the hurried search of which the flat showed traces. Efforts to induce Norris to insure his life had plainly been made by the evidence of the policy found in his rooms, and the careful limitation to accidents hardly likely to be caused purposely suggested, too, considerable suspicion and uneasiness on his part. But such policies so limited are not uncommon, and no jury would see anything there out of the way, or feel forced to accept the theory that Norris might have been testing Beale's reaction to an insurance so carefully limited.

"If Beale sits tight," Bobby told himself gloomily, "he's safe as houses—and so he is even if he doesn't. There's not a thing against him a smart K.C. wouldn't make rings round as easy as winking."

There would even be the testimony, tending to establish an alibi, of the local police set to watch Beale—for his own protection and safety from that threat of murder Bobby was so certain was his own. They had already reported that to the best of their knowledge and belief he had not left his house on the evening of Norris's death. Not that Bobby attached much importance to that evidence. Easy enough for Beale to direct his wife to take his place in the study, to work the typewriter so that its rattle could be heard, to switch on the light at the proper time, to let an unidentifiable but accepted shadow appear on the blinds. That Mrs. Beale was so much under her husband's control as to obey implicitly any directions he gave her was certain enough, and he would have found little difficulty in leaving the house unseen, bicycling to some neighboring station where he was not known, taking a train to town, and returning in time to show himself in person when the local sergeant of police came to make inquiry about the car accident Dr. Beale might have witnessed had he been on the spot at the time as, the sergeant explained, was understood might possibly have been the case.

But once again all was conjecture—probable, even certain in a way, but yet far from the solid, unequivocal proof British law requires.

To Bobby it looked very much as if the man guilty, as he was well convinced, of this long series of murders would escape all human punishment, escape with the rich profit of his crimes, escape perhaps to begin again elsewhere.

In this depressed mood he returned to his rooms from Paddington, to write out there his report in surroundings more comfortable than the crowded conditions at Scotland Yard permitted. As soon as he got in, his landlady appeared to say that Miss Yates was in her room upstairs and wanted very urgently to speak to him, if he would spare her a few minutes. He sent up word accordingly that he would be glad to do so, and she came down at once, blinking, hesitating, nervous. He noticed that she was carrying a small attaché case. She said without preamble of any kind:

"A woman called Magotty Meg stole this for me. I expect you know her. She said she had been seen and she has been keeping out of the way or I should have had it before. It was in a bus. There was a woman there. She was half asleep and she had an attaché case just like this. Meg changed it for this one. It was Dr. Beale's. I mean this one. He kept his hand on it tight, but Meg is very clever. She jerked his hand away somehow, and before he put it back she changed his for the woman's and put his on the woman's seat. Neither of them knew, and then in a minute or two she picked it up from beside the woman and got out with it, so when it was missed the woman thought it was hers had gone. But Meg thought the bus conductor had seen her, so she had to keep out of the way till she could get it to me safely. It's locked, and I haven't tried to open it. I want you to do that."

CHAPTER XXIX

CHRIS'S STATEMENT

BOBBY TOOK the attaché case Alice was offering him, and held it on his knee.

"I don't think we will open it now," he said. "I think we had better take it along with us to the Yard and let them open it there." He added: "You mean Dr. Beale?"

She nodded.

"What made you suspect him?"

"I always knew," she answered slowly, "there was something queer going on. If a man is starving on the Embankment one night, like Mr. Lawrence was, and then he is put in charge of an office, you know there's something behind, something secret. And if it's secret, then it's crooked."

"Yes. Yes," agreed Bobby thoughtfully. "Yes, I expect that's so."

"If it was crooked," she went on, "then there was a crook to make it so, and there were only three of them—Dr. Beale, Mr. Norris, Mr. Lawrence—unless it was someone else nobody ever heard of. But I soon got to be sure there wasn't anyone else—only those three. And it wasn't Mr. Lawrence, because he didn't care enough—a crook has to be wide awake, and he was living in a dream. Besides, he had only been brought in after the thing had been started; I felt sure he was meant just for cover. At least, I did till I found out they had him insured for a lot of money. They thought nobody would ever bother about what happened to an exconvict picked up on the Embankment. I knew very well that was why they had chosen him. For a long time I thought it was Mr. Norris, but then I found out he was worried, too, and was asking questions about things. He did that on the Embankment, and he tried to get out of me what I knew, but I didn't tell him anything, because I didn't trust him. Only, especially because he seemed to suspect Mr. Lawrence, that meant he wasn't the one who was doing it all."

"If he was suspicious something was wrong, why didn't he come to us?" Bobby asked. "He knew I was working on the case."

"I think," she answered slowly, "because he saw there was a lot of money concerned, and he hoped to get hold of it for himself. I think he hoped to be able to say: 'I know all about the game that's going on here, and I'm going to the police about it, but, if you hand over enough of the money you've got, I'll let you have warning in time for you to get away first.' "

She paused, as if inviting comment, but Bobby made none. The explanation seemed to him plausible enough; it fitted in with what he knew of Norris's character, and his association with the Berry, Quick Syndicate explained his recent affluence. He might have suspected he had been selected as a victim of the future, but in the interval he was receiving more money than ever before, and he might easily have thought himself clever enough to run with the hare and hunt with the hounds, so securing a large share of the booty for himself before taking action to expose the conspiracy he suspected.

Alice went on:

"That left only Dr. Beale. I hadn't thought of him at first, because it looked more as if he were one of the people they were planning to rob. But afterwards I felt sure it was he, only I couldn't be sure he and Mr. Norris weren't working together. So I got Meg to watch and see if Dr. Beale went to visit Mr. Norris's flat. If they were partners, they would have to meet there—they were never both at the office at the same time. And, from the way Mr. Norris had asked me questions, I was sure something was going to happen. Meg watched Dr. Beale go to the flat, and then she saw Mr. Lawrence. She saw Mr. Lawrence leave, and afterwards Dr. Beale came away, too. He was carrying an attaché case he hadn't had with him when he came, and he looked all worked up and funny, as if something had happened. She thought she would follow him and try to get hold of his attaché case. And she did, and there it is; and I don't know what's in it—nothing perhaps," she added, with sudden discouragement.

Bobby, nursing the attaché case on his knee, wondered, too, what it held—nothing of interest possibly, or it might be the evidence needed. He said:

"You had never met Lawrence, had you, before that night on the Embankment?"

"No."

"How was it you were there? There was a man who was looking for you?"

"Does that matter?" she asked wearily. "Step by step—there was a book in the sitting room at home: *Step by Step* it was called—that's how I got where I was that night—and birth control," she added. "When I was a girl," she went on—she could not have been much more than twenty-five, but she spoke of her girlhood as might have done a woman of eighty—"I thought birth control made everything just the same for girls and men, too. They all said it did. It doesn't—nothing ever makes it the same for a girl and for a man; and after a time nothing seems to matter any more; and you have to live, or you think you have, and you don't care much—only, one day you are with the others, standing in the street, for sale. And I got to know Sandy—Sandy Watson. I thought he was sorry for me. He used to say I was such a kid. He promised to help me. He said he would see I got a square deal. I was glad to have someone who seemed a friend, and he was good to me at first; only, presently, he began to show he was a devil, really. He knocked me about, too. I didn't mind that so much—you expect that—but there were other things he wanted me to do, and one night I went down to the Embankment. I meant to jump off the steps when no one was looking—they said it was quite easy once you were in the river, and no one could interfere. But Sandy followed, and he found me, and he was putting the lighted end of his cigarette on my wrist when Mr. Lawrence stopped him. I've never seen him since. Mr. Lawrence spoke to me, and what he said showed what he really felt. If he had said anything nice or kind or comforting I shouldn't have noticed so much. He just thought of me as a bit of dirt that he had trodden on, and yet he had done that for me. I hated him worse than anyone ever hated before, and I followed him, and I watched, and I found out he had got a job in an office. There was one girl in the office and no one else, and it was quite plain there was something funny going on. I made up my mind to find out what, and I borrowed some money from Meg and I scared the girl who was there into going away and letting me be there instead. Mr. Lawrence hardly even noticed. He was like—like what I had been the first time I stood in the street. You just feel nothing matters because nothing's real any more—it's not you, only a kind of doll that's there. Mr. Lawrence might have been dead."

"You wanted to make him come alive again?" Bobby asked.

"Yes," she said.

"When you thought something was wrong at the office, why didn't you come to us?"

"A street woman, an ex-convict," she answered simply, quite without bitterness, merely as stating an incontrovertible fact. "They don't go to the police so easily as that." She added: "Besides, I was not sure what Mr. Lawrence had to do with it."

Bobby supposed that was the real reason. She had been afraid, had probably at first believed, that Lawrence was involved or at least had guilty knowledge.

"You would never have believed or understood how dead he was to everything," she continued. "How little anything mattered to him any more." She stared at Bobby, and was silent. Then she said: "Did you know they had flogged him?"

Bobby nodded.

"It killed all feeling in him," she said. "Whipping people isn't any good except for people it doesn't make any difference to. All it did to him was to make him go dead all over."

"He told me once it was being treated like a thing, not like a man," Bobby observed. "I don't quite know what he meant. I think he must have realized after a time what the Berry, Quick Syndicate was up to."

"Yes," she agreed. After a pause, she let fall the one word: "Murder."

She was silent then, and so was Bobby. Somehow that one word had dropped into their talk like a prohibition. Bobby got to his feet to go. He looked across the table at her. He said:

"Are you ready?"

She seemed then to think there was another question in his eyes. Answering it, she said:

"Yes, he knew after a time, but I knew first. If I had told you, you would have been sure he was doing it all; the only thing you would have thought of would have been getting him hanged. He would have had no chance when there was so much you thought you knew about him. So I waited and watched, and that's why I got Meg to watch, too, and some of the other girls. And that's why I had to have money—I had to have money to pay them, and pay Meg what she had lent me, and to have some, too, for Mr. Lawrence to go abroad with, if it turned out he had to."

"That's why you were working yourself blind, then," Bobby said. "Your sight wouldn't have lasted another week."

Her gesture put that aside as of no importance.

"My eyes were always bad," she remarked, "but they would have lasted more than a week. They only said that at the hospital to frighten me. They would have lasted till it was over. I would have made them."

It was Bobby's turn to stare at her now, for she had uttered that last sentence almost casually in a way, and yet with such an accent of tremendous will it almost seemed as though she could at her wish have compelled the natural event to her obedience.

"I suppose all this means," he said, half to himself, "that you're in love with Lawrence."

Again her gesture waved aside a detail without importance.

"He was dead, as I once had been," she answered, "and I knew it was my job to make him come alive again."

"Oh, well, now then," Bobby muttered, and it seemed to him these were waters of emotion and of feeling too deep for his plumbing.

They went out together, and, on their arrival at the Yard, Bobby explained their errand and surrendered the attaché case to be opened with all due form and ceremony. During the delay while the preliminaries were being accomplished Bobby was summoned to the phone, and found it was his cousin, Chris Owen, who was ringing up in considerable agitation.

"Is it true Dick Norris has been murdered?" he asked "And what's the trouble about the piece Lady Endbury bought? Hang it, man, you don't suppose—?"

"I don't think so," Bobby answered, "but it's true enough Norris has been found dead in his bath. Murder has not been established yet. I think it might be as well if you came round here. Some of the chiefs might like to see you."

Chris agreed, and soon made his appearance, still very agitated and disturbed.

"Lady Endbury told me," he said. "What's that piece she bought got to do with it?"

"We hope you'll tell us that," Bobby answered. "We've

been trying to get hold of you the last day or two. The man in your shop said you were cataloguing Lord Westland's collection, but now we find all his stuff is packed away for the time."

"That's right," Chris answered. "I've been over in France with him. He didn't want it known. He's buying a lot of stuff from a johnny near Bordeaux—a big wine merchant who's hard hit, and wants to realize without anyone knowing what he's doing, or else all his creditors will be getting the wind up. Westland wanted expert advice, so I went along. You can ask him."

"That's all right, then," Bobby said. "By the way, Norris told me once you were on the board of the company owning that block of flats—he said you had been investing rather big sums?"

"No business of his," grumbled Chris. "Nosing round in what didn't concern him. It's Westland's money, really —I'm acting as his nominee. You can ask him that, too, if you want to, only don't go telling everyone. He wants it kept quiet. "

"That's all right," Bobby repeated. "There is one thing turned up we rather wanted to ask you about—a bit of Chelsea china you sold Lady Endbury?"

"What about it?" asked Chris sharply. "I happened to see it in a flat in the building where Ronnie was living. Nothing to do with him, or with what happened afterwards. I saw it there and liked it, and bought. In my line, you have to keep your eyes open. Why?"

"You didn't tell us you knew where Ronnie was living? I suppose you did know? It wasn't chance you were there?"

"No-o," answered Chris hesitatingly, very much as if he

would have said "Yes" had he dared. "I knew where Ronnie was all right, but only by accident, and I never dreamed it was murder or any suspicion of it, or anything like it. The verdict was 'Death by Misadventure,' and that's what I thought it was, and, anyhow, buying a bit of china in the flat underneath his couldn't have anything to do with it one way or another."

"I don't see why you didn't say something when you knew murder was suspected," Bobby said. "If people hold things back, they can't complain if we wonder why."

Chris muttered something inaudible. He got up and took a turn or two about the room. Finally he said:

"I suppose it doesn't matter so much now. I was seeing rather a lot of Mrs. Barton at the time—you know—awfully nice woman, but somehow we've drifted a bit apart recently. It's Scales Barton who is her husband, the K.C. Well, it was this way. She took a little flat on her own round about where Ronnie was living. The idea was, her friends could visit her there without any gossip going on. In the afternoon, you understand, or at the week-end, when she was supposed to be visiting her sister in the country. The thing is, everybody knew we were great pals, and if it came out I had been wandering round a place like Islington where nobody ever goes—well, Scales Barton had been asking questions already, and he might have put two and two together and misunderstood things and then there would have been hell to pay. I promised her I would hold my tongue. And I didn't see why not. I hadn't an idea in the world there was anything behind the verdict or anything queer about poor old Ronnie's death. Look here, hang it all, it won't have to come out about Mrs. Barton, will it? There wasn't anything to come out, you understand, but—well—you know how people talk."

"So they do," agreed Bobby. "I don't see that anything need be said now—and I suppose it really wouldn't have made any difference at the time. It was all done so neatly, and so cleverly, I don't know even yet there's any proof we can dig up. Always, it's not the knowing but the proving that we trip over. But I think the man who killed Ronnie may hang for another job, and, if it turns out that way, there'll be no object in carrying on. A man can only hang once."

Chris looked, and was, very relieved. He added, with a touch of defiance, that, if he had to, he was fully prepared to deny on oath all he had just told Bobby about the Mrs. Scales Barton adventure that was now ancient history.

"I hope it won't be necessary," Bobby said, "but if it is, and you try that, you will probably tie yourself up in awful tangles. By the way, have you seen Cora recently?"

Chris shook his head.

"She's at Torquay," he said. "Didn't you know? Been there some days now."

"I wanted to be sure," Bobby said, "she had no idea whereabouts Ronnie was living in Islington."

"I am sure she hadn't," Chris answered. "After she put her advertisement in the paper she told you about, it was Charing Cross where they met."

"They did meet, then?" Bobby asked quickly. "She didn't tell us that."

"She told me long ago," Chris answered. "You mean she didn't say anything about it that day she told us she thought he had been murdered. Why should she? There was no connection, was there? She was a bit overwrought, too. After the advertisement he put in in reply to hers, he rang her up and asked her to meet him at Charing Cross, to talk. And she did. That was when she gave him the signet ring. He took nothing with him when he disappeared, you know—nothing at all. But she brought the ring with her when she went to meet him that day, and gave it him as a kind of token, and that made it all the worse when after that she never heard anything more."

Bobby frowned. He felt he ought to have noticed the tiny discrepancy between the statement that Ronnie had taken nothing away with him and his possession of the signet ring, and have endeavored earlier to clear it up. Not that it mattered much, only it would have saved certain faint, troubling doubts that had thus been unnecessarily added to his worries; and then, before he could say anything more, word came that he was to present himself at the opening of the attaché case now about to be undertaken in the Assistant Commissioner's room.

CHAPTER XXX

THE ATTACHÉ CASE

A LITTLE group of senior officers had assembled for the opening of the attaché case, most of them eagerly expectant, one or two plainly incredulous. The Assistant Commissioner himself presided. A portly superintendent, who had not altogether forgotten certain exploits of his younger days, enjoyed himself with a bit of bent wire and the locks, and had little trouble in getting them open. Within were various bundles of papers, neatly tied up and docketed, and—what took the eye more dramatically—a rubber truncheon. With careful precautions it was lifted out, and the Assistant Commissioner said:

"Sort of thing you could lay anyone out with and nothing much to show. Better have it examined—we have Beale's fingerprints, haven't we? The doctors had better be asked to take another look at Norris's body, too; they may spot something if they know what to look for."

The truncheon was duly taken off for testing and examination, and the Assistant Commissioner turned his attention to the papers. They were in folders, neatly endorsed, and the Assistant Commissioner whistled softly as he picked each up in turn.

"Details of how Beale worked it all, apparently," he said. "This one, marked 'A,' deals with the Ronnie Owen affair, apparently, and the other folders with the other cases. They'll have to be gone through and checked. Hullo, here's one with nothing in it marked 'Percy Lawrence.' "

"There's an endorsement, sir," someone pointed out.

"So there is," agreed the Assistant Commissioner. He read it aloud: " 'P. L. seems half-witted, apparently neither knows nor wants to know anything.' Um-m. Where is Lawrence, by the way?"

"He was told he might go home, sir, but to stay there and be ready if we wanted him for further questioning," answered a chief inspector. "It was thought best, if you remember, sir."

The Assistant Commissioner nodded. He knew well, he shared it himself, that the one nightmare of Scotland Yard, the one thing calculated to reduce all there to dithering despair, was the thought that possibly they might have arrested an innocent man. The mere suggestion was enough to set them all positively grovelling. Nothing is too good for anyone believed to have been unjustly suspected: Lawrence, for instance, had been taken home in one of the Yard's cars in the company of an officer who had positively oozed friendliness and affection the whole way, though Lawrence himself, lost now, not in apathy, but in a tumult of conflicting thoughts, had remained quite unaware of any change in the official atmosphere.

"Looks," said the elderly superintendent who had opened the attaché case, "looks as if Norris had the goods on Beale all O.K."

"Looks," commented someone else, "as if that was why Beale did him in."

"If Norris suspected what was up," asked the Assistant Commissioner, "why didn't he come to us? There's more than enough here to take action on."

"The insurance companies have paid out something like £60,000," the elderly superintendent pointed out, repeating independently the explanation Bobby had already heard. "That's a lot of money, sir, and though overheads were pretty high, no doubt, there must be a good share left. I suggest Norris may have meant to blackmail Beale into parting with some of that money."

"Look at this other folder, sir," another man said, holding it out. "It's endorsed: 'Notes of attempts to get me insured and to take charge of L.B. & S.C. office. Getting warm. Got to look out. R. N.' "

"He evidently had his suspicions," agreed the Assistant Commissioner. "The same old idea, I suppose—insured to cover risk of loss to partner if death occurred. Evidently Norris had tumbled to it, and it does look as if he thought he could fleece Beale and get a share of the plunder. Played with fire, did Mr. Norris, and got burned. Only, if Beale knew, and knew himself cornered, and went to such lengths to get possession of the evidence Norris had collected, why is he so calm about it? He must have found out by now he has the wrong attaché case, and that the right one may be opened and examined any minute. Yet he doesn't seem at all uneasy. How's that? A bit of a snag, isn't it?"

As all his seniors seemed to think so, too, and none offered any explanation, but only looked doubtful and worried, Bobby ventured to say:

"Isn't it on the cards, sir, that he actually does not know? There is a report of a man having been seen to drop an attaché case over Southwark Bridge into the river. The bus Beale and Meg were in was going to Cannon Street. Southwark Bridge isn't far. Beale would be keen on getting rid of such compromising material at once; it must have felt like a bomb in his pocket with the safety pin drawn. He may have never spotted the substitution Magotty Meg managed, and he dropped the attaché case into the river in the full belief that he was getting rid of all Norris's evidence forever."

"It might be that," agreed the Assistant Commissioner, who had listened attentively. "He may believe all Norris's evidence is at the bottom of the river."

"And, instead, it's on the table here before us," commented somebody in an undertone.

They were interrupted by a report from the Fingerprint Department to the effect that fingerprints within the attaché case and on the rubber truncheon were identical with Dr. Ambrose Beale's, and a further note was added that on the truncheon there appeared to be human hairs of a color corresponding to Norris's hair, though closer examination would be necessary before identity could be established with absolute certainty.

"Hardly necessary to wait for that," said the Assistant Commissioner. "Quite enough to bring in Beale; better not wait either. Slippery gentleman, by all accounts. The sooner we get him, the better."

Late though it was by now, an expedition started out at once, by car, to effect the arrest. Bobby was allowed to accompany the party—he was the only one who had met Beale and could identify him—and on arrival the party went first to the local police station, already warned by phone to expect them. The inspector in charge seemed a little worried.

"I've got three men watching Beale's place," he said.

"I had one there, and I sent two more when your message came through. We had just had a report in that a visitor from London had arrived. He seems to answer the description of Lawrence, and our man thought he heard that was the name he gave when the door was opened after he knocked. It rather looked to me as if he might have come to warn Beale and they might be meaning to clear off together."

The little party from Scotland Yard exchanged uncomfortable glances. It was a most disturbing suggestion. If it turned out to be correct, and the story got about that there had been released from custody a suspected person who had immediately taken advantage of that indulgence to convey a warning to his associates, then a whole lot of things would be said, mostly unpleasant.

"If the papers got hold of a yarn like that . . . " murmured one man, wriggling at the thought.

"It isn't the papers, it's the Commissioner," murmured another man, wriggling still more as he pronounced that last dread word, and everyone looked very hard and very severely at Bobby.

"What you said was that Lawrence had nothing to do with it, and nothing to do with Beale, either?" they accused him, almost simultaneously.

"If it's like that, what's Lawrence rushing off to see Beale about?" demanded the third of the party.

"If they've made a getaway together . . . " said the first speaker, and had no need to add in words what his manner made so plain—that the fault and full responsibility would be Bobby's alone.

The others all agreed with him wholeheartedly, and, if

looks could have done it, the glances bestowed on Bobby would instantly have reduced him to no more than a mere shrivelled remnant of humanity. "Immediate return to uniform duty," was the least thing their looks suggested.

The local inspector, by way of cheering them up, chimed in:

"A million to one, as they've had everything so carefully thought out, they've got some nice little hide-away all ready where they'll be as safe as houses."

They all agreed that that was more than likely, and then they all tumbled into the car again, with the local inspector as guide to direct them to Dr. Beale's house, and the disgraced Bobby, making himself as small as he could, in the back seat.

The distance was not great, and, late as the hour had grown, there were still lights burning in the house, one in the study, one in the room to the right of the front door—the drawing room, Bobby thought—and another in a smaller window just above the entrance.

The car drew up on the gravel drive before the front door. Their arrival must have been heard in the quietness of the night, but no notice was taken. Before the car had well stopped, one of the party was out and beating a loud summons with the knocker. There was no response. Bobby said:

"What's that? Do you hear?"

They listened. The local inspector said:

"No. Why? There's water running, that's all. Someone having a bath."

He spoke carelessly, but to Bobby's ear that last word had grown to have a dark significance.

The man at the front door began again his loud hammering with the knocker, and Bobby, staring at the small lighted window above whence came that sound of running water, saw that, by gutter pipe and waste pipe and porch, access to it was possible. He took a short run, a leap; he began to climb desperately. He heard someone below shout, asking him what he thought he was doing. He heard with a queer distinctness his trouser leg rip as the cloth caught on a projecting nail, but he never knew till afterwards that it had torn the flesh as well. The gutter pipe tore away beneath his weight. He had only time to clutch desperately at the sill of the window above as the pipe bent slowly to the ground. He hoisted himself up to crouch on the sill, and, there belancing himself unsteadily, he smashed the window with his elbow. The tinkling glass fell inwards, a cloud of steam came out; through the opening he had made, he tumbled, scrambled, fell into the room.

Through wreaths of steam he could see Lawrence in the bath, staring blankly at him over its edge, half conscious, half fainting. Both the hot water and the cold were turned on, filling the bath from the taps, running off again by the overflow pipe, but not so quickly but that the floor was flooded. Vaguely, in his state of semi-consciousness, Lawrence was trying to lift himself above the lapping water. Twice his head had gone under. A third time, as Bobby projected himself through the window, it disappeared. Bobby seized him under the arms and dragged him up. His senses had again left him, and he sagged unconscious, unable to help himself. From below the clamorous knocking on the door sounded and then ceased. Bobby thought to himself that the door would not be opened, and that his companions could not follow by the way he had taken, since now the gutter pipe had broken away from its supports. With an effort that took all his strength, he dragged Lawrence from the bath, jerked him out to the slippery floor. The door of the room smashed open, and Beale stood there, a transformed, unrecognizable Beale, with wild, pale face, and eyes desperate and strange behind his heavy, gold-rimmed glasses. At the corners of his mouth had gathered a little scum of froth, and in one hand he held an automatic.

He fired—fired twice. But the steam in the room gathered on his glasses, baulking him, making his vision indistinct. One bullet grazed Bobby's left shoulder, and another, aimed lower, scored Lawrence's cheek with a long red scratch. They did no other harm, and for a split second Beale stopped to snatch off the glasses with the gathered steam on them that prevented his clear sight. In that moment Bobby grabbed at something near—only later did he know it was a jar of bath salts—and flung it almost at chance. It struck Beale on the shoulder, a glancing blow, but so far effective that his third shot was jerked sideways, and then Bobby, stooping so that the fourth shot went over his head, caught Beale in a Rugby tackle. On the floor, slippery with water, they both went down, and the automatic jerked from Beale's grasp and splashed into the bath.

For a moment they fought there on the swimming floor. The water had overtaken the capacity of the overflow now and was pouring out on the floor in a small steady stream. Behind them lay Lawrence's naked body, from which, now, all conscious life had gone. With all his natural, swift agility of movement Beale wriggled, fought, twisted. He got a hand to Bobby's throat, a knee to the pit of his stomach. Uttering a scream of triumph he wrenched himself free, rolled away, got to his feet again, ran from the room and across the landing to the stairs, still screaming, as he went, his hate and his despair. Close behind raced Bobby, clutching at the other's shoulder, his grasp still failing to connect. A third of the way down the stairs, when Bobby's hand was actually upon his shoulder though it had not yet closed, Beale seized the banister rail and flung himself over it and down into the passage beneath, miraculously alighting on his feet.

Bobby, unprepared for this maneuver, shot on, lost time before he could leap after him. The front door was beginning to give way under a roaring cascade of assault, but its lock still held. Beale, he had gained a second or two, dashed across the hall and into the drawing room. Bobby was scarce two yards behind. In the room, between a small occasional table and a large bureau in a recess by the wall, Mrs. Beale sat, her knitting in her hands, mechanically turning the heel of the sock she was at work on, as though all this clamor and sudden tumult into which the night had broken meant nothing to her. As busily, as evenly as ever, her long steel needles clicked as her hands moved to and fro, and the thought flashed into Bobby's mind:

"Did she know what was happening in the bathroom while she was sitting knitting here?" And the certain answer, "Yes," responded on the instant.

Ignoring her utterly, as though she had been but another piece of furniture, Beale darted by her. He tore open the upper drawer of the bureau, snatched out two big automatics with one simultaneous gesture, turned snarlingly, a pistol in each hand. Bobby was so close behind, that, when Beale turned, the muzzles of the automatics nearly touched him. The front door lock had yielded to the attack upon it, and Bobby's companions were pouring into the hall, were even now upon the threshold, witnesses of what was about to happen before they had time to play their part. Bobby found himself vividly aware, as with actual physical vision of what was about to be, that, with the aid of those two big automatics he handled as a man well accustomed to their use, Beale could easily shoot them down in succession and then make his escape in safety to the hideaway it had been truly said he was certain to have prepared and ready.

From sheer voluptuous delight in the position, in the power of life and death he held in his outstretched hands, Beale hung back for the fraction of a second from pressing the triggers of his weapons. Well he knew, and gloated in the knowledge, that with the crooking of his fingers death would leap to his will, inevitable and plentiful and sure. With a look of such awful hate as Bobby had never known human features could display, Mrs. Beale half rose from her chair and dashed her knitting, needles and all, full in her husband's face.

CHAPTER XXXI

CONCLUSION

THAT ONE instant of respite was all that was necessary. Before Beale had a chance to recover himself, even while his fingers on the triggers of his automatics began to send a double stream of bullets hopelessly astray, he was seized, tripped up, a prisoner.

"Close shave," gasped one of the others of the party.

Mrs. Beale turned again all her attention to her knitting, straightening its somewhat tangled strands.

From the floor where he knelt by the side of the prisoner, gripping one wrist, tearing the second pistol from his other hand, Bobby said:

"The bathroom . . . quick . . . it's Lawrence there."

He was unconscious when they found him, sprawling on the floor with the water still splashing over the bath's rim. They pulled him out, wrapped him in dry blankets, and the hastily summoned doctor declared that all he needed was rest and warmth; there was no sign of any serious injury. He was removed, accordingly, to the local hospital, where he was in fact only detained twenty-four hours, and Beale also was removed—though his detention was destined to be longer—while Mrs. Beale, having got her knitting straight again, resumed with care her task of turning the heel of the sock she was busy with.

Lawrence's story, when he was in a condition to tell it, was simple. He had come to give Beale that warning which he believed was necessary, the delay in giving which to

Norris had been, he felt, holding himself morbidly responsible, the cause of Norris's unhappy fate. Dr. Beale, to whom he had never given a thought save as another prospective victim, he had decided must not be exposed to the same risk.

But Beale had failed to understand the motive for the other's visit. Lawrence's stumbling, confused explanation had been interpreted by him as a repetition of the hints of knowledge Norris had given, and Beale had supposed that underlying them was the same intention of forcing a share of the booty.

On his side, too, Lawrence had begun to catch glimpses of the truth in Beale's startled and menacing reaction to the warning the other was trying to give him.

"He said things I couldn't make out," Lawrence explained, when he was questioned later on, "and he looked at me in a queer sort of way. I think I was beginning to understand, and then he said he would explain; and he told Mrs. Beale to bring some sherry and the whisky. I said I would have some whisky, and he poured it out. I felt queer at the first taste. I thought it was because it was so long since I had had any. I remember his saying I must sleep it off. I didn't want to, but he got hold of my arm and we went upstairs. The next thing I knew was someone hauling me out of the bath and water splashing all round."

For a time Beale tried to maintain a defiant attitude. Lawrence, he protested, had merely come on a business visit and had asked to stay the night. He was having a bath before retiring, and possibly he had been affected by fumes or had fainted. At any rate, he, Ambrose Beale, knew nothing about it, and was not responsible for the state of his guest's health. When he heard the crash of breaking glass and knew intruders had broken in, naturally he supposed they were burglars, and he had attempted to defend himself, his wife, his goods, as any householder was entitled to do. For any misunderstanding, the violent entry made by the police was entirely to blame. That he had adopted the name of his late dear and intimate friend, Dr. Ambrose Beale, who had died in Australia, he would fully admit. It had been by his friend's own special request, since that friend had not wished a name he believed was destined to be illustrious to die out, and it might be added at once that the silly rumors about the manner of the genuine Dr. Beale's death—by drowning, while swimming in the open sea somewhere off the Queensland coast—were entirely without any foundation whatever. In any case there was no legal offense in adopting another name. As for the Berry, Quick Syndicate, he acknowledged freely his interest in it, and that the tranactions entered in the books were all imaginary. The reason for that was that he was working out an elaborate system by which speculation on the Stock Exchange would be rendered scientifically certain so that enormous gains would infallibly result. For that, it was desirable to have machinery in readiness for instant action. Indeed, the man had an answer for everything, he waxed confident with the sheer unbelievable audacity of his statements —the secret by which acceptance and belief are often gained, since it is felt difficult to suppose that such claims can be made unless they are well founded—and only when he got to know that it was the wrong attaché case he had thrown into the river, and that the contents of the one he had taken from Norris's flat were in possession of the police, and held in testimony against him, only then did he perceive the hopelessness of his position and so fell into a sullen silence and a refusal to utter another word.

That evidence was in fact so strong that the trial became little more than a formality. The other charges against him were not proceeded with, the verdict of guilt in the Norris case being considered sufficient, and, that verdict once returned, he was sentenced and duly executed without even making an appeal.

Many rumors and stories were of course circulated concerning his activities, and for months no Sunday paper dreamed of going to press without some fresh "amazing" or "sensational" or "exclusive" disclosure of his past, generally hopelessly inaccurate, though once or twice fairly complete and correct accounts were given. But the papers were badly handicapped by official reticence, and by the firm refusal, in spite of the most tempting offers, of both Lawrence and of Alice to utter a single word. Chris Owen was more obliging, but then he knew very little, and Mrs. Ronnie went on a long cruise under an assumed name, and so avoided the attentions of the crime experts.

"If it hadn't been for the attaché case that the Magotty Meg woman got hold of, and for the proof that the hairs on the rubber truncheon were identical with those of Norris," the Assistant Commissioner told the Home Secretary, who was still taking a personal and somewhat embarrassing interest in the case, "I don't know that we should have been able to prove a thing against Beale. He had taken the most careful precautions. It was certainly he who appeared as a witness at the inquests, growing beard and moustache for the occasion, and then shaving afterwards—a most effective form of disguise. That yarn he invented, too, of a friend of his, threw us completely off the track. We wasted a lot of time and energy over that, kept some of our best men busy when they ought to have been concentrating on what had happened here. We are so terribly short of staff," said the Assistant Commissioner, with intention, reinforced by a heavy sigh, "we do need more men so badly."

But the Home Secretary, who had heard that tale before —was used to it, indeed, as the accompanying chorus to every report every departmental chief made to him—offered no comment, and the Assistant Commissioner continued:

"Even the panic attempt on Lawrence's life and the shooting on his arrest, he might have got away with. There was his wife, of course. We might have got something out of her, but I doubt it. It's plain she was the woman who passed as Mrs. Oliver, got up as much as possible to look like Mrs. Ronnie Owen. But she was entirely under her husband's control; it's doubtful how much she understood; and there's always the fact that she was his wife. Lord, how she hated him—hated and feared him. Yes, she might have talked, but I don't think so, and, if she had, it's an open question whether she would have been able to give us the legal proof the law will admit and a jury accept. Anyhow, we were all glad to leave her out. After all, she saved the lives of our men. Beale could, and would, have shot them all down but for her. No," he concluded thoughtfully, "it's a fifty to one chance most of her evidence would have been ruled out as inadmissible—lawyers never enjoy themselves so much as when they're showing that the truth is inadmissible."

"What about that leopard-skin coat?" the Home Secretary asked. "Wasn't that traced to her?"

"No proof of identity; no way of nailing it down as the same coat," declared the other. "Oddly enough, though, it was that coat made Alice Yates first suspicious of Beale—a case of fearing the Greeks when they offer gifts. She spotted it had come through Beale, and she felt there was something behind. Fur coats aren't given away to typists without a reason. By the way, we have evidence, now, Beale had a nice little hideaway all prepared and ready. With a bit of luck he would have been safe enough in it if he had managed to get away."

"Just as well he didn't," commented the Home Secretary, and the Assistant Commissioner warmly agreed.

Chris Owen's antique business is still flourishing, and Bobby was glad to put in for a month's special leave after the strain of so much doubt and worry, culminating in an escape so narrow. Lawrence, his identity becoming known through the publicity the papers gave him, was informed that he was entitled, as the sole heir to his mother's estate under her will, to a legacy of a few thousands she had received from an uncle of hers. Part of it Lawrence invested to bring him in a small weekly income, part of it he used to buy a tiny fruit and poultry farm, and part he kept in reserve as additional capital and to meet the inevitable losses till he should have learned his job. He also sought out Alice Yates, and informed her of his intention to marry her. She refused passionately to hear of such a thing, so he went away to have the banns put up in church and give notice at a register office, then returning to explain that the only choice left her was that between church and register office.

She persisted in her refusal; he persisted in his preparations, calling for her quite regularly in a taxi to take her to church or register office as she preferred, till suddenly one day, appalled at the money she was making him spend in fares and fees, her resistance collapsed, and the ceremony was duly performed, with Magotty Meg as a somewhat scandalized and wholly surprised witness.

"It's not what you might call much in my line," she protested, "but there, the best of us never know what we may come to."

44047789R00166

Made in the USA
Charleston, SC
16 July 2015